NON-HAZARDOUS MATERIAL

Fred Lockwood

ISBN: 9798387003240

The cover photo, taken by David Mark, is of the MSV Krishna Sudama.

The photograph supplied from Pixabay is copyright free.

Author's Note

As you start to read this novel you will immediately notice something is different: the text is 'left-aligned' rather than 'justified'.

The print layout for most novels is justified. This is where the line of text starts precisely at the left-hand margin and ends precisely at the right-hand margin. Justified text stretches and compresses the normal spacing within and between words so they fit on a line of specific length. You will have noticed this when some lines in a novel are severely compressed, and others have words with an odd spacing between them. There are many who believe that justified text looks professional or neater than left-aligned text. However, research evidence reveals justified text is more difficult to read! This is because as we develop as readers we recognise and read clusters of letters and shapes of words rather than individual letters and words. In this book, there are more than 90,000 words – that's a lot of reading – but it's all left-aligned.

I do hope you enjoy *Non-Hazardous Material* and find it easy to read. A description of other novels in the Jack Collier Series is provided in the final pages of this book.

Dr Fred Lockwood

About the Author

© Turtle & Ray Productions (2022)

Dr Fred Lockwood is Emeritus Professor of Learning and Teaching, Manchester Metropolitan University, UK. He is also a PADI Master Scuba Diver.

His career in higher education has involved consultancies in over one hundred universities in more than thirty countries. Fred has travelled extensively and dived in the waters of Central America and Africa, the Middle East and South-East Asia, Australasia and the Pacific Islands.

Once a keen runner and squash player, he is now an equally keen cyclist, walker, skier and diver. He lives in Northamptonshire with his wife, Beryl.

Acknowledgments

I would like to thank the following:

David Mark, photographer, and *Pixabay* (http://pixabay.com) for permission to use Mark's exceptional photograph of the MVS *Krishna Sudama,* as she sank, as the cover of *Non-Hazardous Material.*

Andy Hillier, PADI Master Instructor, for his advice on diving with a rebreather, gas mixes, decompression tables and for generally ensuring the diving sections of *Non-Hazardous Material* are plausible. See http://www.divenorthampton.com

Aakanksha Sharma, Barbara Askew, Bob Flanagan, Kevin O' Regan, Janusz Karczewski-Slowikowki and Andy White for reading through the manuscript and offering numerous improvements. Their insights and attention to detail was humbling.

Midlands Dive Chamber, Rugby, for advice on the decompression of divers working at depth.

Turtle & Ray Productions for permission to use the photograph, taken by Layla Elise Boulema, of the author diving off the coast of Curacao in October 2022.

Other books in the Jack Collier Series

Total Loss (2016) Cambridge: Vanguard Press.

Overdue (2017) Cambridge: Vanguard Press.

Missing Presumed Lost (2018) Cambridge: Vanguard Press.

Unlisted Cargo (2019) Kindle Books.

Gross Negligence (2020) Kindle Books.

Wreck Site (2021) Kindle Books.

CONTENTS

Author's Note i
About the Author ii
Acknowledgments iii
Chapter 1 Sexual assault 1
Chapter 2 Charged with assault and rape 8
Chapter 3 The case unfolds 17
Chapter 4 MV *Asenka* 27
Chapter 5 Rising water 41
Chapter 6 Good news 48
Chapter 7 Unusual evidence 51
Chapter 8 Roberta Fox 54
Chapter 9 Inspections 58
Chapter 10 The cold light of day 71
Chapter 11 Mind made up 84
Chapter 12 The MPA Clinic 88
Chapter 13 Ongoing assessment 97
Chapter 14 Working in the dark 103
Chapter 15 A proposition 105
Chapter 16 The next phase 112
Chapter 17 Thorpe Investigations 118
Chapter 18 B&H Limited 123
Chapter 19 Doubts forming 128
Chapter 20 The partnership 132
Chapter 21 Revelations 135
Chapter 22 Reinforcements 144
Chapter 23 Plan of action 150
Chapter 24 Curiouser and curiouser 157
Chapter 25 Working for the EMSA 168
Chapter 26 Fast-tracked 175

Chapter 27 A routine salvage ... 180
Chapter 28 Wrong place, wrong time ... 189
Chapter 29 A combination of factors ... 195
Chapter 30 Gruelling routine ... 211
Chapter 31 Race against time ... 216
Chapter 32 On station ... 222
Chapter 33 Expert witnesses ... 225
Chapter 34 New lines of enquiry ... 229
Chapter 35 Mutual disclosure ... 233
Chapter 36 Kunz Laboratories ... 242
Chapter 37 Disturbing disclosures ... 245
Chapter 38 Last-minute evidence ... 248
Chapter 39 Final jigsaw pieces ... 259
Chapter 40 A fairy tale ... 270
Postscript ... 276
Future Reading ... 288

Chapter 1

Sexual assault

The night porter slowly returned to his seat behind the high reception desk. He was carrying a mug of steaming coffee. It was freshly made by the gleaming chrome machine in the breakfast room a few metres away. He touched the mug to his lips. 'Still too hot,' he said under his breath as he made himself comfortable. It was part of his evening ritual. He'd done all his jobs, only three clients were still to return to the hotel, and the midnight movie would start in a few minutes. He knew two guests, a middle-aged couple, were visiting friends on the other side of Manchester. He wasn't expecting them for at least another thirty minutes. He glanced again at the clock behind him and switched on the small TV that was hidden from guests. Just as the opening sequence of the film rolled across the screen, car headlights turned into the hotel entrance. He could tell from the shape of the yellow light on the roof that it was a local taxi. 'Shit, I'm going to miss the beginning,' he said to himself as he returned to the film and waited for the guests to arrive.

They were slow at getting out of the taxi, presumably paying or collecting luggage. Casually he glanced towards the bank of CCTV screens and the one covering the entrance. He could see a taxi driver and a woman struggling to support a man between them. It looked as though he was ill or drunk; probably drunk. He would make a note in the incident book in case there was a mess to clear up in the morning. There could be additional charges to pay.

The night porter got to his feet as the automatic doors opened and the trio staggered into reception. He recognised the taxi driver and nodded sympathetically to him; he was a regular. He turned his attention to the drunk – not a pretty sight. He looked Mediterranean, young and well dressed. His long, curly, dark hair was dishevelled and despite his olive skin he looked pale. He also had a pronounced five o'clock shadow.

'Gi' us a hand,' the taxi driver appealed as he wedged the drunk against the counter so that the woman could get money to pay the fare.

The night porter's hand hovered over the rack of keys. 'Which room is it?'

'Room 107, first floor, next to lift,' the woman replied in an accent he didn't recognise.

He glanced at the register. It said her name was Anna Kalnina from Latvia. He picked up the key and slipped around the counter to hold the drunk against it whilst the taxi driver collected his fare and turned to leave. The good news for the taxi driver was that his passenger hadn't been sick in the car, and he could get back to the rank quickly and be ready for the next fare.

The night porter knew the rules, he shouldn't leave reception unoccupied, but he had no choice. With one hand he grabbed the drunk's wrist and wrapped the arm over his shoulder and around his neck. He then grabbed his waistband with the other hand and balanced the weight. He lifted and dragged the drunk to the lift and wedged him against the wall until it arrived. Whilst he waited, he looked at the visitor from Latvia. There was no way she would have been able to manhandle this guy. She was at least twenty centimetres shorter and well over twenty kilograms lighter than her friend. She gave him a forced smile in gratitude. It was then that he really looked at her. She was pretty, trim and didn't need the heavy make-up and skimpy clothes to look attractive.

The drunk was heavy, and the night porter was grateful for the brief rest. When the lift door opened, he struggled to follow the woman into the lift and then to room 107. He let her open the door. In a final effort, he manhandled the drunk towards the bed and stood next to it. 'Can you start to take his coat off? Slip the sleeve off his shoulder whilst I hold him.'

She slipped her hand inside the jacket and wriggled it off his shoulder. It was awkward bending the man's arm, but she got it free. The night porter changed his grip from the drunk's wrist to the cuff of the jacket and pulled it off as he let him drop onto the bed. He heard a dull 'ping' and saw a small white button bounce off the bedside table and onto the floor. It looked as though he had lost other shirt buttons because only the one near his neck was still fastened.

The night porter knew what to do; he'd done it several times before. He pulled the drunk onto his side and into the recovery position. He wedged him in place with pillows, checked he was breathing and undid the last button on his open-necked shirt. He wouldn't choke on his own vomit or strangle himself. He went to the bathroom and returned with the waste bin and a towel.

'If he starts to be sick try to get him to use the bin. There's a plastic bag inside and it will save you money on cleaning the room,' he explained. 'If there's a problem, give me a ring on zero; I'll be in reception all night.'

As he returned to his seat behind the reception desk, a high-speed car chase was underway on the TV, but he had no idea who was chasing who. He resigned himself to trying to understand the plot as he watched the film. His coffee was cold.

He heard the screams above the sound from the TV. They were coming from the direction of the staircase to the upper floors and getting louder all the time. Automatically he got up from his chair, TV programme forgotten, and moved towards the sound. The woman in 107, the one he had helped with the drunk, emerged from the staircase and burst into reception screaming. She was waving her arms and running towards him.

He stood, rooted to the spot, as this near naked woman ran towards him screaming. Her small, pale, bare breasts bounced and quivered with each bound she made. His eyes were momentarily locked onto them before being drawn to the tuft of dark hair at the pit of her belly. The skimpy dress she had been wearing hours before was now billowing behind her and in shreds. One, maybe two seconds, and his lust was transformed into concern. There were vivid red scratches on her chest, breast and hip. Her long fair hair had been tidily combed when she arrived, but it was now a mess. Blood from her nose and lipstick were smeared around her mouth and tears were washing away the make-up around her eyes.

'Help me, help me,' she blurted with tears flowing down her face. 'He raped me.'

She almost knocked the night porter off his feet as she slammed into him, threw her arms around his shoulders and clung onto him. He could feel her whole body shaking as she sobbed. He held her tightly: 'You're OK, you're OK, you're fine, you're safe.'

He wasn't sure how long the tight embrace lasted, probably less than a minute, before he started to walk her out of the reception area and towards the rear office behind reception. At first, she was reluctant to let go of him, but he kept telling her she was OK and safe as he gradually guided her behind the counter and into the rear office. He helped her to a chair and knelt beside her. He gestured to move but she wouldn't let him go.

'Don't leave me!' she begged.

'I'm just getting you a coat, to keep you warm, I'm not leaving you. I also need to phone the police. I must make a report.'

She relaxed her grip on his arm and let him go. He picked up his raincoat from the stand and held it open and high as though shielding her from view. He could feel her arms slipping through the sleeves as she wrapped the old coat around her. As they made eye contact, he gave a forced smile, reached across the desk, lifted the phone from its cradle and dialled. When he recalled the events later, he was disgusted with himself. His first thoughts should have been for the welfare of his guest, but instead they were lustful; but he'd tried to make amends.

The few minutes they waited for the police felt like an age even though he knew they would arrive shortly. He recalled the annual health and safety course he had attended the previous month and could still remember the basic advice about comforting a possible rape victim; he was following it now.

'The police are on their way. They'll be here in minutes and will want to talk to you. Unless you are thirsty you shouldn't drink anything whilst we wait. You shouldn't try to clean yourself up – best if we just wait.'

'I'm OK. I feel much better now. Thank you for helping me. He went crazy...'

'Don't upset yourself. Let's wait for the police. They have specially trained officers. They will look after you and I will look after your room.'

Lights from the police patrol car shone through the office window.

'The police are here. I need to meet them. I'll leave the door open so you can see me at the reception desk,' he explained as he rose to meet the police.

Moments later, a burly policeman and an only slightly smaller policewoman strode into the hotel; they seemed to fill the foyer. Their yellow high-viz waistcoats, festooned with equipment and with bulging pockets, made them seem even bigger. The muscular and hairy arms of the policeman contrasted with the slender, pale skin of the policewoman. Before they could say anything, the night porter told them what they needed to know.

'The woman who has been attacked is in the back office. She's been injured. She's got a bloody nose and mouth, scratches on her chest and her dress is in tatters. I gave her my raincoat to keep her warm. She's in room 107, first floor. I helped her carry a drunken friend to her room about midnight. He couldn't stand. I thought he'd be in a drunken stupor 'til morning. I never thought he'd attack her. I'll be in reception if you need me.'

He knew from his training that the police would check on the physical health of the woman first, arrange for her to go to hospital and then make a statement. He'd make sure all the right entries were made in the incident book. It was the policeman who came out of the office first.

'An ambulance is on its way; should be here in a few minutes. I need to check out Room 107 and see if the suspect is still inside. What are the ways out of the hotel from the room?'

'Main staircase, lift and emergency exit at the end of the corridor; the emergency exit is alarmed. It's not been used.'

'Can you switch off the lift and do you have a passkey for the room?'

The night porter retrieved the passkey from a side drawer and gave it to the policeman. They walked to the lift and the porter disabled it. The only way out of the hotel was via the main staircase or emergency exit.

The door to Room 107 was wide open when they arrived. The suspect was slumped on a crumpled bed, close to the headboard. He looked pathetic. His trousers and underwear were caught around one of his ankles and his bare backside was exposed. The woman's shoes and ripped underwear littered the carpet.

'He's breathing and not about to make a run for it,' said the policeman. 'I'll radio for forensics to come and process him. If he's got skin cells under his fingernails and other DNA on him, I don't want to compromise the evidence. I'm going to stay here. You can go back to reception. Afraid this room is now a crime scene – it's sealed until further notice.'

It took over two hours for the forensic team to arrive; Friday nights in Manchester were always busy. The drunk was still unresponsive as the forensic team bagged his hands and put the woman's underwear and the bedding in evidence bags. With the deep red lipstick smeared across his lips, the drunk looked like a sad clown. When he sobered up it would be no laughing matter.

Chapter 2

Charged with assault and rape

Alessandro Calovarlo slumped in his chair in the interview room. His head was in his hands, his elbows on the table. With half open eyes he stared, unfocused, at the table-top before him. He looked worse than when he had arrived at the police station in central Manchester. His long, curly, black hair now looked lank and greasy. The five o'clock shadow looked more pronounced and there were distinct dark patches under his eyes.

He looked down at the disposable blue all-in-one suit he was wearing. He vaguely remembered being woken, undressed, and being annoyed at seeing his clothes rumpled and creased as they were forced into plastic bags. Although still confused, he knew he was in a police station. He felt grubby and could smell the sweat from his body. There was a sound at the door and he slowly turned his head towards it. The police officer who had brought him into the room was still standing by the door, back against the wall, with his hands clasped behind him. Two people came into the room: a man and a woman in normal clothes, not uniform. The woman put a folder on the desk in front of Sandro and they both sat down.

Sandro looked up and made eye contact with the woman. His first impression was that she looked young, but the wrinkles around her eyes suggested she was in her late twenties or early thirties. She smiled and switched on the electronic equipment fixed to the tabletop. It bleeped and lights flashed before she started speaking. It took a few moments for Sandro to realise what she was saying as she began to recite the classic police caution. He'd heard it dozens of times on TV and in films but never when it was directed at him. Before she had come into the interview room, he had felt queasy. He now felt as though he was about to be sick and struggled to control the urge. She had finished reciting the police caution and opened the folder in front of her.

'Could you please tell me your full name, age, address and nationality?'

A note in the file indicated the arresting officer had failed to record this information because the suspect was barely conscious when he was brought in. She noted that Alessandro Marcus Calovarlo was an Italian national, living in an upmarket apartment block in Manchester. A practised eye, coupled with a prior inspection of his clothes and personal possessions, told her that this suspect wasn't the usual Friday night rabble rouser. His clothes and shoes were expensive. The heavy, multi-functional watch also looked expensive. He was well-groomed with non-calloused hands and clean fingernails; these observations set him apart. 'What was he doing in a seedy nightclub, picking up a tourist and raping her?' she asked herself. The next few hours and days would answer that.

'Mr Calovarlo, I'm Detective Inspector Coleen Latchem and this is Detective Sergeant Alan Herman. You are currently in the Greater Manchester Police city centre station, being held on charges of assault and rape...'

'I didn't do anything,' Calovarlo interrupted.

'Mr Calovarlo, may I call you Alessandro?' Inspector Latchem asked in a respectful tone that was almost motherly.

Coleen Latchem was the youngest detective inspector in the Greater Manchester Police Force. Her colleagues predicted she would be the youngest chief inspector in a few years' time – unless she burnt out. She had the heaviest case load in the station, inherited the most difficult cases, yet had a high clear-up rate. Coleen was ambitious and aware it wasn't always the most dedicated and successful officers who were promoted. It helped to have friends, rather than enemies in high places; she had both.

Detective Inspector, DI, Latchem had a disarming personality. She acted and sounded like your friend, sister or mother – depending on the circumstances. Calovarlo responded as she had hoped.

'Please, call me Sandro.'

DI Latchem and her team had spent the last few hours urgently collecting witness statements, reviewing CCTV footage and arranging for the forensic analysis of numerous samples taken from Calovarlo and the victim. The preliminary evidence was so strong she could afford to have her concerns for the suspect on record. If, and when, the case came to trial, the prosecuting council could confirm that everything had been done to protect both victim and suspect.

'Sandro, I must tell you that you could be in serious trouble, very serious trouble. I need your help in finding out what happened last night and in the early hours of this morning. I also need to ensure your rights are protected whilst you are interviewed.

'The charges are so serious you may wish to get advice from a legal representative. You can ask your own representative to be present or you can ask the duty solicitor for advice before and during any interview. You may, of course, decide to answer my questions without a legal representative being present. It's your choice. What would you like to do?'

The fuzz of confusion was clearing rapidly, and he no longer felt sick, just unwell. Sandro quickly reviewed his options and decided he wouldn't call the lawyers his company used. It wasn't that he didn't respect their ability – he was simply embarrassed by the thought that anyone would regard him as a rape suspect. He asked to speak to the duty solicitor. DI Latchem gave Sandro a friendly smile and said: 'I think that's a wise decision. I asked the duty solicitor to be available in case you wanted to speak to him. I'll fetch him now.'

Sandro lost track of the time between the policewoman leaving the interview room and a smartly dressed young man walking in. He introduced himself as David Moxon, a solicitor who was working *pro bono;* there would be no charge for his advice. He also informed Sandro of the information the police had shared with him.

'Look,' said David Moxon, 'I'm really a commercial lawyer not a criminal lawyer. I'm doing this *pro bono* work to get more experience. I've never defended a rape allegation in court, but I know people who have. My father is Robert Moxon KC. He's a barrister specialising in criminal law, head of Albert Chambers in Manchester and has a team of experienced lawyers better able than me to represent you.

'From what DI Latchem has shown me, they feel they have a strong case, a very strong case, against you. Quite honestly, the best advice I can give you is to say nothing to the police until a more experienced criminal lawyer has reviewed the evidence against you and given you detailed advice. My advice is to request a specialist lawyer and to say nothing, nothing at all. To all questions just say, "no comment".'

'But I didn't do anything!' said Sandro – almost shouting.

'They believe they have evidence that you did. It's going to take a few days, but we can begin to assemble a case to refute the allegations and apply for bail.'

'I can't stay here!' The realisation was clear in his voice. 'I have to get to the office on Monday, I've got things to do, Jack will be wondering where I am.'

'I can speak to your friend, Jack. I can put you in touch with other lawyers, I... they, can apply for bail... but it's going to take time. I'm afraid for the next few hours, or even days, you will remain here.'

David Moxon shuffled the thin sheaf of papers in his hand.

'Do you want to speak to your own lawyer, or do you want me to contact Albert Chambers? You can change your mind at any time. I'm just keen that you get the best advice available and as quickly as possible.'

The full reality of what was happening eventually dawned on Sandro. His shoulders slumped and his entire body seemed to collapse. He stayed motionless for a moment before sitting upright. He was back in a semblance of control.

'Would you call my business partner, Jack Collier, and tell him where I am and what is happening? I'll give you his number. Could you also call your father and ask if he can arrange for someone to represent me and arrange bail? ... What happens next?'

'I'll do what you ask. As to what happens next – the police will want to interview you as soon as possible. You can agree to do that now or wait until we arrange for a specialist criminal lawyer to advise you. If you do agree to speak with them, I'll prompt you when you should say "no comment". If you do speak to them now, most of what you say will be "no comment".'

'Let's speak to them now and tell them someone else will be advising me.'

It was almost an hour before DI Latchem and her colleague joined them in the interview room. David Moxon explained that his client was happy to answer questions but reserved the right not to incriminate himself and may answer 'no comment' to certain questions. It was also likely that his client would be represented by a lawyer from Albert Chambers, Manchester. Coleen Latchem smiled at them both and thanked them. After a few frantic hours, she was now in no rush. The evidence from witnesses and statements from the night porter and the victim were compelling. It looked like this was going to be a straightforward case; another one to add to her clear-up record. Tomorrow she would have toxicology reports and initial results from the DNA samples collected. From her enquiries she had discovered that Sandro Calovarlo had no criminal record and was part of a successful multi-million-pound business based in Salford. A few more hours, or even days, in a police cell was likely to make him more cooperative. She opened the folder in front of her and looked Sandro in the face.

'Can I tell you what we have discovered so far and the actions we are taking?'

She didn't wait for an acknowledgment. It was merely a ploy to demonstrate that she held the initiative, she would maintain control.

'You are charged with the assault and rape of Latvian tourist Anna Kalnina.'

'I didn't do anything,' Sandro blurted.

DI Latchem glanced at the duty solicitor before replying. 'Please, Sandro, let me do my job. Let me tell you what we've discovered and what we are doing, and then you will have every opportunity to respond.'

She appeared to pause to control herself before she continued; she was in full control. 'We have several witnesses from the Mojito Nightclub who say you were talking, dancing and drinking...'

'I don't drink! I'm a professional diver. I was drinking soda water all night,' Sandro blurted out.

David Moxon leaned across and whispered in Sandro's ear.

'*Scusami,* I'm sorry,' said Sandro – reverting to Italian. 'This is... a nightmare. I can't believe what's happening. I'll be quiet... I'm sorry.'

'Sandro, I completely understand how distressing this must be to you. Let me outline what we know, and we can start to discover what happened,' Coleen said with a sympathetic smile and in a reassuring tone. She was working hard to win his trust.

'As I was saying, we have witnesses who place you in the company of Anna Kalnina, talking, dancing and drinking. In a statement, a security guard at the Mojito says you appear to have collapsed on the dance floor just before midnight and needed help to return to your table. In his opinion, you were drunk. He and a colleague had to carry you from the nightclub to a waiting taxi. The taxi took you and Anna Kalnina to the Wayside Hotel; the departure time from the Mojito was 11.42 p.m.

'The taxi driver says that you were uncommunicative and unable to stand; he carried you into the Wayside Hotel. The night porter carried you to the room of Anna Kalnina. He says that because you appeared so drunk, he placed you in the recovery position on the bed in room 107 and wedged you with pillows. He also put a waste bin by the bed in case you were sick. He believes the time was approximately 12.10 a.m. At this time, he reports that Anna Kalnina was concerned about you but otherwise looked normal. She was fully clothed and hair combed.'

DI Latchem paused as she turned a page in the folder and then continued. 'In his statement, the night porter states that at approximately 02.00 a.m. he heard screams coming from the stairwell leading to the upper floors. As he went to investigate, Anna Kalnina burst from the foot of the stairs, screaming, in clear distress and almost naked.

'Her dress had been almost ripped off. Her underclothes had been torn off. These were recovered from the floor of room 107. She had sustained deep scratches to her chest, left breast and hip. She was bleeding from the mouth and nose.'

DI Latchem paused again to let the full impact of what she was saying sink in. She moved to the final statements.

'Thank you for supplying samples of your DNA and blood as well as other samples from your hands. The arresting officer says you were unable to complete a breath test upon arrival at the police station. However, from the blood tests this morning, the toxicology report will show if there are any drugs or alcohol in your bloodstream. The police forensic team and police doctor have taken similar samples from Anna Kalnina.'

DI Latchem paused again so her next comment would have maximum impact.

'We are currently comparing the samples taken from beneath your fingernails to the skin cells on Anna's body. We are also comparing the samples taken from your hands and body to those taken from Anna's body and her clothes. Shortly we will have scientific evidence to confirm or refute her account.

'I must tell you that if the cells beneath your fingernails match those of Anna Kalnina, and samples of semen taken from Anna's body match your DNA, the case against you mounts considerably. You could be facing ten to fifteen years in prison. Do you have anything to say?'

David Moxon placed a hand on Sandro's arm. 'My client would prefer not to respond at this time. He is seeking legal advice from lawyers at Albert Chambers in Manchester and would prefer to respond to all you have said after he has spoken to his new legal representative.'

With no emotion in her voice, DI Latchem brought the interview to a conclusion. 'Fine, you will be held in custody here for the immediate future. We will interview you in the presence of your legal adviser and then transfer you to another facility or you will be freed on bail. Do you understand?'

Sandro mumbled that he understood. As DI Latchem left the interview room David Moxon turned to Sandro. 'I'm going to go and see my father and get things moving. I'll be as quick as I can.'

Sandro was escorted down corridors, through doors, until he arrived at a high counter; a police sergeant, without a jacket, was standing behind it. He heard the words being spoken but made no attempt to understand them. His mind was still in a whirl. A tug on his arm jolted him back to the present before he was led along a plain corridor to a small cell. The person holding his arm gave him a firm steer that directed him into the cell. A moment later the door clanged shut. He tottered to the stainless-steel toilet that was bolted to the wall, fell to his knees and was violently sick. It seemed the last vestiges of his former self were emptied into the bowl.

Chapter 3

The case unfolds

Jack Collier, Sandro's business partner, was escorted to the meeting room by a police officer. They stopped outside the door and the officer issued a warning. 'Remember, no contact, do not attempt to give the suspect anything – anything at all. Do not attempt to accept anything from him. Your meeting is being recorded on video. Do you understand?'

Jack nodded and said he understood before the door was opened and they entered. Sandro was sitting at one of six plain plastic-topped tables. Jack was visibly shocked to see his appearance. Sandro was always vibrant, with bright flashing eyes and a warm smile on his face. He had lost that vibrancy. His eyes were bloodshot, there was no warm smile and he looked despondent. The disposable all-in-one suit had transformed him into a non-person. Even after shaving, Sandro still had a five o'clock shadow, which now looked like the start of a beard. His rich olive complexion looked sallow. He had dark rings under his eyes and his normal long, black, curly hair looked greasy. Sandro looked up and muttered, *'Sono disperatamente dispiaciuto'*. Jack wasn't sure what he'd said but could interpret the sentiment.

'Sorry to drag you here – but thanks for coming.' Sandro's voice was deadpan and lifeless; it mirrored his posture.

'No problem. How yer doing buddy?'

Jack and Sandro were the same age, similar height, weight and build, both divers and joint owners of the *Marine Salvage &*

Investigation Company. That is where the similarity ended. Where Sandro was flamboyant and gregarious, Jack was conservative and reserved. They looked and acted like opposites. Sandro would stand out in a crowd – Jack would blend into it. Today their personalities seemed reversed.

'Not well. I just need to… understand what's happening and how to end this nightmare.'

'OK, let me tell you what I've done – you can decide what you want to change. As soon as David Moxon contacted me, I phoned our company lawyers. Bill Watts told me that McKnight, Lewis and Watts don't take on criminal cases, but he had a high regard for Robert Moxon and his team at Albert Chambers. He said they have an outstanding reputation in Manchester. He phoned me on my way here and told me one of their top lawyers, a woman called Roberta Fox, will be representing you. It seems she and her team are reviewing all the preliminary evidence against you and are arranging an application for bail. They are confident that bail will be granted. You're innocent until proven guilty,' Jack stressed. 'However, the court may want a sum of money or security to ensure you do not abscond.'

Jack paused for a moment because he felt he was talking like a lawyer rather than a friend. 'We can meet any bail conditions. We just need to get you out of here and everything sorted.'

'Police say I beat up and raped a woman, a woman I met last night… I wouldn't do that. You know I wouldn't do that.' The appeal was clear in his tone. 'I felt strange at the nightclub but can't remember anything until later when they took samples and tried to interview me… All I remember are sounds and sights… it's all confusing. I… vaguely remember being put into this suit!'

Jack nodded his head sympathetically before replying. 'Moxon said he expected the lawyer to come and see you sometime today. I doubt anything is going to happen until then. Is there anything you want me to do?'

Suddenly Sandro was more concerned about work issues than his own predicament. 'What's going to happen about the inspection of the MV *Asenka,* the wreck? We were due to fly to Aberdeen… then to Esbjerg to complete the inspection. They may not let me leave the country!'

'Don't worry about it. If you can't make it for any reason, I can arrange for others to help me. It's not a problem,' Jack replied.

They chatted for another ten to fifteen minutes – switching between the charges Sandro was facing and the salvage contract that their company had secured. Just when Jack was wondering whether to stay or go a policewoman entered the meeting room. She looked down at the note in her hand. 'A Ms Roberta Fox from Albert Chambers is here to meet with Alessandro Calovarlo. I can ask her to wait or come back...'

Jack started to get up from his seat and spoke to Sandro. 'It's important that you speak to her. I'll check with her office and arrange when I can see you again. I'll also check with the people here. Hopefully I'll see you tonight… or… sometime…'

Sandro's head dropped and they lost eye contact as silence followed the last stumbling words Jack had uttered. It had been the wrong thing to say. He now desperately tried to think of something positive to say as the policewoman moved to escort Sandro from the meeting room. 'Oh, by the way, Penny is coming this weekend. Shall I book us a table at the Mughal Palace?'

Sandro didn't respond as he was ushered out of the room, then along corridors and back to the interview room he had been in earlier. He sat on one of the chairs around a nondescript table and waited. As he looked down, he noticed the table was bolted to the floor.

As Jack retraced his steps, a forced smile was replaced by a grimace. Just when the company's fortunes were changing for the better, the life of Sandro was changing for the worse. When Jack thought of Penny he also wondered if his own life may change for the worse soon. There was an awkwardness in her voice the last time they spoke.

The door into the interview room was opened and three people walked in. Sandro recognised David Moxon immediately, but it was clear who was the most senior of the group. Roberta Fox was small and slight but exuded a presence. Short dark hair framed her thin, pale face. The dark trouser suit and simple high-necked white shirt completed Sandro's image of a barrister. At a distance it looked as though she wasn't wearing make-up but when she held out her hand and introduced herself, he noticed it was light and barely visible. Her voice was certainly not light and delicate; it was loud, confident and suggested 'no nonsense'. She seemed to dominate the room to such an extent that it took Sandro some time to even acknowledge her colleague. She introduced him as Daniel Fowler, her paralegal. He looked significantly older but in the same dark suit and white shirt uniform. He smiled weakly, put a large case next to his chair and waited for Roberta Fox to sit down. Without turning to look at him she merely held out her hand and waited until he placed a thin file into it.

'Mr Calovarlo, how would you like me to address you?'

'Call me Sandro.'

'Sandro, I will be leading your defence team. My paralegal will be providing administrative support; Mr David Moxon will be merely an observer.'

In seconds she had made the pecking order in the room clear. Daniel Fowler continued to look subservient whilst David Moxon gave a weak, self-conscious smile.

'Detective Inspector Latchem has made an initial disclosure, er, she has given me copies of all the preliminary evidence associated with the charges against you. It is likely that other evidence will be collected over time, and this will be shared with me in due course. You have stated, under caution, that you did not assault or rape Ms Anna Kalnina. If this case comes to trial, can we assume you will be pleading not guilty?'

'I didn't do anything,' Sandro replied in frustration. 'I don't remember anything.'

'I've reviewed the witness statements and police reports against you. We will be seeking other witnesses who may offer different evidence. We will also be conducting a background check on Ms Anna Kalnina in Latvia and her movements whilst in the country.'

Roberta Fox turned over pages in the file and renewed eye contact with Sandro. 'DI Latchem tells me that toxicology and drug screening reports are now available. She wishes to interview you, under caution, at the end of this meeting...'

Sandro interrupted and leaned across the table. 'I didn't drink any alcohol last night! I'm a professional diver, I don't drink. It was hot in the nightclub, but I was only drinking soda water.'

'Sandro, I'm merely alerting you to what evidence is being collected. The results from these tests may be presented in court. There are at least four witness statements that say you appeared drunk, unable to stand and communicate.'

Roberta Fox questioned Sandro about the hours prior to his visit to Mojito Nightclub, his meeting with Anna Kalnina and the subsequent events. Her paralegal, Daniel Fowler, took copious notes; David Moxon didn't make many. Just when Sandro was getting frustrated at the repeated questions, Roberta stopped.

'I think we are ready to meet with Detective Inspector Latchem and hear what she has to say. Remember, unless I nod to indicate you can answer her questions, merely say, "no comment".'

DI Latchem and her colleague entered the interview room. There were no handshakes, merely professional acknowledgment as they seated themselves around the table. DI Latchem switched on a tape recorder, told Sandro he was still under caution, and opened the folder in front of her.

'Sandro, we have the initial DNA analyses and toxicology reports,' she said with a sad tone in her voice. 'The human tissue removed from under your fingernails matches the DNA of Anna Kalnina. It appears you scratched her chest, breast and hip when you raped her...'

'I didn't rape her. I didn't do anything!' Sandro shouted as he started to rise from his chair.

'Sandro, please sit down, sit down,' Coleen Latchem said firmly. 'You will have plenty of time to reply to these accusations. Your DNA was detected on the dress and underwear of Anna Kalnina. Your DNA and semen were also detected on and inside her body.'

'This is a set-up. I didn't do anything,' Sandro answered in frustration.

'I can assure you this is not a set-up. If you have any evidence to suggest it is, please tell me now...'

DI Latchem folded her hands and sat back in her chair, wating for Sandro to comment. When he looked down and shook his head, the Detective Inspector continued: 'Apart from admitting, and I quote, "I don't remember anything," do you have any reason to believe Ms Anna Kalnina, who you only met on Friday night, wishes you harm?'

There was silence in the room as Sandro continued to look down, shaking his head as he began to understand the significance of the findings.

'A blood alcohol concentration of 0.215 was recorded in samples of your blood. At this level, men of your age and weight would be so drunk they would be unable to walk unassisted.'

DI Latchem returned to the file in front of her and removed a large photograph. With exaggerated care she placed the photograph on the tabletop, directly in front of Sandro. It was a full-face photograph of Anna Kalnina. She looked as though she had been in a fight – and lost. There was dried blood around her nose and mouth. The dark colour of the blood contrasted with the bright lipstick that was smeared over her face and mixed with the blood. It looked as though her lip had been cut and was swollen. The photograph captured the trails of mascara and tears that had run down her face. There was the hint of bruising on her cheek. However, the most striking part of the photograph was her eyes; she looked terrified.

'This photograph was taken of Anna Kalnina on her arrival at the Greater Manchester Police station. This is the photograph the jury will see at your trial for the assault and rape of Anna Kalnina. What happened Sandro? Did she signal "yes" and then say "no". Was it a combination of drink and frustration? I must tell you, the case against you looks overwhelming. You need to talk to me. You need to tell me your side of the story.'

Coleen employed a tone that suggested to do so would make his problems disappear. She had successfully exploded the bomb over Sandro. Over the next couple of hours, she engaged in the painstaking process of taking him through every aspect of the evidence against him and invited his comments. To many of the questions, Roberta Fox shook her head and Sandro answered "no comment".

Detective Inspector Latchem was drawing the first formal interview to an end. She had closed the file and was about to stand when she appeared to remember something. She hadn't forgotten, it was merely a ploy to get the suspect to relax before she dropped the final bombshells. 'Sandro, are you a diabetic? Do you have any medical problems for which you are receiving treatment? Are you taking any medication?'

Roberta Fox knew the police could obtain this information and to attempt to hide it could compromise her client; she was about to signal to Sandro to answer when Latchem added another question: 'Are you an alcoholic Sandro?'

Sandro's reaction was quick. He leaned forward in his chair and almost shouted at Coleen Latchem. 'I don't take drugs. I'm not taking any medication. I have six-monthly medicals and an annual one for my diving insurance… Check with my doctor – he'll tell you I'm fit. I don't need alcohol to perform – either underwater or in the bedroom.'

Detective Inspector Latchem was pleased with the outburst. She would check, of course, but she had wanted to jolt and unsettle him. She had succeeded. 'I ask because the blood tests revealed an abnormal spike of aldehydes and ketones in your blood. Aldehydes are produced when alcohol is broken down in the liver. However, the levels are abnormally high. They are consistent with the levels in alcoholics. I've asked for further tests to explore the spike in ketones. I trust you are willing to provide further blood samples.'

Having dropped her bombs, she was happy to end the interview and return to collecting more evidence.

Sandro's head was reeling from the barrage of questions and their implications. He heard Roberta Fox saying something but couldn't focus on what it was. Daniel Fowler simply followed in Fox's wake. At least David Moxon gave him a reassuring pat on the shoulder and whispered. 'Try not to worry – she's good.'

Sandro wasn't the only worried person. David Moxon was desperately trying to remain calm and act like an interested observer. However, coming face to face with Alessandro Calovarlo, and seeing another phase of his plan underway, was unnerving.

Months earlier, before the lawyer had even heard of Alessandro Calovarlo, he and his property development business partner had received an email from Baltic Marine Services. It was buried amongst a dozen others. At the time, David had regarded it as a low priority, and it was early afternoon by the time he got to it. The message was short and precise. The ship carrying their cargo of plastic beads and machinery towards Riga, Latvia, had foundered in the North Sea. Forms to initiate an insurance claim were attached and they would welcome early completion. He read that the underwriters were arranging for the wreck to be inspected as part of a possible salvage operation. If a decision was made to salvage part of the cargo, owners would be given the option to purchase these goods.

David Moxon had been stunned by the message but recovered quickly and began to consider the implications. As he thought through them, he became more and more agitated. If their cargo was lost, they had a valid insurance claim; they wouldn't lose out financially – but this would be the least of his worries. Did the ship break up during the sinking or when it landed on the seabed? Was their cargo damaged in the sinking? Was their cargo leaking into the sea? The authorities would be checking for leaking fuel oil, and other contaminants from the ship and its cargo. As a commercial lawyer he knew they would be sampling the seawater around the ship.

If they decided not to salvage any of the cargo, perhaps the ship would remain intact for decades. Perhaps long enough for him to be dead and buried before any of their cargo was detected and traced back to them. What if the underwriters decided to salvage parts of the cargo? Part of their merchandise was packed in cardboard drums. Weeks, perhaps months, in the water and they would collapse. What if the drums collapsed or were ruptured during a salvage attempt? It would be a disaster.

David and his business partner, Tony Levens, had pooled the information they had gathered. David had summarised it. They had discovered that a Danish marine agency had sampled the water around the wreck and reported there were no current contaminants. David explained that EU directives required recent wrecks to be checked for leaking fuel oil, chemicals leeching out of cargo and so on. The authorities were not concerned about any of the cargo but were considering trying to pump out any remaining fuel oil inside the ship.

David also explained how another Danish company had conducted a sonar sweep over the wreck. They had constructed a digital image of the wreck. It was going to be used to assess the amount of damage and inform possible salvage. They would know in weeks if there would be an attempt at salvage. Both were aware that this was when their problems would start.

Chapter 4

MV *Asenka*

Jack was in the office early as he had a lot to do. He had spent the weekend liaising with Bill Watts, senior partner of McKnight, Lewis and Watts, their company lawyers. Last night Bill had confirmed that he had assembled all the financial documents Roberta Fox needed to support the request for bail. He was confident that bail would be granted this morning and Sandro should be released from custody. Between talking to Bill Watts, Jack had waded through all the outstanding emails and paperwork. Normally Jack and Sandro would share the day-to-day office jobs and talk through any decisions that needed to be made. However, Jack had already decided he would take responsibility for everything until Sandro was able to contribute. He guessed Sandro would be preoccupied with the charges against him and unable to focus on day-to-day office work.

Jack logged on to the company email and immediately abandoned his long-held practice of working through his emails in order. He scanned the long list of new messages in case there was one from Moxon & Associates, Bill Watts or anyone connected with the case; there wasn't. He had spotted an email from Baltic Marine Services and guessed this was about their salvage of cargo from the *Asenka*. He decided not to open it but to return to his previous habit of working through the emails methodically. Over the next two hours, Jack went through them all, annotating and adding action notes. He'd go through them all with Lesley, the company secretary, and at some time in the future he'd bring Sandro up to date with his actions. Eventually he got to the Baltic Marine Services email. It informed the *Marine Salvage & Investigation Company* that two additional items of cargo on board the MV *Asenka* had been promoted to *priority salvage items*. It seemed the owners of the cargo were prepared to revise their insurance claim if the items were salvaged. The news was not what Jack wanted to hear.

A few weeks ago, he would have been delighted. It would be more work and a bigger fee. The job was their first successful tender since the one committing their search and recovery ship, the *Stavanger,* to a year in the Gulf of Mexico. However, today it seemed like an unwanted distraction – especially considering the related timescale. Several months ago, he and Sandro had received an email from Carib Oil, the oil production consortium that was employing the *Stavanger* as a standby vessel to three of their oil rigs. It wasn't a lucrative contract, far from it, but the ship and crew were working, not rocking at anchor in a backwater. It had been a last-resort, rock-bottom bid to keep the ship working. If it had been a last resort for Jack and Sandro, it had been a triumph for Carib Oil. The presence of a ship like the *Stavanger* in the Gulf of Mexico massively increased their profile. Impressive photographs of the *Stavanger* in the industry press, coupled with extravagant announcements from Carib Oil, represented great publicity that they didn't have to pay for. It had generated lots of interest in the company.

The email from Carib Oil told them of a major change of rig support policy. They had undertaken a risk assessment of their oil production and concluded that they did not require a standby vessel as sophisticated, and expensive, as the MV *Stavanger.* Whilst they greatly appreciated the reassurance and support the *Stavanger* provided, the current standby contract would not be renewed. However, the *Marine Salvage & Investigation Company* were invited to bid for the new tender. A note said their tender 'would be looked upon favourably'. Jack and Sandro had looked through the documentation and concluded that Carib Oil were severely downgrading their rig protection – big mistake, but their decision. If they assembled a tender they would be competing with much smaller vessels, with greatly inferior specifications, and which could be offered at a fraction of their cost. They simply couldn't compete and would need to find new work for the ship at the end of the contract and after salvaging cargo from the *Asenka*. Jack was also resigned to doing it on his own and felt a sudden flare of irritation and resentment. 'Why couldn't he keep his trousers on?' Jack asked himself and then immediately dismissed the thought. Although he didn't know the details of the charges against Sandro, he was sure he wouldn't have done anything unwanted.

Some hours later, Sandro self-consciously climbed the stairs of Whitworth Mansions in Salford. The recently renovated Victorian building contained the company offices and he needed to head to the second floor. He was certain that the two people he met on the stairs looked at him differently – as though the whole world knew he was charged with assault and rape. Roberta Fox had arranged bail and he had signed one document after another. He knew he should have read each one in detail but was so keen to get out of the police station he would have signed anything. With his head bowed he made his way quickly to the office and was relieved when he found sanctuary. At least Lesley greeted him with a broad, genuine smile and friendly welcome.

'Good to see you… I believe in you,' was all she said.

'Thanks, it's appreciated… And I like the new hair style – *è bella*,' he said with a smile. 'It suits you. Is Jack in?'

Nothing about Lesley was conventional as the short and brilliantly blue hairstyle illustrated.

'Yes, I think he's waiting for you and planning to go over the inspection of the *Asenka*.'

Sandro turned and moved towards Jack's office, tapped on the door and walked in. In the last forty-eight hours Sandro's life had been turned upside down. He still felt the weight of the allegations hanging over him – and it showed. He had lost that sparkle, that bounce in his step, glint in his eyes and smile on his lips. His clothes still gave the impression of flamboyance and confidence, but his body language shouted the opposite. The dark rings under his eyes suggested he wasn't well. He flopped into a chair and took a deep breath before continuing.

'Thanks again for agreeing to put up company assets for my bail,' Sandro stammered.

He was still acutely embarrassed at the thought of being charged with assault and rape. 'Roberta Fox says it provides strong support for my plea of not guilty.'

'No problem. If there's anything else I can do, just say. If you need to spend more time with Ms Fox, there's no problem. We all want this business sorted – but realise it may take months rather than days or weeks...'

Sandro interrupted: 'I've done all I can. I'm leaving Roberta and her team to get on with the case and have agreed to meet her on Friday. She's going to check on the woman who accused me... It must be a set-up... but I can't think how. There's going to be a regular, weekly progress report. We've also agreed that I should carry on as normal – so let's get back to the *Asenka.* I'll feel better once I'm working.'

It was a relief for both of them.

The successful tender to salvage cargo from the MV *Asenka* would be the first time their state-of-the-art search and recovery ship, the MV *Stavanger*, would be deployed in European waters. They had bought the ship for a knockdown price at auction. What Jack and Sandro hadn't known at the time was that the main salvage companies in Europe had secretly colluded not to bid for the ship. This had depressed the selling price at auction, ruined the ship's original owners and removed a leading competitor from the market. Ownership of the MV *Stavanger*, of course, elevated the *Marine Salvage & Investigation Company* to the status of a major competitor within the industry. However, the other major players didn't expect this to last long.

Their solution to the challenge of the newcomer had been easy. Continue the collusion and slowly destroy Jack and Sandro's company. With their informants within the industry, the major players could simply submit more competitive bids for every tender Jack and Sandro made and rotate the loss-making tenders between them, sharing the financial burden and slowly bleeding the newcomer dry. A bonus would be that one of them would eventually buy the *Stavanger* at the resultant bankruptcy sale.

The strategy had nearly worked but they now had encouraging news. A contact had informed them that unofficial government discussions, coupled with reduced profits due to cut-price tendering, had resulted in the industry-wide collusion against them being abandoned. Their successful tender to salvage the *Asenka* could mark a change for the better. All they had to do now was complete the salvage.

On the Monday morning after Sandro's arrest, Jack had completed his inspection of the plans of the *Asenka*, and read the ship's log for the last three years, the last three surveyor's reports and the account of the sinking. He had summarised it all in a series of bullet points on sheets of paper.

'OK, let me give you a summary of what we know about the ship,' said Jack as he leaned over the pile of papers on his desk and began.

'The MV *Asenka* was a mixed cargo freighter and typical of thousands of seagoing workhorses around the world. Built in 1979 by the Liejaja Shipyard in Riga, Latvia, the ship was 3232 deadweight tonnes, eighty-seven metres long, had a beam of thirteen metres and a draft of five metres. Three holds – for'ard, mid-ships and aft, separated by fixed bulkheads. Three derricks mounted above these dividing bulkheads. After over forty years of hard work, the *Asenka* was reaching the end of her working life.

'She had an experienced Filipino captain and a crew of twelve. The notes in the file said the *Asenka* had an ice class rating of ID. It's the lowest rating and would mean the northern Baltic Sea ports would be closed to the ship in winter. However, it seems this didn't stop the owners trying to access these ports during the winter as we'll see in a moment.'

Jack looked up from his notes. 'It seems for the first 29 years of her life she operated solely in the Baltic Sea, shuttling goods between all the main ports. However, increasing maintenance costs and containerisation resulted in the sale of the ship in 2008 to a Lithuanian company. The company operated in northern Europe – Germany, The Netherlands, Belgium, France and Spain. The waters were ice free, even in winter, but grim winter weather in the Bay of Biscay and North Sea would be challenging.

'The log records that prior to the sinking there were three reported groundings. Each one occurred when the ship attempted to force its way through thick ice and became stranded on top of it. Each time the ship had to be towed off. Whilst damage was recorded as "superficial" we both know the groundings would create stresses within the ship's structure. It's interesting that there are no entries about being stranded on top of the ice – and getting off unaided. My guess is that the ship suffered multiple groundings.

'The last inspection reported high levels of water in the bilges. The pumps were keeping pace with it, but the conclusion was that it was seeping through dozens of cracked welds and buckled hull plates. As a precaution, the ship was also carrying two auxiliary pumps – should they be needed. There was also a recommendation to ensure loads were correctly distributed across the holds. I phoned the inspector...'

Jack looked down again at his notes until he found the name. '...Inspector Otto Weller believes the cracked welds and buckled plates were probably a result of the groundings but made worse by continual haphazard loading that failed to distribute the weight of the cargo across the holds. He told me that the company typically accepted last-minute cargo. He also suspected it was placed where there was space – irrespective of weight distribution!

'The captain was interviewed after the sinking and mentioned all of this to the investigators. He also told them that the last trip had been in poor weather through the Bay of Biscay and the English Channel. Here's a transcript of the account he gave to the investigators of events leading up to and including the sinking. You can visualise what happened.'

Sandro started reading.

Investigators: 'Captain Cabrera, thank you for agreeing to talk to us about the sinking of the MV Asenka. We would be grateful if you could answer the following questions in as much detail as possible…'

Captain Cabrera: 'I want to help.'

Investigators: 'Captain, what was the position of the MV Asenka when you first noticed a problem with the ship?'

Captain Cabrera: 'We were on the last leg of the trip to Riga via our home port of Klaipeda in Lithuania. Our position is marked on the chart as you can see. (*Background noise and unintelligible)…* you've got a copy. We were here… about 110 nautical miles north of Wilhelmshaven and about forty-five nautical miles due west of the Danish coast.'

Investigators: 'What first alerted you to a potential problem with the ship?'

Captain Cabrera: 'I'd woken up just before the alarm clock was due to ring for my watch. After over thirty years at sea, and thousands of watches, I was always awake in time for my watch. As soon as I got out of my bunk, I felt it. The motion of the ship had changed. It wasn't the normal roll and twist through the swell. It was a sluggish motion, with a split-second delay before the ship recovered…

'I could sense something was wrong and didn't even bother to shower. I pulled on my clothes and made my way to the bridge. I remember the navigation officer greeting me but I was concentrating on calling up the electronic log… he said nothing about the motion of the ship.

'I scanned the log entries but there was no mention of a change in motion. I spoke to the helmsman, Edwardo, and asked if he'd noticed any change in the motion of the ship. He gave me a confused reply – it was obvious he hadn't noticed any change. By this time the navigation officer had joined us. I asked him if he'd noticed any change in the motion, but he said he hadn't.'

Investigators: 'What did you do then?'

Captain Cabrera: 'I told them I was going on deck and for'ard. The weather was fair but there was a heavy swell as I made my way down the stairwell and onto the deck. I walked to about mid-ships and leaned over the side. I had already sensed it before I heard it. The ship was sluggish and nose heavy. I couldn't understand how the helmsman and the navigation officer had failed to notice it.

'I could see the pumps were pouring streams of dirty brown water into the sea; I listened. I could cut out the engine vibration, the flapping of stays and lines as well as the rattles and groans of the old ship. There was the unmistakable regular, high-pitched squeak and dull grind of metal on metal as the ship rolled and twisted. I knew the hull plate welds were failing and we were taking on water. I didn't need to see it; I could feel it. I pushed off the rail and made my way across the deck to the other side of the ship. The starboard side pumps were working, and I could hear the same high-pitched squeaks and dull groans.

'I ran back to my cabin, quickly changed into my boiler suit, and ran back to the bridge. I'm not as young and fit as…'

Investigators: 'Why did you return to your cabin and change before you returned to the bridge?'

Captain Cabrera: 'I'd already decided. I was going to call the chief and tell him the motion of the ship had changed and that I was going to check the water levels with him. I was going to do it immediately – and I did.'

Investigators: 'What is your assessment of the chief engineer, er, Vergara?'

Captain Cabrera: 'I don't like or respect him. The man is lazy and does just enough to avoid direct criticism… *(long pause)* After the last grounding, the ship had started to take on small amounts of water. It was seeping through the hull plates. There wasn't enough for expensive remedial work on the whole hull, but enough to monitor. I ordered Chief Vergara to check the water levels inside the hull on every watch… *(long pause)* I now believe that neither the chief nor any of the engine crew were monitoring the water levels.'

Investigators: 'When did you instruct Chief Engineer Vergara to monitor water levels inside the hull?'

Captain Cabrera: 'Er, it was just less than a year ago – at the time of the last inspection – the office has the date – it's in the log. High water levels were recorded in the bilges. It was suggested that I monitor the levels…'

Investigators: 'How did you instruct Chief Engineer Vergara to monitor water levels? Was it just a verbal instruction, was a record made in the log? Were there any witnesses to your instruction?'

Captain Cabrera: 'Er, I told him in the engine room, straight after we re-joined the ship after the inspection… after I'd read the report and discussed it with the owner… The owner will confirm that I said I would order Vergara to monitor the water levels. It's in the log.'

Investigators: 'Were any of the crew witness to this conversation?'

Captain Cabrera: *(Long pause)* 'I don't think so – but I made a note in the log – there'll be a record of it… you must have seen it already.'

Investigators: 'How often did you check that the monitoring of the water level inside the hull was being undertaken?'

Captain Cabrera: 'I checked the log every time I returned to the bridge. It always said, "water levels normal" … every officer would check the log each time he came on duty.'

Investigators: 'Did you ever check the water levels yourself – inside the bilges?'

Captain Cabrera: 'No, as captain I issued the order and expected it to be carried out.'

Investigators: 'Fine, can you talk us through the trip from the pick-up in Liverpool to discovering the high levels of water inside the hull?'

Captain Cabrera: 'After Liverpool we thought we were on our way home via a drop-off in Hamburg… A message came through as we cleared Land's End and were about to enter the English Channel. The message was from the owner's son, Dapkus. We were to divert to Santander in northern Spain for an unscheduled pick-up; it wasn't a surprise. Since young Dapkus joined the company, last-minute changes were common – he had us going backwards and forwards, wherever there was a pick-up that would make money… *(unintelligible)*

'The change in route had us sailing south, through the Bay of Biscay… rough seas. However, with more weight in the ship, it'd make the passage more comfortable on the way back…There'd be more paid days at sea; the extra money would be useful to me and the crew.'

Investigators: 'Were you concerned about the pick-up in Santander? We understand the consignment was of 720 metric tonnes of zinc ingots.'

Captain Cabrera: 'No, the holds were only part full and so plenty of room. Even with the additional weight we were well inside the permissible cargo weight. It was the position of the cargo that troubled me. I sent a message to the owner saying it would be necessary to redistribute the existing cargo to ensure the additional weight was correctly positioned. There'll be a record of the message. However, young Dapkus vetoed the request. He replied *(background noise and delay)* saying "Redistributing existing cargo didn't make sense" and that "It's a waste of time and money... plenty of space on the ship". Dapkus is an accountant not a sailor; he's never been to sea! ... You learn quickly not to cross Dapkus – he's not a nice person as other captains have found out.'

Investigators: 'What was your reaction to being told not to redistribute the cargo?'

Captain Cabrera: 'I felt powerless to do anything... *(long pause)* If I took the time to rearrange the cargo, Dapkus would find out – he'd be checking. He'd deduct pay from me and the crew. *(pause)* I was captain of the *Asenka* not Dapkus. I should have insisted we take time to redistribute the cargo and accepted the additional cost...'

Investigators: 'What was the condition of the sea during your passage through the Bay of Biscay and onwards?'

Captain Cabrera: 'Rough... we were battered, but the additional weight had us riding lower in the water... a bit more comfortable. The weather eased as we passed through the English Channel to Hamburg. The drop-off in Hamburg was routine but as we entered the North Sea, on the last leg of the trip, we encountered a heavy swell.'

Investigators: 'Can we return to your inspection of the bilges and the water level with Chief Engineer Vergara? Can you describe what happened once you entered the engine room?'

Captain Cabrera: 'Vergara and one of the crew, Emile, were waiting for me. They had battery-powered inspection lamps and I asked Vergara, "When was the last time you checked the water levels?' He said it was the last watch, but I didn't believe him. He looked nervous and had a forced smile on his face. I also knew there was no way I could challenge him; I'd just have to check myself.

'It's cold, dark and noisy in the bilges. The noise from the engine seemed to be magnified in the space between the engine room bulkheads and the steel plates of the hull. The heat from the engine room warms the bulkheads. It was hot and humid when we climbed into the cramped space. It was oppressive… I could see why Vergara and the others would avoid checking the water level if they could. As you move for'ard it gets colder.

'I let Vergara lead the way along the narrow gantry. We had to negotiate a short stairwell to the walkway that stretched to the bow. I remember that the inspection lamps were bright and it was easy to see the walkway and heavy metal hull plates around us. We hadn't gone far on the walkway when Vergara stopped. I bumped into him and we both looked down. As the ship rolled, water was lapping over the walkway and over our shoes. *(pause)*

'I felt sick in my stomach. We were taking on lots of water; we could be in danger of losing the ship. I was angry and shouted at Vergara. I said something like, "What was the time you checked the level here? How far has the water risen since you checked?" He said he hadn't checked it yet on this watch. I reminded him that his entry in the log said it was checked on the previous watch. I challenged him. "Who checked it? What was the level?" I remember exactly what he said. He said, "We were busy, I thought it would be OK" – he admitted no one had checked it, but in the log, he'd said the water level was normal.'

Investigators: 'What did you do next?'

Captain Cabrera: 'I told him to get help to check the water levels along the whole hull – port and starboard. I told him to make sure they checked the inspection valves before they opened any watertight doors. If there was water in a forward section, we didn't want it flooding through the ship!'

Investigators: 'What did Chief Engineer Vergara say or do next?'

Captain Cabrera: 'Nothing, he just stood there and looked terrified. His mouth was open and his hands were trembling as he held the inspection lamp. I could see that he was shocked but I had to ensure action was taken. I grabbed his arm and held my hand directly in front of his face. I used my fingers to emphasise my orders...'

Investigators: 'What were your orders?'

Captain Cabrera: *(Gesticulating)* 'One, to go back to the engine room and get two men. I said I would send two more in the next few minutes. Two, get them to record the current water levels at fixed points along the walkway and in each section. Three, get the two auxiliary pumps working. Four, report to me on the bridge as soon as possible. I told him to get going and gave him a shove.'

Investigators: 'What did you do next?'

Captain Cabrera: 'I went back to the bridge, contacted the owner about the rising water levels and requested a diversion to the nearest port to assess any damage. I also told the other officers on the bridge of my actions and made an entry in the log.'

Investigators: 'Did you get a reply from the owners?'

Captain Cabrera: 'Yes, within minutes. Young Dapkus ordered me to maintain the revised schedule and said, "Checks would be made in Klaipeda" – our home port in Lithuania.'

Investigators: 'What was your reaction?'

Captain Cabrera: 'I knew it was a mistake but … *(long pause)* I was too weak to insist… I just hoped that the extra pumps would control the water… that we'd be able to make port… I lost the ship. *(sobbing)*'

Investigators: 'Are you OK? Would you like a break?'

Captain Cabrera: 'No, no, I'm OK. Just give me a minute.'

Jack and Sandro were silent for a few moments. They'd heard similar stories of ships taking on water and owners unwilling to take the action needed. They'd also seen the effect on captains and crew who had a lost a ship under similar circumstances – it was devasting.

'Remind me what the *Asenka* was carrying?' asked Sandro.

'The main salvage item is the consignment of 720 metric tonnes of zinc ingots, split between the three holds. According to the shipping notes, there are two stacks of ingots per US standard pallet. Each stack is bound by metal tape and weighs one thousand kilos. We should expect most of the pallets and stacks to be intact. A subsidiary of Lloyds of London insured the ship and cargo. The note says the current price of zinc, 99.99% pure, is US$3620 per metric ton. The value of zinc on the ship is about US$2.6 million; it's definitely worth recovering. There are also four new JCB backhoe loaders – also well worth salvaging. Together they're worth more than a couple of Ferraris. There are twenty-three crates of machine parts, four hundred pallets of fruit and vegetables – they're going to be mush. Manifest says there are another 240 pallets of animal feed... and two hundred drums of plastic pellets – two hundred metric tonnes.'

Sandro returned to the report and continued reading.

Chapter 5

Rising water

(Interview resumed)

Investigators: 'Captain Cabrera, you've told us that you gave Chief Engineer Vergara orders to monitor the water levels in the bilges. Can you describe what happened at the time of his first report?'

Captain Cabrera: 'There was a tense silence on the bridge as we waited for Vergara. When he eventually arrived on the bridge, sweat was gleaming on his face. He told us the main pumps were working and he had the two auxiliary pumps working at maximum. He said the rate at which the water was rising had slowed – but it wasn't going down.

'I knew this was a guess… without reference points, over a period, it would be impossible to know if the level was going up or down. If I'm honest I was angry with Vergara for letting this situation arise but it was my ultimate responsibility.

'I thanked him and ordered him to pump water ballast from the for'ard holding tanks to the rear tanks to correct the trim of the ship. I also told him to keep the water levels under hourly watch and tell me immediately if there was any major change. I also said I would reduce speed to ease the strain on the hull as we rolled over the swell. I made a note of this in the log.

'He was back on the bridge one hour later; again, he was breathless and agitated. He confirmed that ballast had been pumped aft to correct the trim but the water had risen ten to twelve centimetres in the last hour. I remember him saying he couldn't control it and that in another twelve hours the engine room floor would be awash.

'It wasn't the news I wanted... but I'd already planned for such a worsening situation. I gave the crew an update and informed the owner. In my opinion the situation wasn't immediately life threatening so I issued a Pan-Pan rather than a May Day... contacted the Danish authorities... You already have a record of all of this. *(pause)* I asked if they could get one or more high-volume pumps to us. If they could, we may be able to pump her out and make port.'

Investigators: '*What was your plan?*'

Captain Cabrera: 'We were about seven hundred nautical miles from our home port of Klaipeda; over three days sailing. At the rate water was rising we could have another couple of metres of seawater inside the hull in twenty-four hours. The weather was set fair but we'd never make our home port without help.

'I ordered the crew to assemble their personal possessions and wear life jackets but continue to work as normal. If I judged the *Asenka* was in danger of sinking, they would have plenty of time to get into the lifeboat. The Danish coast was less than fifty nautical miles away and the weather was good. I asked the first officer to transfer navigation and survival equipment, food and water, to the lifeboat. I continued to monitor the situation.'

Investigators: 'What was the message to the owners and what was their reply?'

Captain Cabrera: 'I told the owners the *Asenka* was taking on water at an alarming rate. Unless emergency pumps could restrict the water level, the *Asenka* was in danger of sinking. I told them a Pan-Pan had been issued and Danish authorities alerted with a request for emergency pumps. Dapkus merely acknowledged the message... I'm sure you already have a copy of all of this.

'Within minutes of issuing the Pan-Pan we were receiving

messages from ships in the area. The shipping lanes were busy, and ships were passing and approaching all the time. A message from the Danish authorities said they were sending two high-volume submersible water pumps by a patrol boat. They said they should arrive within a couple of hours. I was told they could pump over thirty cubic metres of seawater per minute from the hull. It was probably over-kill – but better safe than sorry. The problem was the pumps were heavy and it would take three or four men with hoists to get them in position.'

Investigators: 'What happened next?'

Captain Cabrera: 'Pumping ballast aft had corrected the trim but the ship was still sluggish as she rolled over the swell. I'd reduced speed to the minimum, just enough to maintain steerage and to take us towards the Danish coast. It was a race between the rising water and the arrival of the high-volume pumps.

'I waited two hours but they never arrived – nothing, so I contacted them again. They said the patrol boat had been delayed on a previous emergency. They were going to do a helicopter drop but their two helicopters were both on other emergencies. They told me the pumps were on their way and would arrive in the next hour – it was about the time of Vergara's next report.

'I heard him running up the stairs before he burst onto the bridge, he was losing it, he looked scared. He blurted out that the engine room was awash… three pumps had failed and there was no way he could get to them. He said the water was rising faster than before and that it would get into the electrics any minute. He said we would soon be dead in the water.

'I'd never lost a ship but I knew what needed to be done. I told the crew that we were going to prepare to abandon ship and issue a May Day. I said the first officer would launch and take command of the lifeboat. I told Vergara that he and I would stand by with two of the engine room crew and wait for the pumps to arrive. If the ship remained stable, we'd manhandle the pumps below and start pumping. If it looked like the ship was about to founder, I'd give the order to abandon ship. I asked him if he understood and he nodded.'

Investigators: 'Can you describe what happened between your second contact with the Danish authorities and the final message from the Danish patrol boat delivering the pumps?'

Captain Cabrera: 'We'd been heading east, towards Esbjerg, the nearest port on the Danish coast. We were also heading towards the boat carrying the pumps. However, I decided to change course towards the north-west… I told the Danish… I told everybody our position in the May Day… gave the bearing…'

Investigators: 'Why did you change course – away from the boat delivering the pumps?'

Captain Cabrera: 'I wanted to be in deep water… If the *Asenka* did go down, I didn't want the ship to become a shipping hazard… I'd gone below, to the engine room, to reassure them and to see conditions for myself…The *Asenka* was slowing and had developed a laborious roll and twist over the swell. You could hear the hull plates grinding and scraping.

'They'd closed the inspection hatch to the bilges but water was covering my shoes... it was seeping through the bulkheads… *(long pause)* Years of neglect and cut-price maintenance were catching up with her. You could see water bubbling through the bottom of paper-thin rusty bulkheads – it'd be like that throughput the entire ship. A trickle would become a spout as the water searched for a way through the ship. The watertight bulkhead doors may be as firm as ever, but the water was finding a way around them.

'I'd sent the navigation officer to check the for'ard and central holds; they were awash. He reported that seawater was finding its way past welds, through repairs and fittings and gushing through voids that had never been sealed. It was about this time that we heard from the Danish patrol boat – the *Jacob Ulfeldt.* They said their ETA was twenty minutes… You'll have a copy of my reply. I said we were preparing to abandon ship. Water was rising rapidly and was about to flood the engine room. I told them three crew and myself would remain on ship and that I'd be standing by on Channel 16. *(prolonged silence)*

'I remember looking at my watch and wondering what would happen in the next twenty minutes. *(unintelligible)* ...it was answered. The engine stopped and there was an eerie silence on the bridge The rising water must have shorted the electrical circuits – we'd lost all power and were dead in the water. There was no power to operate the pumps, even if they arrived now. We had battery power for the radio and navigation, emergency lights and things a little longer but not enough for the pumps. *(heavy sigh)* I used the PA to tell everyone we were abandoning ship – she was going down – it was time to leave.'

Investigators: 'Can you recall the sequence of events immediately after your decision to abandon ship?'

Captain Cabrera: 'I spoke by radio to the first officer in the lifeboat and told him we were abandoning the ship. I told him that I would stay on board with Vergara and two engine crew and wait for the pumps to arrive. I ordered him to leeward where we'd dropped a rope ladder. I watched as the lifeboat pressed against the hull and the crew clambered down into it.'

Investigators: 'How long did you wait on board the Asenka before you abandoned ship?'

Captain Cabrera: 'Not long – minutes. Vergara came to the bridge. He said water was gushing into the engine room. It was pouring through vents and the level was rising all the time. He said it was up to his knees when he and the last of the engine crew left.

'There was just me and Vergara left on the bridge. I could sense the ship was going down. We lost the pitch and roll and were... heavy and still. *(pause)* I spoke to the first officer... he'd done a roll call and confirmed everyone was accounted for – except Vergara and me. I told Vergara to go and watched as he climbed down to the lifeboat.

'It was a sad end to a ship that had given good service. But, as I climbed over the rail, I thought it was probably better than the ignominy of being dismantled for scrap and laid bare on an Indian beach.'

Investigators: 'What actions did you take when you boarded the lifeboat?'

Captain Cabrera: 'I shouted to the helmsman to pull away… in case the ship went down quickly. I did a visual check to make sure everyone was strapped in. As we eased away from the ship I remember looking back. It looked tired and forlorn. I couldn't recall seeing it from such a position… It looked like the for'ard and rear watertight sections were holding but she was only down slightly at the stern. I imagined seawater flooding between the hull and hold bulkheads and racing through the ship. I thought the sheer weight of the rear tower and engine, together with the seawater and ballast, would drag her down, stern first. I could see ribbons of encrusted rust around the bow waterline, weeping trails of red, orange and brown along welds, seams and around the scuppers. As I watched, I noticed the trim was changing. She was becoming level in the calm waters as seawater rushed to fill every nook and cranny. I guessed the for'ard hold was filling. The ship was also starting to list to port.

'You'd never guess that at one time the rear tower had been painted white. Over the years it had been transformed into a patchwork of rust. It seemed to glow orange in the faint sunlight. The ship was no longer a thing of beauty – but I knew it would become a haven for others… *(long pause)*

'I asked the first officer to set a course for Esbjerg. In calm seas we'd be able to maintain six knots and be in port by early evening. I contacted the *Jacob Ulfeldt* and told them we'd abandoned ship and she was going down. *(long pause)* I knew the real drama would start back in the office… but in front of me, one drama was reaching its conclusion – but it wasn't spectacular.

'The stern didn't plunge below the waves. The bow didn't rear out of the water. It was a calm and dignified death as the ship simply slipped under the water. The for'ard and rear watertight bulkheads must have strived to maintain buoyancy, but the water had simply swirled around them and flooded the holds. One moment the ship was low in the water, the next she tilted to port, slipped through the surface and was gone. I could see boiling water marking the spot... but it would slow within minutes. I checked the GPS trace I'd ripped off the machine before I left the ship. I had the coordinates of the wreck. She was resting in approximately fifty metres of water and wasn't a hazard.'

Sandro stopped reading, looked up and commented: 'Sad business... now it all depends on whether the ship rolled as she sank and how she hit the seabed.'

Chapter 6

Good news

Jack and Sandro had two ships: the MV *Sultano* and the MV *Stavanger.* The first, the *Sultano,* was an ex-Italian patrol boat they had discovered in a Croatian backwater. The thirty-three-metres-long, one-hundred-ton boat had been owned by an Italian financier who had started to convert it into a luxury cruiser. When they first saw the boat, it looked derelict – but it had been built to a high naval specification. The financier had had new Caterpillar engines fitted at the start of his renovation but had not lived to see the conversion completed. Identifying his assets and liabilities had taken time – hence the deterioration of the boat. Jack and Sandro bought the patrol boat and a Croatian boatyard transformed it into a fast and agile diving platform. It was currently detecting shipping containers on the bed of the Irish Sea.

The *Stavanger* was a completely different ship. At eighty metres long and almost two-thousand tonnes it was a floating powerhouse. Massive engines allowed it to tow a vessel many times its own size whilst dynamic positioning allowed it to maintain its position in even the roughest of seas. It provided a stable platform for a deep-sea diving bell and offered both firefighting and water-pumping capabilities. It represented a formidable ocean-going resource – but was costly to use and maintain. The successful tender to salvage cargo from the MV *Asenka* would keep the *Stavanger* working – but only for a few weeks. In practical terms, it involved sailing six and a half thousand nautical miles from its standby position in the Gulf of Mexico to the wreck site in the North Sea. At an economical speed of eighteen knots, it would take fifteen days. Go faster and fuel consumption and cost would go up. What's more, after a year on standby, there was routine and preventative maintenance work to be completed. Two months had been scheduled for this work and this would severely cut into the preferred timescale specified in the *Asenka* tender.

The message from Baltic Marine Services respectfully asked the *Marine Salvage & Investigation Company* to acknowledge their email, to inspect the attachments provided and not to hesitate to contact them should further information be required. They also asked for regular updates on progress so they could keep their clients informed. Jack was mulling over what to do next when his phone rang. He picked it up automatically.

'Good morning, *Marine Salvage & Investigation Company*,' he announced with a forced smile in his voice.

'Good morning,' said Charles St John Stevens in his characteristic upper-class accent. 'How's business?'

Jack had met Charles six years ago when he and Sandro were seeking information about a container ship, the MV *Rockingham Castle,* that had disappeared. Jack had gone to Lloyds of London's headquarters for a meeting with Charles. His first impression was of a public school educated, arrogant and privileged man only three or four years older than himself. Over the next few hours Jack's impression was drastically revised. Charles was smart, shrewd and efficient. He also had an extensive network of contacts that kept him informed about everything happening in the shipping and salvage business. Amazingly, Jack, and later Sandro, formed a close friendship with Charles.

'We're still in business and always looking for more,' Jack replied, intrigued by Charles's question. 'How can I help you?'

'I think it's more a case of how I can help you, but firstly let me congratulate you on winning the tender to salvage cargo from the *Asenka* in the North Sea.'

'Yes, it's going to be our first job in European waters in some time. It's small, and should be straightforward, but it's a start.'

'You will have heard that the review of the North Sea standby model is about to be published. What you may not know is that it will be suggesting a new search, rescue and recovery strategy in the central and northern sectors of the North Sea. The review will recommend a regional approach in which BP and Exxon collaborate. The plan will be based on four new state-of-the-art vessels to be constructed in China. I should add that these ships will be constructed at great cost. Three ships are to be assigned to the Bruce, Monroe and Thistle platforms in the Fortes area. A fourth ship will provide relief and cover. I understand the design of these ships is to be based on the *Stavanger.*

'I've learned that, in the interim, they want to trial the plan with available and suitable vessels. The call for tenders will be issued next week. You might wish to tender. The specification of the *Stavanger* is on public record. Your recent standby experience in the Gulf of Mexico will be in your favour, as well as your recent history. You should be a front runner in any bid. Oh yes, you will need to include a long-distance helicopter and crew in your tender. I'm sure Piers Lilbourn would be happy to advise you on financing.'

Both Jack and Sandro were aware of the North Sea review but hadn't been invited to contribute and didn't realise the call for tenders was so close. It would be a big job to assemble a tender, but they had copies of previous tenders and no shortage of costing templates to draw upon. They also had the unique services of Piers Lilbourn. It had been Piers who had drawn up the complex financial deal that enabled them to buy the *Stavanger*. If they could secure a well-paid standby contract, even for one year, it would safeguard the future of the *Stavanger* within the company. Suddenly Jack believed he had good news to share with Sandro.

Chapter 7

Unusual evidence

'So, what have you got for me?' asked Detective Inspector Latchem as she sat heavily in the chair facing Dr Simon Scrimshaw across his desk.

She had driven across the city to the police forensic labs to hear the results of the various tests on samples collected from Calovarlo and his victim. The last few weeks had been long and exhausting as the team checked and double-checked statements, followed up lines of enquiry and methodically assembled the case against Sandro Calovarlo. It wasn't the only case Inspector Latchem was working on. She was used to juggling several cases at the same time but was finding Roberta Fox particularly irritating. She steadfastly instructed her client to answer 'no comment' to most of her questions, constantly asked for disclosure of evidence against her client and seemed to use every ruse and technicality to frustrate her. What Coleen wanted now was further evidence to link the suspect to the assault and rape of the victim.

Simon picked up the file on his desk, opened it and glanced at his summary. The first part was a repeat of the initial analyses they had completed shortly after Calovarlo's arrest.

'All the detail is in there. We've rechecked the initial samples taken from the suspect and victim. They confirm skin cells from the victim under the fingernails of the suspect. We confirmed DNA from the suspect on the victim's dress and underwear. The position and concentration of these samples are consistent with clothing being ripped off. We also confirm traces of the suspect's semen and saliva on her body. The diagram on page five notes the position of these samples on the body of the victim. There was penetration. We found traces of saliva and lipstick from the victim on the face of the suspect.'

Simon paused as he glanced down his bullet points. 'We detected microscopic fibres on the hands of the suspect that are identical to those in the dress and the underwear the victim was wearing. We also found blood and skin cells on the knuckles of the suspect that are identical to those of the victim. We are still working on the bedding, but I hope to get the results to you in the next forty-eight hours. You'll also have the latest blood traces and a comparison with the one taken after the suspect's arrest.'

'It's starting to sound like a *slam dunk*... but is there anything that's, er, inconsistent with an assault and rape? I ask because the accused said it was a set-up – but couldn't provide any evidence.'

'No, the traces of DNA, body fluids and semen from the accused on the victim are all consistent with rape. The injuries sustained by the victim, again, are all consistent with a violent assault... but...'

'But what?' asked Coleen.

'It seems she didn't fight back. I couldn't detect any defence injuries... there was a marked absence of bruises on her arms, wrists and thighs... although that's not uncommon.'

'Is there anything else I need to know?'

'A couple of things, but I'll happily get on the stand and say that, in my opinion, all the evidence points to a violent assault and rape.'

Detective Inspector Latchem was now convinced that Sandro Calovarlo did indeed assault and rape Anna Kalnina. She was also aware of the arguments that Roberta Fox would employ to explain this evidence away.

'Er, the aldehyde spike on the blood trace is intriguing," Simon continued. "If the suspect had been binge-drinking, or was an alcoholic, it would account for this spike. However, I understand he claims to be a professional diver and doesn't drink. The ketone spike is also odd. A high ketone level may indicate diabetic ketoacidosis; it's a complication of diabetes. We've checked with his doctor and there is no evidence of diabetes. He sent us a copy of his most recent blood test, it was a couple of months ago, and it is all normal; no aldehyde or ketone spikes.'

Simon sat back in the chair and breathed out heavily through his nose as though in frustration. 'I compared the blood trace for the suspect that was taken several hours after his arrest with the one provided by his doctor and the one taken most recently. The one from his doctor and the latest trace are virtually identical. No aldehyde or ketone spikes. When I looked at the trace taken after his arrest, I also noticed a slight reduction in his glucose level. As you know, a reduction in glucose level and increase in ketones typically indicate the presence of diabetes; the suspect doesn't have diabetes! I'll make a few enquiries and try to come up with an explanation.'

'Could he have taken a drug? Could someone have slipped him a drug?'

'Obvious question, speculation at the moment, but one we can both chase up.'

Chapter 8

Roberta Fox

Roberta Fox had deployed all the resources available to her. Her team had checked and double checked all the statements provided by the police. They had sought other statements from witnesses but there was nothing she could use to undermine or challenge the evidence against Calovarlo. Half a dozen character statements from his former girlfriends had been collected but Roberta knew these wouldn't be sufficient to influence any jury. The private investigator in Latvia had provided a thick file on the background and lifestyle of Anna Kalnina – but there was little she could use in any cross examination. She lived modestly and there was nothing to suggest she was part of a conspiracy. She appeared to have nothing to gain beyond justice for what Sandro had done to her. Ms Kalnina was an attractive single woman working in a small office in Riga with no criminal record and no gossip – nothing special, nothing unusual, nothing she could use.

The recent disclosure about the forensic evidence collected from the crime scene depressed her even further. Blood and saliva, skin cells and DNA from the victim, her clothes and the bedding combined to present an overwhelming case. She had presented this evidence to her client at the last meeting. In her experience, suspects faced with such overwhelming evidence simply confessed. This time her client was different; he refused to accept that he assaulted and raped the woman. It wouldn't be the first time in her career that Roberta Fox had lost a case – but she'd always been able to mitigate the damage. This time she knew she was going to lose a case, and badly, it was just a matter of how long the trial would last. She needed to exercise her professional judgement.

Sandro arrived at Albert Chambers well before the time of the regular Friday meeting with Roberta Fox and her paralegal. The waiting room looked like a Victorian film set. There were large wooden bookcases stretching from floor to ceiling. They covered the walls with metre after metre of large books. There was row after row of green and red, black and grey tomes – all neatly stacked. The gold lettering on the spines had dulled with the passage of time. It looked like a scene to impress the clients rather than a working library. The large wooden chairs, with deep red leather seats and backs, also served to convey the impression of a long-established practice.

The side door opened as David Moxon walked into the reception area and smiled. 'Good morning Sandro, I hope we haven't kept you waiting long.'

'No, it's given me time to think about the case. I'm eager to hear your latest news.'

The expression on David's face changed from friendly and smiling to stern and set. 'My father persuaded Ms Fox to let me sit in on the case; to give me an insight into how the defence team operated. I haven't been involved in any of the work; I've just been an observer. As a friend, I can tell you it's not going well – but I'll let Roberta tell you herself.'

Having delivered that body-blow, David led the way to Roberta Fox's office in silence. Roberta and her paralegal were already in the office and merely nodded to acknowledge Sandro's forced smile. Without any pleasantries, Roberta got straight to the point.

'Mr Calovarlo, we have received further disclosures from Detective Inspector Latchem; one of these is significant. It is a statement from Isobel Downing, one of your former girlfriends. The way Isobel described your brief relationship resembles a *transaction*. You took her to expensive restaurants, in your exotic sports car, to be wined and dined in return for the satisfaction of your, I quote, *"weird sexual fantasies"*. You took her on an indulgent weekend to a spa, paid for expensive treatments in glamorous surroundings, in return for lovemaking that she described as, I quote, "like some sadomasochistic porn movie". According to her statement, when she told you of her dislike for your sexual preferences you lost interest in her.'

'It's not true and I don't know why she said that. We had a brief relationship – a few weeks – but it ended amicably. Yes, we did go to restaurants and had a spa weekend together, but I'm not a weirdo; I'm not into all that sadomasochistic stuff.'

Roberta Fox did not respond but merely glanced down at the papers before her.

'We have reviewed all the evidence the police have disclosed and compared it with what we have been able to collect. We have also discounted any conspiracy against you – there is simply no evidence to suggest this. At this time, we feel we have exhausted any, er, advantageous lines of enquiry. We have also discussed various defence strategies and the arguments likely to be made by the prosecution.'

Roberta paused; her tone and expression wasn't what Sandro had been hoping for.

'I've concluded that, faced with the overwhelming evidence against you, the chance of your acquittal is remote. Furthermore, by pleading not guilty and undertaking the trial, I believe you risk receiving a harsh sentence. The judge for your future trial hasn't been fixed. However, in my experience, judges do not look kindly on not guilty pleas when the evidence available prior to the trial is so strong. In my opinion you should consider changing your plea to guilty. I will do all I can to mitigate the charges against you. I believe it is likely you will receive a custodial sentence but one that is significantly shorter than if you continue with the plea of not guilty.'

Even forewarned, the announcement was devastating. She believed he did it, she believed he was guilty. All the energy and hope he had brought with him drained from his body. He motioned to speak but Roberta held out her hand to stop him.

'I'm aware of what this means to you. All I ask is that you consider this change in plea. I remain prepared to defend you but feel I need to be completely honest and open with you. If you wish to seek a second opinion, or to instruct another barrister, I completely understand. I will cooperate in every way.'

Sandro sat silently in his chair, head bowed.

'I would like to suggest that we end this meeting now and meet again next week. At that time, I may have further disclosures from the police, and you may have come to a decision about your plea.'

Sandro was motionless in his seat. It took awkward seconds for the enormity of what had been said to sink in. Without saying a word or making eye contact with those in the room he rose from his chair and made his way out of the building. A short time later he switched off the car engine. He couldn't remember how he had driven from central Manchester to his apartment. He sat in the car unable to think beyond accepting he was guilty.

He had once driven past HM Prison Manchester, 'Strangeways'. He recalled the imposing Victorian brick and stone towers either side of the huge entrance doors and the massive brick walls that surrounded it. He never thought he would be spending ten years or more inside those walls. He was suddenly overtaken by the thought of going to prison and what his parents and friends would think of him. A deep bellowing sob erupted from deep inside him. Tears began to flow down his face as his shoulders shook with raw emotion.

Chapter 9

Inspections

Sandro's involvement in the inspection of the MV *Asenka* was in doubt. His bail conditions stipulated he must surrender his passport until the forthcoming trial was over. However, Roberta Fox had petitioned the authorities and argued it would adversely affect his ability to conduct his business. In addition, the substantial bond, together with evidence of previous good character, convinced the authorities Sandro was not a flight risk. He joined Jack and the crew on board the *Sultano* after their return from the Irish Sea and after completing the sonar scanning contract. They would use the ship to conduct the inspection whilst the *Stavanger* was undergoing routine maintenance.

The *Sultano* was moored in Portsmouth. Even in a busy port and naval base like Portsmouth, the ship stood out. The pristine sleek white ex-Italian naval patrol boat was the boating equivalent of a classic sports car. She was built almost fifty-years ago to a stringent naval specification. However, modern twin Caterpillar diesel engines, generating two thousand bhp, could power the *Sultano* to twenty-eight knots. The ship could get anywhere, fast, and with modern electronics and dynamic positioning could remain on station within centimetres of a GPS plot. The addition of a vintage water cannon near the bow, and a utilitarian A-frame off the stern, merely reinforced the impression of an extremely capable ship.

The *Sultano* was strategically positioned in Portsmouth. It was in the middle of the English Channel, the busiest shipping route in the world. Westwards it was relatively close to the Bristol Channel and the Irish Sea. A similar distance to the east was the North Sea. Millions of tonnes of shipping passed through these stretches of water every day. The ship was ready for departure. The seas were light and so cruising at eighteen knots they would make the wreck site in just over twenty-four hours. The new member of the diving team, Gunnar, had checked all the diving kit, cameras and torches. They were ready to go.

They had accurate coordinates for the wreck from the print-out ripped off the GPS plotter by the captain of the *Asenka*. The insurance syndicate had confirmed the coordinates and had provided images of the wreck from side sonar scans. However, Jack and Sandro judged it prudent to conduct their own scans; wrecks tend to move or settle in the weeks and months after sinking. They would make multiple passes with their multi-beam side sonar equipment over and around the wreck. It would be time consuming and repetitive as each track, at a different depth, captured thousands of images. The complex electronics would conflate these into a composite picture, a three-dimensional image of the wreck, that they could manipulate. They would be able to enlarge sections and rotate them for detailed inspection. The computer software would allow them to inspect every visible part of the wreck from the comfort of the bridge of the *Sultano* – rather than the grey depths of the North Sea. Previous experience had demonstrated the images were likely to be so good that they would be able to detect wire stays, hatch handles and buckled hull plates. It would also allow them to scope the wreck site before any attempt to penetrate it.

Combined with drawings of the ship, the computer imaging allowed them to identify points on each hold cover that could be cut through thus allowing access to the hold. There had been a debate in Salford about gaining access to the hold. Jack and Sandro had previously invested in a sophisticated ROV, a remotely operated vehicle that could do all that a diver could do and at no risk. The decision was whether to buy a cutting torch to attach to the ROV or to do it manually. Gunnar, a newly appointed diver, had years of experience cutting through steel structures whilst working on the oil rigs in the Black Sea and the North Sea. This was why he had been given the job. He had argued that a Broco cutting torch, the Firewire, was cheap, light, simple to use and effective.

'It's basically a magnesium alloy rod, about forty-five centimetres long, held in a pistol grip,' he had explained. 'There's a cable and a narrow hose attached to the grip. One feeds high electrical current to the rod and tip, the other floods the tip with oxygen. When the rod touches a metal surface the circuit is closed, a spark is created and the oxygen boosts the tip to over ten thousand degrees. Whatever's close is melted. I've used the Firewire hundreds of times – never had a problem. The ROVs can take hours to set up and are a nightmare in current. It's your money, but I'd use the Firewire,' he'd concluded.

Gunnar was about to be given the opportunity to demonstrate his skill. Kev Donnelly, captain of the *Sultano,* had activated the dynamic positioning system and had the ship positioned directly above the wreck and fixed on the GPS coordinates. Propellers and thrusters would ensure the *Sultano* didn't move from this spot. A shot line had been lowered onto the wreck. It would guide the divers down to the *Asenka* and be their lifeline back. One of the engineers provided Gunnar with the Broco cutting torch and clipped a bag full of cutting rods to his harness. Three powerful torches were clipped onto Jack whilst Sandro carried the video camera. A crew member was ready on the hoist and basket to lower the divers into the water. It should be a routine dive.

Low grey clouds cut out the sun as the basket and divers touched the water and disappeared below it. The water was choppier than it looked from the ship but there should be little current, and the drysuits would keep them warm and dry. Diving with a rebreather, even at fifty metres, would give them plenty of bottom time. Instead of expelling air underwater, in the form of bubbles, the rebreather not only recycled the gases being breathed but automatically mixed them to give the optimum gas mix at all stages of the dive. The rebreather would give them more than enough time to cut entry and exit holes in the hold covers and survey the hull and the holds. The downside would be a lengthy decompression time – it would take over an hour to rise to the surface through a series of decompression stops. The divers signalled to each other, and to those watching, before they disappeared below the surface and started their descent.

Drifting down a shot line is always slightly disorientating. There is no sound from the rebreather, no reference point, just the vast backdrop of the ocean. The only sense of movement is the passage of small particles in front of you as you let a hand glide over the shot line. It's a line that disappears into the gloom. Jack was checking the diving computer on his wrist. They were well within the decent rate as a green segment on his dive computer confirmed. Eventually a grey mass started to form below them and as they got closer, the rear tower of the MV *Asenka* emerged through the gloom. Ariels reached upwards but would never again receive a message. The visibility was good, probably at least fifteen metres, and they were dropping almost in the middle of the rear hold, close to one of the loading derricks. Jack and Sandro both flared in the water and dumped some gas from their drysuits so they could drop and kneel on the deck. Between them they pulled the shot line to the centre of the deck and secured it to a cleat at the foot of a derrick. The shot line was their route back to the surface, the ship and safety. Lose the shot line in a current and in a very short time you could be a long way from the ship, lost, cold and praying someone comes to find you. Gunnar secured the Firewire to the same cleat and signalled his intention to move towards the stern; it was to be the starting point for their inspection of the hull.

The gentle current was behind them and flowing right to left as they finned to the starboard side of the wreck close to the stern. They assembled in a line by the rear rail – each grabbing it in their hands. The once smooth white painted tubular steel rail was now rough and mottled grey. Jack swept the torch over the rails and down the side of the ship. As far as he could see the rails were damaged – ill treatment, accident and general wear and tear. Years of exposure to the elements had corroded the metal. It had bubbled slowly under the paint, dislodged rusty flakes and eventually made its way through the thin metal tubular walls. Slopping more paint on the rust hadn't slowed it. The hull was no more inviting. At some time, thick, tar-like black paint had been daubed over the hull. Jack could see the rough brush marks. However, scratches and scrapes, dents and gouges bore witness to the hard life the *Asenka* had endured. In the torchlight, streaks of rust flashed orange, red and brown amongst the buckled hull plates.

'Makes you wonder how it passed the last inspection,' said Sandro. 'Ready to go?'

With a single heave, Sandro, then Jack and finally Gunnar pulled themselves over the rail and towards the seabed. They had previously agreed that Sandro would swim just above the seabed, Jack along the middle of the hull and Gunnar along the rail. They could fin towards the bow and be sheltered from the current by the bulk of the ship. As they inspected the hull, they would be able to detect any structural damage that could influence the salvage. It was Sandro who spoke first:

'Gee, just look at the hull... when was the last time it was scraped and anti-fouled? It looks like an overgrown garden. It's going to be tricky spotting any damage through all this lot.'

'The main plates aren't much better,' said Jack. 'Lots of evidence of rough treatment – buckled plates, gouges and heavy corrosion... but it shouldn't affect the salvage.'

'I'll concentrate on trying to spot any distortion between the hull and deck... but looks OK so far,' added Gunnar.

Sandro was hovering just above the seabed and to the starboard of the stern. He was sheltered from the gentle current and had a clear view of the rudder and propeller. The leading edges of the propeller were still bright but short lengths of weed waved in the current.

'There's a clear gap between the stern and the seabed. She must be resting on the for'ard and mid-section of the hull. It'll be worth checking along the bottom of the hull to see how fast she is. There's been plenty of time for her to settle but we don't know what effect salvaging a significant weight may have on her stability. If she does move, I doubt it will be much.'

In the shelter of the hull the trio finned around the stern, each giving a running commentary of what they could see. Kev Donnelly would be recording the conversation and Sandro was taking lots of photos. Between them they would have plenty of information to assess the state of the wreck.

'OK, let's start making our way along starboard, towards the bow. We'll be in the shelter of the ship until the bow. Once we clear the bow the current will push us along the port side and back towards the stern.'

Moments later it was Gunnar who made the first significant observation.

'Whoooow, guys, come and look at this.'

Jack and Sandro drifted upwards to where Gunnar was hovering in the water. His torch picked out an area of the hull close to the rail. The steel plates had been mashed together, welds ripped apart, hull plates bent as though starting to fold. It was as though some giant had tried to bend the ship. As Jack and Sandro joined him, he explained what he could see: 'Part of the deck is distorted... it's like a huge ripple between the end of the rear hold and the start of the rear tower. Looks as though she nose-dived... hit hard... then came to rest. I'll check across the deck.'

Moments later Gunnar confirmed: 'No major damage on the port side area.'

This wasn't the news Jack and Sandro had been hoping for. The account of the sinking had said it was a gentle capsize in calm water. The ship simply 'slipped beneath the surface'. Both Jack and Sandro had seen the result of ships 'slipping beneath the surface'. On their way to the bottom, ships rolled and twisted and often caused massive destruction on impact. But it wasn't the ship they were bothered about – it was the cargo. If the ship had rolled and twisted, the thousands of tonnes of cargo could be in a heap. If they had to salvage the zinc, ingot by ingot, it could take months not days.

They finned steadily along the hull but there was no other sign of damage until they reached the bow. As they moved out of the shelter of the ship, the current hit them. It had increased but they could fin against it and still inspect the bow. It was Sandro who gave the verdict.

'Well, it looks like she hit the seabed bow first... almost upright but with a slight tilt to port. The bulbous nose has been pushed upwards and to starboard. I was expecting to see much more damage – especially if she hit the seabed hard. I'm now thinking that perhaps it wasn't such a hard hit... just structural weakness at the point between the hull and the rear tower. This is always a weak spot in old ships. We'll have a better idea when we look inside the holds.'

They gathered at the bow but had to fin steadily to maintain their position because of the current. It was trying to flush them along the hull.

'Ready for the port side?' asked Jack as he finned upwards to his inspection position.

They drifted along the hull, made no further discoveries, and rendezvoused in the shelter of the stern before finning to the rear-most hold covers.

The *Asenka* had three holds that ran the length of the ship. They were separated by bulkheads, reinforced by ribs with derricks mounted above. A series of overlapping hold covers, between the derricks, allowed access to the cargo. Each cover consisted of a box section support framework covered with thin sheets of steel. Attached to the edges of the port and starboard side hold covers were steel wheels that allowed winches to pull a hold cover open and closed. It was possible to uncover a different section of the hold just by winching covers into place; but the ship's winches would never work again. To try and attach a steel cable to pull the hatches open risked merely jamming them in place. The ship may look intact but if it had twisted and moved out of alignment during the sinking the steel wheels wouldn't run true. The solution was to support a hold cover with a heavy line from the ship above, cut through the axles of the hold wheels on one side, lift the cover and let it fall over the side of the ship – crude but effective. The remaining wheels and cover may break free from the guide channels that ran along the hull or merely crumple. Either way they would have access.

Gunnar had collected the cutting gear, found the spot on the rearmost hold cover, dumped some gas from his drysuit, and knelt on the steel plate. Jack could appreciate the economy of effort as he used a marker to draw a rough metre and a half circle around him. They knelt, up current, on the hold cover.

'Look away or close your eyes. I'll give you a count of three, ready?'

Jack and Sandro merely said "ready" as they bowed their heads. Gunnar flipped the black narrow visor in front of his eyes and was poised to start cutting.

'Cutting in three, two, one...'

Even with his eyes closed Jack could tell a bright light was close – he moved his hands in front of his mask. Gunnar had simply leaned to his left, pulled the trigger and touched the Firewire to the cover. There was an explosion of light and a cloud of tiny particles as he slowly drew an arc around his body. The cutting rod shortened and Gunnar leaned a little more until the rod was down to a stump. He was halfway through the cut.

'Have a look,' Gunnar invited and Jack and Sandro quickly finned to see the result of his work. Gunnar had cut a clean arc all the way through the cover; he'd missed the box sections.

'Impressive, just as you said,' Sandro commented, as Gunnar fitted another rod to the pistol grip.

'Ready for the next bit?' Gunnar asked as he repositioned himself.

He cut the remaining arc but left two small sections; they stopped the steel plate dropping free into the hold whilst he was kneeling on it. A quick adjustment to one side and he cut the two remaining sections. Within minutes the hole was cut and the egg-shaped plate simply disappeared into the hold. With Jack and Sandro guiding the cables and hose that fed the cutter, Gunnar cut five more holes in the hold covers and ended close to the bow. They had already decided that Gunnar would remain on deck with the cutting equipment as he shadowed their passage inside each hold. No one wanted to think about the implications of cutting a diver free from fallen metalwork – but it was prudent to have the kit readily available.

'Time to take a look,' said Jack as he pushed his torch inside the wreck and gingerly followed it with his head and shoulders.

The three divers were anxious because penetrating a wreck for the first time is one of the most dangerous things a diver can do. The notes said the MV *Asenka* had 'settled deeper and deeper in the water, developed a list to port, and in calm seas simply slid beneath the surface'. The computer images suggested the ship was intact, sitting upright on the bottom with a slight list to starboard. The inspection had confirmed there was no evidence of catastrophic damage. However, it was possible that the ship had rolled and twisted under the surface. Thousands of tonnes of cargo could have been thrown free and piled together. The ship may appear benign but could be a deadly trap, waiting to be sprung. Cargo may be balanced so carefully that the slightest movement could bring it crashing down. A deadly web of cargo nets and ropes, cables and debris could be waiting to ensnare or fall on the unwary.

In the darkness, a nightmare labyrinth stretched before Jack. The capsize had stirred up forty-plus years of dirt and dust as well as that from hundreds of stacked sacks. It had also released anything that would float – wooden pallets and battens, ropes, bottles and cans as well as bits of rubbish. It had all drifted towards the surface, only to be trapped under the hold cover. Sheets of discarded newspapers, magazines and plastic bags were suspended in the water. One length of rope looked like a long thin snake. A lot of the dirt had settled but the powerful torch still cast a searchlight beam through the gloom. Jack slowly moved the beam away from the floating debris to the abandoned cargo. As the torch beam passed over the grey landscape, a vivid yellow shape burst into view. A rush of adrenalin immediately raced through his body, his senses on high alert.

'Oh no!' Jack muttered into the voice comm before correcting himself. 'It's OK, just a yellow waterproof hanging in the water. I thought for an awful minute it was a crew member.'

He spoke to Kev Donnelly on the ship above them. 'Kev, there's a lot of rubbish in the water but it looks like we may be lucky.' Jack's torch beam continued its search of the scene just below him. '...it looks like the pallets are still in place. There's a clear space between the cargo and the floating debris. Reckon it's safe to penetrate.'

He turned to Sandro and signalled that he was ready to enter the ship. Sandro switched on the video camera, signalled AOK, and followed Jack inside the hull. Dozens of pallets were neatly stacked in rows, one on top of another. Heavy cargo nets were stretched around them and secured to recessed cleats on the deck; they had held everything in place during the sinking. According to the manifest this was the animal feed. All that it would be feeding once they opened the hold covers would be fish – until it turned to mush.

'Looks like the crew left a pathway between the two blocks of pallets,' Sandro explained. 'Guess it was to allow access during loading and unloading.'

Sandro finned gently over the stacked pallets and swung his torch and camera in gentle arcs to record the scene.

'Arr, part of the top row of pallets from one side slipped during the sinking. There's a jumble of pallets and sacks blocking part of the pathway. There's no problem… we've no plans to salvage the animal feed.'

Jack skimmed over the stacks of animal feed and glanced into the darkness ahead of them. He could see a broad column of dull light penetrating the hold. It helped to orientate him in the darkness. As he continued to fin towards the light, his torch picked out row after row of squat stacks of zinc ingots. He finned closer to them to get a better look at the stacks. The manifest said they were ingots, but they looked more like slabs. Each one was as long as his arm and a full span of his fingers wide. He immediately saw that they were stacked close together. The comments from Otto Weller sprang to mind. It looked as though the pallets of ingots had been squeezed into any space that was available.

'Jack, I'm going to swim a pattern over the stacks of ingots and get a detailed picture. They look pretty close together. Getting the first stack out is going to be tricky but once the first one is out it will get easier.'

Jack hung in the water, directly under the column of dull light shining through the hole in the hold cover. This was their exit point from the hold. Sandro swam methodically across the hold and recorded the layout of the stacks. It all looked stable and readily accessible. Jack and Sandro were careful to avoid the tangle of floating wreckage above them as they exited the hold. Gunnar was waiting for them and gave them an AOK hand signal.

A quick check of the diving computer and Sandro led the way into the mid-ships hold. The notes had told them that the *Asenka* had a capacity of over four and a half thousand cubic metres of cargo. It sounded a lot but only a small proportion was being used – and most of this was one or two pallets high. Jack and Sandro worked their way aft from hold to hold as they inspected the cargo. They moved their torch beams, lazily seeking stacked pallets of zinc ingots. Dark grey shapes emerged from the gloom; they were the JCB backhoe loaders. Jack could see the broad strips of webbing holding the wheels in place. He could also see a large crate in the bucket of the front loader. He guessed these were accessories or spare parts. At fifty metres, all the surface colours are lost, and you are left with shades of grey. It was only when the torch beam caught the paintwork that Jack could see the trademark yellow of the equipment. A further glance told him it would be easy to salvage and had a resale value.

Beyond the backhoe loaders was another part of the main prize – more zinc ingots. In the gloom, the stacks of ingots stood like silent sentinels, stack after stack, row after row. This was the major prize and it looked ready for salvage. All they had to do was remove the hold covers and systematically hoist out pallet after pallet and transfer them to the waiting freighter. It was looking like a profitable salvage. They checked the dive time, still plenty of time, as they finned along the hold, just beneath the hold cover. It was clear that the crates of machine parts had tumbled during the capsize. It was likely the crates contained a lot of air and would have been buoyant for minutes or hours before coming to rest in a heap. Unfortunately, they were a priority salvage item and would be awkward to handle.

In the hold, dozens of pallets stacked with drums came into view. It looked as though the crew had started to stack them two pallets high but had stopped after half a dozen or so. The rest of them were lined up on the deck. Jack guessed they had not been expecting the consignment of zinc ingots and so had not needed to pile pallet upon pallet – there was plenty of room in the hold.

From a distance, the drums looked intact, but Jack knew the thick cardboard would be waterlogged and would start to disintegrate as soon as it was touched. This was going to be a problem. The drums had been made a priority salvage item despite being a relatively cheap item on the manifest.

Beyond the drums and towards the end of the hold, the remaining cargo was stacked. The crates of fruit were swathed in plastic sheeting. It had been clear but now looked like a thin grey blanket, held in place by more cargo nets. It wasn't worth the time and effort to salvage them. Jack winced as he glanced at the remaining pallets of zinc ingots. Several of the stacks had slipped during the sinking and loose ingots were strewn around the deck. It wasn't a disaster – just more time consuming to collect and bring to the surface.

'Time to go,' announced Gunnar as he pointed to his wrist computer.

Breathing trimix, a mixture of oxygen, helium and nitrogen, allowed them extended bottom time – time to inspect the cargo. However, every minute spent at depth added to the time they would spend holding onto the shot line as they completed decompression stops. It would take them over sixty minutes to gradually make their way to the surface.

Chapter 10

The cold light of day

An inspection of the wreck was over. Fair weather and calm seas were a bonus as the *Sultano* cruised at eighteen knots back to Portsmouth. There had been time to consider the disposition of the cargo for salvage, and the techniques and time required to get it on board the rented freighter. During the time he was busy, Sandro forgot about the cloud hanging over him. It was in the quiet moments, when he was alone, that it all came flooding back. Strangely, he wanted to be alone; apart from work, he suddenly didn't know what to say to his friends.

Their accountant had persuaded them to lease a company car; he'd explained it was a tax efficient way to provide company transport. They'd settled on the Land Rover Discovery. With the rear seats folded down, the boot was cavernous. They could ferry enormous amounts of kit from place to place. Sandro drove as they negotiated the crowded dock-side car park and soon had them cruising up the motorway network to Manchester. They had chatted easily about work for the first hour or so of the journey but as the miles passed, conversation stopped and they drove in silence. When Jack tried to initiate conversation, Sandro barely responded; he'd retreated into his own thoughts. Conversation resumed as they turned off the motorway and drove towards Manchester city centre. Sandro dropped Jack off at his apartment and discovered someone had parked in the numbered space outside his own apartment. He deliberately blocked the car in and left a message under their windscreen wiper. If they wanted to leave before him tomorrow, they would have to contact him. He knew it was petty – but he wasn't feeling magnanimous!

His mood didn't improve when he checked his mailbox. In addition to leaflets advertising fast food there was a large, thick envelope. The embossed address on the front told him it was from Moxon & Partners, Roberta Fox. A few weeks ago, he would have rushed to open it. Today he looked at it with trepidation and decided he would wait until he had unpacked and made a sandwich. Eventually Sandro could put it off no longer. He ripped open the envelope and found an invoice for a large amount of money and another document which he started to read.

It was essentially a report that started with a summary of the charges against him and then systematically addressed them in turn. He was tempted to skip over some of the legalese but forced himself to read it carefully. The more he read the more depressed he became. Detective Inspector Latchem had described the evidence against him as "overwhelming"; Roberta Fox seemed to agree with her.

The later parts of the report outlined possible defence strategies. They suggested how mitigating circumstances could be marshalled to counter the evidence. The file gave a long list of business colleagues and former girlfriends who could be approached to provide written statements of his character. It was clear to Sandro that this was damage limitation, not a strong counterargument. With increasing dread Sandro worked his way to the concluding comments. It wasn't a surprise that the advice was to plead guilty. Neither was he surprised when Roberta suggested he may wish to seek a second opinion. She had written: "Be assured, should you decide to ask others to act on your behalf I will provide all the information I have accrued and will cooperate fully with them."

Sandro glanced again at the invoice. The charging period was up to the end of the week; she was bailing out. It was as though the last strand between him and avoiding prison had been cut.

Sandro dropped the folder, closed his eyes and sank back into the chair. He thought of his mother and could visualise a look of anguish on her face when told her son was guilty of rape. His father would be angry. He would shout and curse before collapsing in a heap of self-recrimination. What would his friends say and do? Would they quickly drift away – not wanting to be contaminated? If he was in prison he couldn't contribute to the company. Would his share in it be frozen or would Jack want to buy him out? He would enter prison as a young man. He'd come out as a middle-aged man – if he came out. He'd heard stories of how sex offenders were ill-treated in prison – brutal stories. Tears welled up in his eyes and his throat grew tight. 'Think, think,' he told himself. He couldn't use his passport, but he had money. With money he would be able to buy a fake passport and get away. For a brief instance there was the prospect of escape.

If he fled the country, the bond Jack and the company had raised for his bail would be lost. He may have a fake passport and credit cards but how long before these cards were cancelled? How long could he go undetected? If he tried to register in a hotel, they would want his name and his credit card. He wouldn't be able to find work using his qualifications. He'd be relegated to menial work on the black market. The prospect of escape was dashed as quickly as it emerged. He tried to think back to the events at the nightclub, but the nightmare of the police interrogation and the aftermath dominated everything.

Sandro racked his brain, trying to think of a person or a company that would wish him harm or wish to damage the Marine Investigation & Salvage Company. He couldn't think of any. The tenders for contracts were impersonal, there had been no confrontations with clients, with insurers... with girlfriends. Eventually Sandro fell into an uneasy sleep.

The piercing chime from his mobile phone woke him up some time later. He was cold and it was dark outside, but he quickly opened the text from his current girlfriend, 'U R disgustin' was all she had written. He hadn't told her about the charges against him and now regretted it. For a moment he tottered on the brink. Perhaps he should just accept what everyone was telling him and take his punishment. 'I didn't do it,' he shouted out loud and a spark was struck inside him. In seconds the anger inside him fanned the spark into flames that grew and grew. He wasn't going to give up, he would fight but he needed help.

The company had a 24/7 direct line to McKnight, Lewis and Watts, their legal representatives in Manchester; he'd call the number now. A sleepy voice answered the phone, but Sandro cut through the questions. He was aware he was being brusque but didn't care. He'd apologise later. He just wanted to speak to Bill Watts as soon as possible. It took a few minutes, but Bill answered the phone. Whilst he was waiting, Sandro realised how late it was. He felt awkward at probably waking Bill – realising there was little he could do immediately.

'Sandro, how can I help?'

'Bill, I'm sorry it's so late... but I've just had a letter, or rather a report from Roberta Fox, the barrister handling my... case.' Sandro was still embarrassed at using the word 'rape' in any conversation. 'Her advice is to plead guilty, to… er, reduce the sentence. I didn't do it!' Sandro shouted down the phone and then immediately apologised. 'She's sent me an invoice and suggested I get a second opinion. It looks like she just wants to take her fee and bail out. Can you suggest someone else I can talk to, a second opinion? I've got to fight this.'

'Of course,' Bill replied in a tone that was business-like and reassuring. 'I've been giving some thought to a possible second opinion – just in case it was needed. There's a barrister in London called Reginald Melton-Barr. I don't know him, but I know of him. He's a criminal lawyer and as such our paths seldom cross. I did hear him speak at a Law Society event in London several years ago and was impressed. My contacts speak highly of him. No, not just highly, very highly. He has recently represented, successfully, some high-profile defendants. Sandro, barristers like Melton-Barr do not like to lose. If you wish I am happy to contact his chambers and ask if he is prepared to give you a second opinion. If he is, I will contact Roberta Fox on your behalf and ask her to assemble all the evidence available at this time. One of our juniors will take the files immediately to him. Sandro, people like Melton-Barr typically have a full diary. Even if he is prepared to give you a second opinion we may be talking about weeks or months before he is able to deliver it. What do you want me to do?'

'I'd be grateful if you could contact him and let me know what he says; thanks Bill.'

'I'll get back to you as soon as possible,' was all Bill Watts said.

There were regular updates, but it took almost two weeks before Melton-Barr agreed to offer a second opinion with a meeting over three weeks later. The train from Manchester to London took just over two hours and did little to calm Sandro's nerves. He was early for his appointment and so decided to catch the underground train to Temple Station, just north of the River Thames, and walk to the chambers of Melton-Barr. A modest, highly polished brass plaque outside a grand Victorian entrance announced Themis Chambers. Large wooden double doors guarded the entrance to a brightly lit foyer. A wall of glass, etched with the name of the chambers, was surmounted by the stylised head of some Greek or Roman figure. Its significance was lost on Sandro; he merely looked for a receptionist. She was seated behind a large modern desk and appeared to be surrounded by computer screens, monitors and electronic equipment. She smiled warmly as she made eye contact.

'Are you Mr Alessandro Calovarlo?'

'Yes, I've an appointment with Mr Melton-Barr.'

Sandro noticed that her hand glided over a small keyboard and pressed one of the buttons.

'Mr Melton-Barr is expecting you. One of his colleagues is on her way to escort you to his office. If you would care to take a seat she will be here in a moment.'

Sandro had no sooner sat on a surprisingly comfortable chrome and fabric chair when a slim young woman pushed open one of the glass doors and held out her hand. 'Good morning, I'm Samantha Elliot, one of Mr Melton-Barr's colleagues.'

Sandro was getting used to the dress code of female lawyers, simple black skirt and shoes, white shirt and a minimum of jewellery. Samantha was attractive, looked closer to forty than twenty, and had an aura of confidence. Her hair was short, almost masculine, but it was the wrinkles around her eyes and mouth that said she wasn't a teenager.

'If you would like to follow me,' she said and led the way out of reception, along corridors, up staircases to Melton-Barr's office.

Sandro had been surprised at the offices of Moxon & Associates. He was equally surprised now. The room was enormous. An overweight man with long grey hair wearing a white collarless shirt rose from a large cluttered desk by the window. His dark pinstripe trousers were in stark contrast to the scarlet braces that held them up. Around the walls were hundreds of books; it was like working in a library. There were several large tables with piles of paper, stacks of books and computers. He could see at least four electronic whiteboards on walls. One was on and displayed a number of colour photographs with arrows, notes, scribbles and numbers all over them. It looked like an open plan office for a dozen people, not one. The man walked briskly towards him, held out his hand and smiled.

'Ah, Mr Calovarlo, delighted to meet you. I see you've met my colleague, Samantha. We will be working together on your case.' Melton-Barr was aware of the initial impression Samantha had on clients. 'Samantha has one of the sharpest legal brains in London – if not the whole UK. Please, please, take a seat,' he gestured.

Reginald Melton-Barr led the way to a table near the bright

electronic whiteboard. It was piled with books, some of them open, and several thick files; three chairs were arranged around it. He picked up a sheet of paper from an open file, glanced at it and sat down. Looking first at Sandro and then the whiteboard he began to speak.

'We've studied the evidence against you. Initially it can be grouped into three areas: forensic evidence, testimony from the alleged victim and other witness statements.'

Sandro could now see the significance of the whiteboard and the information on it. It was a summary of the case against him. The photograph that caught his eye, then his whole attention, was the bloody face of Anna Kalnina. Sandro switched his concentration back to Melton-Barr.

'At a superficial level one can see why Detective Inspector Latchem and even Ms Roberta Fox believed the combined evidence was "overwhelming". In my opinion any defence should accept all the forensic evidence presented...'

'But Roberta Fox believed it was the forensic evidence that was the most damning...'

Melton-Barr raised his hand in a gesture that asked Sandro to be silent. 'In my experience there is nothing to be gained in challenging forensic evidence – but everything to be gained in how it is interpreted. The Crown will want to bring expert after expert to testify that your DNA, your blood, saliva and semen are on the clothes and body of Ms Anna Kalnina. We merely accept this evidence. However, our interpretation is that they are present due to consensual, rough sex that perhaps went a little too far.'

Samantha Elliot continued: 'This would be consistent with a young, attractive, single woman enjoying a midweek break in a vibrant city like Manchester. She was on holiday to "have a good time". Going to a nightclub, alone, to dance and drink with a stranger, a virile young man, is not unusual. I suspect it would not be difficult to establish that Ms Kalnina was not a virgin, has had several partners, and was an "active" partner.'

Melton-Barr interrupted: 'In our experience, previous boyfriends can be forthcoming and graphic when describing the sexual behaviour of a partner who has discarded them.'

'What about the scratches on her body, her bloody nose and cut lip?'

Samantha answered the question. 'I can bring a dozen medical and behavioural experts to the stand who will confirm that it is not unusual for an aroused woman to demand their partner bite, scratch and beat them. Equally, I can elicit testimony from eminent psychologists on the practice of *displacement* – the defence mechanism in which a person redirects responsibility for a particular emotion or action from themself onto another. Such behaviour is not uncommon.'

Melton-Barr took up the conversation. 'I believe the basis of your defence should be in creating an alternative scenario for what happened that night. We would need to place doubt in the minds of the jury. Whenever there is doubt there cannot be a conviction...'

Sandro raised his hands and interrupted. 'You haven't asked me if I'm innocent. You haven't asked me if I beat and raped that young woman.'

Melton-Barr reached across the desk for a file. He opened it, extracted a sheaf of papers and flicked through them until he found what he was looking for. 'You told the police, and I quote, "I didn't do anything". Throughout your entire statement you maintain you did not assault and rape Ms Kalnina. You also said, repeatedly, that you did not remember what happened between your collapse and arrival at the police station in Manchester. You also pleaded not guilty.'

'But it sounds like you would systematically destroy the reputation of Ms Kalnina.'

Melton-Barr paused and took a deep breath as though irritated.

'You can't both be telling the truth... but it is not important what I think, it is only important what I can prove or demonstrate is beyond reasonable doubt.

'Mr Calovarlo, I'm not sure you understand what is at stake here. In the court room, you will be fighting for your life. If you are found guilty of these charges you will go to prison. You will have a criminal record and be on the sex offenders' register. You will spend the best years of your life in a cell. When you leave you will no longer be the person you are today; you will be an old man. Whatever life you have today will have been changed forever.'

Samantha took up the conversation: 'Since the kidnap, rape and murder of Sarah Everard by a policeman last year, the police are under pressure to bring charges against suspected rapists. The Crown Prosecution Service and judges are also under pressure to increase conviction rates and award stern sentences. If you do not allow us to conduct what we believe to be the strongest possible defence, you may spend a long time in prison.'

Sandro slumped in the chair and for a moment held his head in his hands. Drawing his hands across his face, he made eye contact with Melton-Barr and asked him to continue.

'Witness statements: Detective Inspector Latchem has provided witness statements to say you were drunk and collapsed on the dance floor. We do not challenge the fact that you collapsed, that you had to be helped to a chair, to a taxi and to a hotel room. The Crown has to provide evidence that you were drunk at the nightclub.'

Samantha Elliot took up the argument: 'They have provided no evidence that you drank alcohol; none was ordered for your consumption whilst you were in the nightclub. A search of your apartment discovered several full bottles of champagne but no empty bottles with your fingerprints on them. I suspect Inspector Latchem will have checked with bars and off-licences in the area between your apartment and the nightclub in case you bought alcohol that evening. There's no mention of this in the file and so I suspect they failed to find any evidence.

'We can provide ample evidence to show that extremely high proportions of young women drink before entering nightclubs. They want the effect that alcohol brings but at supermarket prices. Ms Kalnina's blood tests, taken at the police station, indicate she did have significant amounts of alcohol in her bloodstream. Our experts will confirm that concentrations at this level lower or entirely remove inhibitions.'

She turned to Melton-Barr who took up the conversation. 'You are a successful professional diver and have repeatedly stated that you do not drink. We will be able to bring a succession of witnesses to court – business associates, friends and colleagues – who will state, on oath, that you do not drink. We can parade former girlfriends who will all say you do not drink. Blood tests from your doctor and dive medicals will confirm that no alcohol was ever found in your bloodstream.

'Drunks typically smell of alcohol. However, in all the witness statements to date, there is no mention of you reeking of alcohol. The security guard at the nightclub, the taxi driver and the night porter all *assumed* you were drunk – but without any evidence.'

Melton-Barr stopped speaking, looked up and smiled at Sandro. 'Mr Calovarlo, can you describe the symptoms of hypoglycaemia and ingesting flunitrazepam?'

Sandro looked at the questioner in puzzlement. 'I've never heard of flunitrazepam, but I think hypoglycaemia is related to eyesight...'

'Don't worry, you are not alone in not knowing about these conditions. Flunitrazepam is a date rape drug and hypoglycaemia is related to a drop in blood sugar. A common symptom of both would be total collapse – just like what happened on the dance floor. But did the nightclub offer first aid? Did they call for medical help? No, and neither did the taxi driver. At least the night porter, thinking that you were merely drunk, put you in the recovery position to stop you choking on your own vomit!'

'Why would anybody spike my drink with a date rape drug?'

Samantha leaned forwards in her chair: 'If you think only women are given date rape drugs, think again!'

'But how do we account for the alcohol in my bloodstream?' asked Sandro.

'Perhaps you drank it involuntarily. In a collapsed state, perhaps you thought it was water. Perhaps it was pressed upon you whilst in a vulnerable state. Again, the focus would be on creating doubt in the minds of a jury. There is no evidence of alcohol consumption prior to your collapse. It is possible that, unknowingly, you drank it whilst in the company of Ms Kalnina. There is no mention in the files of the police finding an open or empty bottle of alcohol in the hotel room, or even outside the window. After midnight, the corridors of the hotel would be quiet. It would be easy for Ms Kalnina to dispose of an empty bottle if she so wished.'

'I, I... I'm starting to understand how you plan to sow doubt and offer an alternative explanation.'

'Mr Calovarlo, during your first police interview you claimed the complaints against you were "a set-up" but were unable to provide any evidence. We will explore this possibility and Ms Kalnina is the obvious starting point.'

Melton-Barr continued. 'A jury consists of ordinary members of the public who are generally worldly-wise. They listen to the arguments and reasons and are seldom swayed by character assassination. In my experience they are also reluctant to convict. In this country less than two percent of reported cases of sexual assault end in a conviction. I think you have every chance of being acquitted.

'However, there is an important point I need to mention. If I were to judge the case was going badly, you would need to consider pleading guilty to a much lesser charge, like common assault. The maximum penalty is six months in prison but if this charge was accepted, I would expect merely a fine.'

'But I'd still have it on my record.'

'Yes. However, from my assessment of the evidence, I believe there is every chance of a complete acquittal.'

Samantha picked up a large envelope from the table and slipped out a thin bound document. 'This report represents our professional opinion on your case and the strategies we would employ in your defence. It is strictly confidential and *for your eyes only.* Should this report fall into the hands of others it would seriously compromise not only your case, but our ability to represent you. It indicates the investigations we would conduct on your behalf, the expert witnesses we would call, the re-analyses of forensic samples and so on.

'We also include an invoice which represents the cost of assembling this report as well as an estimate of the cost of your defence should the case come to trial. I'm sure you will want to consider the contents of the report, and your other options, before you come to a decision. We will simply wait to hear from you. Is there anything else you would like to ask us at this time?'

With so much to consider Sandro's mind was in a whirl. He just wanted to escape so he could think and decide what to do next. As he walked to the underground station, Sandro could hear the words of Melton-Barr ringing in his ears: 'In the court room you will be fighting for your life.' They were replaced by those of Detective Inspector Latchem claiming the police had 'overwhelming evidence'. He thought of his last meeting with Roberta Fox who had recommended he plead guilty. Even Samantha Elliot was telling him he may 'spend a long time in prison'.

Sandro made his way to the railway station and onto the train. As it trundled towards Manchester, he removed the report and invoices from the envelope. He was shocked. The second opinion cost over twice the amount Roberta Fox was claiming. If Melton-

Barr and his team represented him at a trial there would be three more bills: one upon engaging them as his defence lawyers, a second at the start of any trial and a third at its conclusion. Sandro was amazed at the cost of over £200,000. He could buy another ship cheaper – except he may not be at liberty to buy one.

Chapter 11

Mind made up

Sandro had plenty of time to think about the meeting with Reginald Melton-Barr and Samantha Elliot. On the journey back to Manchester and the whole of the evening he thought of nothing else. He had made his mind up by the time he walked into the office in Salford. Jack and Lesley were chatting; their smiles and welcome seemed genuine. As he made eye contact with Jack he said: 'If you've got a few minutes this morning there's something I want to share with you...'

He didn't wait for a reply but continued walking to his own office. Jack followed only moments later, wide-eyed and with a look of anticipation on his face. 'So, what's the news?'

Sandro leaned forward in his chair and placed his arms on the desk in front of him. 'It's not very good, but I've reached some decisions; decisions that are going to affect you and the company. The lawyers in London think my best defence is to create what they call an alternative scenario for what happened and to create doubt in the minds of a jury. They're suggesting we argue that what happened was "rough sex that went too far". They're also going to explore a possible set-up – but I can't think of anyone who would do it. What have they got to gain – besides destroying me? I'm going to phone the lawyers this morning and confirm I want them to represent me.'

Sandro paused to collect his thoughts. 'It seems the police and the courts are under pressure to prosecute more suspects and achieve higher conviction rates. I didn't know that last year less than two percent of rape complaints ended in conviction. They were talking about mounting a strong defence but said I may have to plead guilty to a lesser charge of assault. When I weigh up all that I've been told, it looks like I'm going to prison. I've been thinking about it, and I've come to some conclusions.

'I'm going to arrange to rent out the apartment – fully furnished – if I'm convicted. It will raise some money whilst I'm in prison. Before I get out, I'll arrange to have it cleared, redecorated and then sold. I'm going to arrange to sell the Alfa. There's no point paying for it to be stored. By the time I get out it will be an antique, a dinosaur. I also want to draw up some legal agreement between us about the company. I don't want to sell my share – I'm happy for you to continue. However, if I'm not contributing, I can't expect a share of any profit. If you want to bring in another partner, I won't object.

'I don't know what happens to prisoners once they leave prison. They may put me on some sort of probation, or I may be completely free – I don't know. What I do know is that whatever the outcome, I don't want to stay in Manchester. I will leave the country as soon as possible. I don't want to return to Italy or Naples but maybe some small Caribbean island where no one knows me. I would still have my diving qualifications. I'd get a job with some dive centre and start to rebuild a life. The lawyers will take all my savings and I'll still owe them money… perhaps we could leave any discussion about me selling my share and leaving the company until then? I'm not sure how much money I'd need to start another life.'

Jack was shocked both by what Sandro said and at the broken man sitting in front of him. In recent weeks he had noticed changes in Sandro. He seemed to be taking less care of himself. Sandro was fastidious about his clothes but seemed to be wearing the same shirt and trousers day after day. His eyes had lost that sparkle and the dark patches under them were becoming a permanent feature. Today, as the sunlight bathed Sandro's desk, he saw his cheekbones for the first time. Sandro had lost weight... and hope. As tears began to well in his eyes, Sandro muttered: '*Ti ho deluso* – I've let you down, I'm sorry.'

Jack could feel his own emotions rising as he moved to Sandro's side and wrapped a consoling arm around him. 'You haven't let anyone down... I can't believe you would hurt anyone. I don't want to lose you as a partner, so please, don't do anything without us talking about it.

'If it makes you feel any better, why don't we ask Bill Watts to make some provisional arrangements about the apartment, your car and the company. Once that's done you can concentrate on what needs to be done on the case. We can also crack on with the salvage of the *Asenka*,' announced Jack as he punched Sandro on his shoulder.

Alone in his office, Sandro phoned Themis Chambers and was eventually put through to Samantha Elliot. He was trying to sound positive when he spoke. 'It's Sandro... I wanted to thank you and your colleague Mr Melton-Barr for your comments and advice regarding the charges against me. This morning I paid your fee by bank transfer and would be grateful if you and staff at Themis Chambers would represent me in any future court case...'

There was silence from the other end of the phone as Sandro waited agonisingly for a response. At first, he had been strangely unconcerned about who would offer him advice when talking to the police. Although he couldn't remember, he never thought for a moment that he was guilty of the rape of Anna Kalnina. He had naively believed it would be sorted out quickly. However, when Roberta Fox advised him to reconsider his plea, he suddenly realised the enormity of the case against him. He had read, and reread, the second opinion by Samantha Elliot and Reginald Melton-Barr and realised they were offering him a lifeline. He was now gripping the phone and praying they wouldn't cast him adrift.

'We would be delighted... if you just bear with me for a moment,' said Samantha as Sandro heard her put down the phone and shuffle files. 'The office will send you a formal contract setting out the terms and conditions of our representation. As soon as we have the signed contract, we will liaise with Ms Roberta Fox and obtain copies of all her information about the case. We will also initiate the various enquiries set out in our submission. Oh, there's one other thing. We would like you to undertake a full medical and psychological assessment. It's to pre-empt any questions about medical or psychological conditions that may have been present at the time of the incident. We would expect a completely normal assessment – but we need to obtain it as a matter of course. We use a clinic in south London; the office will send you contact details. Assessment is made over two days and involves an overnight stay in a nearby hotel. If you could arrange to complete the assessment as soon as possible it would be appreciated. Don't worry about payment. They will send all charges directly to us.'

Samantha fixed a future date for a London meeting and, with enthusiasm that was encouraging, said she was looking forward to working with him.

Chapter 12

The MPA Clinic

Sandro decided to spend the night before the assessment in the hotel Samantha Elliot had recommended; it was only a ten-to-fifteen-minute walk to the clinic. The hotel was comfortable and impersonal. It was just what he wanted at the present time; he wasn't feeling sociable. He had checked the location of the clinic but almost walked past it. He'd been expecting bold signs announcing it, perhaps an ambulance, parked cars and the bustle of pedestrians. Instead, he walked alone alongside a modern, low-rise building that could have been an insurance company or apartment block. A shallow ramp led him from the pavement to two sets of double glass doors and a discreet stainless-steel plaque. It simply stated MPA CLINIC and gave the address as 147 Southam Street, SE7.

Inside, the impression of an insurance company rather than a medical clinic continued. It was bright, modern and decorated more like a business-class airport lounge than a reception. He was greeted by pastel green walls, numerous paintings, downlights, Scandinavian-style furniture and carpet rather than the harsh, utilitarian equivalent he had been expecting. He scanned the room. There were probably ten or more people sitting around, presumably waiting for appointments. On his left he noted a coffee machine, jugs of fruit juice, bottles and cans. It looked like there was a glass display case holding snacks. Closest to him was an elderly man reading a newspaper. He was about to raise a cup to his lips.

'Mr Alessandro Calovarlo?' he was asked by a young woman who had sprung from nowhere.

Sandro was initially taken aback. He wasn't sure at first if the woman was a receptionist or a doctor. She had a bright, friendly, engaging smile, soft American accent and long, straight, cherry-red hair. The white jacket, different-coloured lanyards with electronic keys attached and metal badge that announced 'Dr Esther May' that confirmed who she was.

'Yes, yes, but call me Sandro,' he replied, returning the smile.

Sandro now realised that Dr May had been hidden in a small alcove when he walked in. She had been standing by a counter and talking to what seemed to be the official receptionist.

'I'm Doctor Esther May, one of the assessment team. I'm also your assessment coordinator. I'll be leading you through the next two days so if you have any questions, anything you're unsure about or want to clarify, just ask me. The medical team are waiting for you but there are a few administrative things I need to confirm.'

Dr Esther May glanced at the computer tablet she was cradling in her hands. 'We don't seem to have received your registration information or agreement to our code of practice and recording system. Have you brought the documents with you?'

Sandro hesitated for a moment and then recalled the email. He'd forgotten to respond and apologised.

'No problem,' replied Dr May. 'If you'd like to follow me, we can complete them now and get started on the assessments.'

She led Sandro to a small office, complete with table-top computer. A few deft strokes and the first online form was ready for completion. 'The registration document is merely for our records. Some of it is already filled in but it would be good if you could check and complete the rest. The other document explains our code of practice and recording system. It's quite long and rather complicated. Basically, it says we collect your personal data at each stage of the assessment process. We also make audio and video recordings during each assessment. All this data and all the recordings remain your property. You can suspend or cancel the assessment and recordings at any time.

'It also explains that you will receive the original documents and recordings; we will retain a copy and a copy will be sent to your legal representative. You can request these copies at any time to preserve your privacy.'

Dr May grimaced as she continued. 'It also says that if you decide not to accept our code of practice and refuse to sign it, we cannot conduct the assessment. It's important that you read the whole document and decide whether to sign it or not. I'll leave you to decide and come back in a few minutes.'

Sandro was annoyed with himself for letting things slip. He pounded away at the computer keyboard and quickly completed the registration form. It took longer to wade through the legalese of the code of practice. However, he had nothing to hide. Melton-Barr and Samantha Elliot believed the assessment would support his case and he completed the form and sat back to wait. Dr May returned shortly, forwarded the forms to some place in the clinic computer system and led him off to yet another room.

A white jacketed doctor and uniformed nurse were standing next to an examination couch waiting for him. The nurse directed him to a cubicle to change and produce his first urine sample of the day. He emerged, plastic container in hand, and dressed in a green T-shirt, matching shorts and short socks. Blood tests and an ECG were followed by a thorough physical examination from top to toe. Many of the tests were like the ones he completed regularly as part of his fitness to dive medical. The doctor tested his balance, reflexes and coordination. He conducted detailed hearing and sight tests as well as applying a row of sticking plasters on his forearm to test for allergies.

As the assessment continued, Sandro started to feel that both the doctor and the nurse were trying too hard to be pleasant and reassuring; the smiles started to look forced. They were repeatedly asking if he was comfortable, had any questions, wanted a break and so on. It was only when Sandro had completed the 'step-up test', rhythmically stepping up and down from a bench in time to a metronome for several minutes, that the doctor sounded spontaneous and genuine.

'I'd say you're pretty fit,' he commented with a smile. 'Minimum body fat, a resting pulse rate of fifty-five and still under ninety at the end of the assessment.'

The nurse gave Sandro another forced smile and told him the morning assessment was complete. He could shower, change and have lunch before the afternoon sessions.

Sandro was emerging from the change cubicle just as Dr Esther May entered the examination room. 'That was good timing,' she said with a broad smile. 'One of the perks is that I get a free lunch if we have it together; you hungry?'

Despite missing breakfast Sandro wasn't particularly hungry but was happy to accept the invitation. Esther led him through a series of corridors and up a staircase to a modern-looking refectory. The décor and furniture were in keeping with what he'd seen already. It was almost empty, but Esther explained: 'We're early, give it ten minutes and the place will be crowded. It's a simple set menu. Just choose what you like, and we'll find a table.'

The food was simple and wholesome and the smell made him realise he was hungry. He'd no sooner started eating when Dr May asked: 'Your notes say you are a deep-sea diver. That must be exciting and dangerous.'

'We do everything we can to make sure it's not exciting and not dangerous; but it is another world.'

'Tell me about it; what's your most memorable dive?'

'Simple question but difficult to answer because there have been so many.'

'Which one would encourage me to learn to dive?' she asked.

Sandro's thoughts flicked through hundreds of dives. He recalled once losing a shot line that had been attached to a wreck and being swept away by the current. Jack had probably saved his life by using the current to feed him a line attached to a remotely operated vehicle. He'd been trapped by falling rocks in an underwater maze inside a volcanic worm hole. It had been almost zero visibility. Jack had lifted a huge volcanic slab and pulled him free. The more he thought about it, the more he realised he owed Jack so much. Yet he was in danger of destroying himself and taking Jack and the company with him. He didn't want to visit these dark places and so recalled a truly memorable dive.

'My business partner, Jack Collier, taught me to dive when we were both on a master's degree course in Portsmouth. At the end of the course, the university dive club took a cheap and cheerful trip to dive in the Seychelles. We booked a small guest house close to the beach and one of the local dive boats. One of the early dives was to a site called Shark Bank. It was a couple of kilometres off the coast and between the main island and a rocky outcrop. It wasn't a particularly deep dive, probably twenty-five to twenty-seven metres. We'd been told to expect a moderate current and to go down a mooring line and into the shelter of a large underwater rock.'

Sandro paused as he remembered the dive. 'It was the colour of the water, the corals and the viz,' he recalled. 'The water was a crisp, clear blue. I could see to the seabed. I could also see the stream of bubbles from divers below, and off to the side was a massive shoal of yellow snapper. I'd never seen such a big shoal; I'd never seen yellow snapper! At one point we swam through the shoal – so close we could have touched them. Sunlight was catching the silver of their bodies as they moved in the water. There were graceful shapes of reef sharks cruising a couple of metres above the seabed.

'Near the bottom we sheltered by the large rock for a few

minutes and just let the parade continue around us. I remember small groups of yellowfin tuna flashing past as though in a race. They were leaving bubbles in their wake like the pictures of penguins on the TV. The current was catching the soft corals and they swayed gently. I'd been so preoccupied I'd forgotten the time. It was Jack who tapped his dive computer to signal it was time to surface.'

For a few moments, Sandro had been transported to happier times. He wasn't sure if Dr May had done it on purpose or if he was merely reminiscing. He would have liked the feeling to continue but changed the subject and kept the rest of the conversation to trivial topics.

The afternoon sessions were conducted by Dr May and were unlike any he had experienced. During the first session he sat in front of a computer screen and completed dozens of multiple-choice questions about his interaction with people. At first, he found it easy to reply but as the session continued, he found it harder and harder to choose a single answer. When he queried one of the questions, Dr May merely told him he should select only one answer, the one that he thought was the most appropriate.

In another session, a type of blood pressure machine was fitted to his arm. Electrodes were attached to some of his fingers and to his palms. Once he'd been 'wired up' she fired words and phrases at him and asked him to reply with the first word or phrase that came to mind. He guessed this was some sort of lie detector test. All it did was make him more nervous.

Later, pictures replaced the words and phrases and he became aware that intermingled with innocuous photographs were pictures of naked men and women, boys and girls. At the start of yet another assessment, a technician put a tight-fitting skull cap on his head. Spots of gel were squeezed through numerous holes in the skull cap and electrodes fitted. He was bombarded by a whole new set of words and phrases, photos and sounds. The whole thing seemed to last hours and he felt drained at the end. It was a relief to escape into the changing cubicle and have a long, hot shower.

That evening, in his hotel room, Sandro typed the name Dr Esther May into his computer search engine. He was surprised by the number of hits. Esther May was the only daughter of Colonel George May and Lieutenant Colonel Jean May, two doctors in the US Medical Corps. At sixteen she had won a scholarship to the Johns Hopkins University School of Medicine and was one of the youngest ever doctors to qualify. However, instead of joining a lucrative practice in the States she had joined Médecins Sans Frontières and volunteered to work in war zones, from Afghanistan to Beirut, Ethiopia to Sri Lanka. Later she had moved from emergency medicine to working in the field of mental health.

As Sandro jumped from one account to another, he came across a summary of a recent conference presentation. She had presented a paper entitled 'The psychological diagnosis and treatment of sexual offenders'. The phrase on the computer screen stopped him in his tracks. A cold shiver of realisation swept over him. 'They think I'm a sex offender. She's assessing me as a rapist.' His first reaction was to rebel, to phone Samantha Elliot and demand an explanation – to ask why he had been sent to a clinic to be assessed as a rapist. No sooner had he reacted than he acknowledged the reality. Detective Inspector Latchem had told him the case against him was 'overwhelming' and Roberta Fox had agreed. Samantha Elliot and Melton-Barr were simply collecting evidence and would decide how they could interpret the data. It took Sandro hours to get over the shock and to decide what to do. In the end it was simple. He wouldn't confront anyone, he would act as normal, complete the assessment and wait to learn the results.

Sandro felt strangely calm as he changed into the green T-shirt, shorts and socks in readiness for another day of assessment. He would play his role and let the medics play theirs.

The doctor told him more blood, urine and saliva samples would be taken, followed by a complete MRI scan of his body and a CAT scan of his head. Sandro had forgotten about the row of sticking plasters on his arm. It was only when the doctor asked to inspect the sites of allergy tests that he remembered; there had been no reaction.

In the afternoon Dr May conducted more assessments but Sandro felt detached from them. He recalled arranging coloured cards and symbols into groups, small odd-shaped tablets into mini constructions and even recognised one of the assessments as the Rorschach Inkblot Test. Throughout, he was calm, relaxed and no longer anxious, merely compliant. It came as a surprise when Dr May announced that the assessment was complete.

There were regular trains from London to Manchester so there was no rush to collect his overnight bag and make his way through corridors towards the exit. But it was a surprise when he almost bumped into Dr May in reception. He didn't recognise her at first. The maroon hoody was hiding her hair and was much too big for her. He also wondered how she had managed to get to the reception area ahead of him.

'I've finished for the day,' she said with a smile. 'If you're in no rush to get back to Manchester perhaps we could grab a coffee or even a beer.'

In the last few minutes Sandro had abandoned his compliant, detached mode and returned to normal. Suddenly he was on high alert. 'Why is Dr Esther May showing me so much attention?' he asked himself. 'She was waiting for me in reception yesterday, took me to lunch and is waiting for me now. This is not a chance invitation.'

Sandro returned Dr May's broad smile and switched to compliant mode. 'A coffee would be great – but I'll pass on the beer, I don't drink.'

Sandro wasn't sure where he was going but was happy to walk

along the street, down side roads and eventually to a quiet coffee shop. It was almost deserted. As they made themselves comfortable in a cosy booth Sandro smiled warmly and decided to take the initiative. 'Well, you've spent the last two days finding out all about me; so tell me about Dr Esther May.'

Chapter 13

Ongoing assessment

It emerged that Esther's parents were career soldiers, or rather medics in the US Army. She had been born in a US Army hospital and moved from one military post to another, one home to another, one school to another. Her early life seemed to be completely different to Sandro's. He had played in the narrow streets and alleys of Naples with his friends. He had been surrounded by aunts and uncles and learned from all of them. He'd never really thought about a career or what he might do when he left school. He'd assumed he would join the family boat-building and repair business.

In contrast, Esther had few opportunities to make friends. Those she started to form were lost when her parents were transferred to another post. Instead, she described how she lost herself in books and in her studies. All the discussion around her was about medicine and so it seemed natural to read about it. 'I remember being confused when Mom told me I'd won a scholarship to Johns Hopkins to study medicine. I wasn't even aware I'd applied. It had just been another test or quiz alongside dozens of others.'

Sandro found it easy to talk to Esther, she put him at ease. He found himself lowering the emotional barriers he'd erected earlier. He also realised it was more than simply 'putting him at ease'. In Italian she was *vivace*, in English she was vivacious. He found himself attracted to her and began to bask in the feeling. In recent months, he'd withdrawn from those around him, especially women. For the first time in his life, he had questioned the way he related to women, how he regarded them and treated them. His first reaction was to assess them sexually rather than consider their intellect or potential. Was he normal? Would the assessment reveal exactly who he was and conclude he was merely driven by sexual desire and prowess?

Could that be changing? He had a respect for Esther – who she was and what she had achieved. He enjoyed listening to her as she talked about studying in Baltimore, working in the university hospital, and deciding to join Médecins Sans Frontières. Esther was recalling a tale of her work in Eritrea when the café door slammed. It broke the spell and Sandro checked his watch as he shuffled in his chair.

'Look at the time. You should be thinking of going home and I've a train to catch.'

Esther checked her watch as well. 'I can drop you at the underground station, but rush hour has already started. You're going to be fighting to get on a tube and will probably end up standing most of the way to Manchester. If you're not in a rush, we could grab tapas from my local takeaway and I could drop you at the station later – up to you.'

Sandro wasn't about to turn down the offer. They strolled back to the clinic and took a side road to the car park. Esther clicked the remote control and the lights on a vivid yellow VW Beetle flashed.

'Easy to find in a car park,' Sandro commented.

The traffic was heavy and there seemed to be one traffic light after another. Esther switched between a commentary about living in London, visiting her parents and wondering about what to do next. Sandro was happy to listen.

'We're here,' she announced as she signalled to turn off the road and down a broad concrete ramp.

Esther must have triggered a switch because a heavy metal

screen started to lift and reveal the entrance to an underground car park. Lights came on and bathed the space in light; it reflected off the white painted walls. What immediately struck Sandro was how clean and organised it was. The floor was painted grey, and the tyres squealed as Esther drove through the maze-like space. Dark blue rectangles marked individual parking bays with service pipes and ducting painted red, yellow and green. Esther parked in her bay. Sandro grabbed his overnight bag and followed her to the front of the car. He was just about to ask which way when an elevator door opened. The door was white, the same colour as the walls, and it looked like a shallow recess. Sandro followed her into the elevator as she fiddled with her phone.

'Just switching the lights on,' was all she said.

Moments later the lift door opened and they stepped out into her apartment. It was large and open. Soft downlights and shaded table lamps created a cosy glow. Directly in front of him was a large picture window. It was getting dark outside and lights from houses and streets below were starting to twinkle and stretched into the distance. There was a waist high kitchen unit to his left. It separated a modern-looking kitchen from the lounge area in which he was standing. A couple of large light-brown leather sofas and two equally large leather chairs surrounded a low table and looked out over the city. The subtle lighting, paintings and bookshelves made it look more like a film set than a place someone lived.

'You get used to it... make yourself comfortable. I'm going to change out of the uniform,' Esther said as she made her way towards a corridor.

'Could you pour me a glass of white wine? There's a bottle in the fridge... try the cupboards until you find what you need.'

She was out of sight by the time she shouted: 'There are cans of soda water in the fridge.'

Sandro froze when he heard the phrase. An involuntary shiver washed over him. 'There are cans of soda water in the fridge,' she had said – but how did she know he drank soda water? He hadn't mentioned soda water at any time over the last two days. Esther had said, 'We could grab a coffee or even a beer' but apart from saying he didn't drink, he hadn't said anymore. How did she know he typically drank soda water? It couldn't have been a guess. The only way she could know was if she had read about it in the police files or in notes from Samantha Elliot.

Suddenly the polite and friendly questioning over lunch, the conversation in the coffee shop and in the car made sense. The assessment was continuing. If it was continuing, it was probably being recorded. Sandro realised he had drifted out of his compliant mode; he returned to it now. He walked over to the kitchen area and stared at the cupboards; they were all plain fronted and white, they all looked the same. Hidden lights lit the rows of tiles between the work surface and cupboards. He touched one of the cupboard doors and it opened – plates and saucers, wrong cupboard. The next was cups, mugs and bowls. Eventually he found the glasses and picked out a wine glass and a tumbler. All the crockery looked new; it didn't look used. The fridge was easy to spot. It was the only large-fronted cupboard and had a small blue light glowing near the top. As he grabbed a can of soda water, he noticed that the fridge was almost empty, no partly used jars, no opened packages, no milk. Sandro concluded that this was indeed a film set and he was about to be auditioned. He took his place on the couch, sipped the soda water and gazed over the roof tops.

Sandro was composed by the time Esther returned. She'd been transformed. The hoody and clinic uniform were gone, and she was wearing a large grey T-shirt with a life-size head of Minnie Mouse on her chest and tight grey leggings. His immediate reaction was that the colour of the bow in Minnie's hair clashed with Esther's red hair. The second was that Esther was bra-less. The natural movement of her breasts beneath the T-shirt was unmistakable. She bent forwards to pick up the glass of wine, smiled and said 'cheers' as she raised her glass in a toast. The material across her chest stretched revealing the clear shape of a nipple.

On another evening, on another day and with another attractive young woman he would have been aroused. Instead, he raised his tumbler and said '*saluti'* with the most genuine smile he could muster. Sandro had already decided to continue the game he had played whilst at the clinic. The conversation was relaxed and pleasant. Sandro was happy to respond to the questions Esther posed and tried not to appear guarded. He returned to asking about her work with Médecins Sans Frontières but avoided anything to do with the clinic and the assessment. He described how locating the wreck of the *Rockingham Castle* had transformed the fledgling company he and Jack Collier had formed. Esther had curled her legs beneath her. A shapely leg and thigh merely added to the desirable image before him. It was one that for once he could easily resist. The minutes passed, they talked easily, but Sandro never lost his composure. Esther had refilled her glass and brought Sandro another small can of soda water.

'Do you fancy tapas?' she asked. 'There's a place just around the corner that can deliver in minutes.'

Sandro glanced at his watch: 'Tempting but I think I'll pass and get off to the railway station. The rush will have eased by now. Is there an underground station nearby? If not, perhaps I can call for a taxi...'

Esther looked surprised at the decision. 'You're welcome to relax here, stay overnight and catch an early train tomorrow...' She let the offer linger, the invitation to spend the night with her was clear.

'That's very generous of you but I'm sure you have better things to do than entertain me… Do you have the number of a taxi company?' Sandro asked as he finished his soda water and sat up on the sofa.

It was an awkward ten-minute wait for the taxi. Esther slipped the hoody over her head and put trainers onto her feet before escorting Sandro to the entrance area. They waited in almost silence until the taxi arrived. As the taxi stopped by the kerb Sandro took Esther's hand, raised it to his lips and kissed it. 'Thank you for the last two days and this evening. I'll look forward to the report, *ciao.*'

As the taxi dodged through the light traffic to the railway station he wondered if he had been right. Was it another assessment or was there an attraction between them? Was he becoming paranoid or was he changing?

Chapter 14

Working in the dark

'He's changed barristers!' David Moxon almost shouted as he burst into the portacabin that formed their low-profile office. It was one of dozens in the fenced compound next to the lorry park.

'What?' was Tony's reply.

'Calovarlo has been dumped by Fox and has teamed up with Melton-Barr in London. It's a disaster.' Moxon shook his head in a gesture of disbelief.

'OK, tell me more.'

'I only discovered this morning. With no new lines of enquiry, Fox came to the conclusion that Calovarlo was going to lose and lose badly. It would be a black mark against her reputation, a cross against her record. She sent him an invoice for the work to date and bailed out. She basically told him to plead guilty or seek another opinion. I only discovered what had happened when I asked about the next meeting with Calovarlo. There isn't going to be one!'

'He's gone with Reginald Melton-Barr; he's a big name and handles high-profile criminal cases in London. I phoned a friend who works in London and he told me Melton-Barr has a fearsome reputation. He's renowned for pulling rabbits out of hats, reinterpreting the evidence... and getting people off.'

'OK, OK, so besides a change in the barrister, what else has changed? The evidence is the evidence. Roberta Fox believed it was so overwhelming that she gave up and invited him to plead guilty. You said that the policewoman thought the evidence was… overwhelming. How does Melton-Barr change this?'

'He can't change the evidence – but suddenly we don't know the strategy or strategies he's going to adopt. We don't know how he will challenge or interpret the evidence. We don't see the disclosures the police and Melton-Barr make. We don't know how Calovarlo will react. It leaves us in the dark.'

Tony sat quietly for a few moments before replying. 'Let's just think for a moment. How does this affect our plan? We wanted the pressure on Calovarlo to increase – and it has! Is he more or less likely to go for it?'

Tony paused for a few moments before continuing: 'Three questions: when do we expect the drums and machinery parts to be salvaged? When could a court case start? How much will Melton-Barr be charging him?'

'I don't know exactly when the salvage is going to start but it's scheduled within the next three weeks. The insurance company said the salvors expect the priority salvage items to be recovered in seven to ten days. A few more days to get to the warehouse in Riga – so five, maybe six weeks at the earliest.

'Even if the case is fast-tracked, I can't see it starting for a couple of months. I'm not sure about the fees. My guess is that they would be staggered over the case – from preparatory work, starting a trial and its conclusion.'

David suddenly realised the reason for the questions. 'The legal fees would be four to five times the "compensation" to be paid to Anna Kalnina. Now would be a good time to let Calovarlo know that he could ensure he never faced the charges against him in court – and at a fraction of the costs if he did risk a trial. It's got to be a no brainer,' he said with a smile.

'I reckon it's time to put the plan in operation,' said Tony as he moved to pick up the phone.

Chapter 15

A proposition

Jack was in his office in Wentworth Mansions, Salford. He was bent over the drawings of the MV *Asenka* and comparing the side sonar trace of the wreck with the manifest and disposition of the cargo. Their own inspection had confirmed the *Asenka* was resting on the seabed at fifty-two metres. The ship was intact and leaning no more than five degrees to starboard. With the three holds uncovered they should have ready access to the cargo. However, he knew it was all speculation until they started to move the cargo. The initial inspection had shown most of the pallets of zinc ingots had remained in place. Luckily, they hadn't moved during the sinking. If they had smashed into the other cargo, it would have been a nightmare. Pallets of two thousand kilograms of metal bouncing around in a confined space could do a lot of damage. The video record confirmed most of the pallets were intact. Jack's estimate was that it would take them well under seven days to haul everything to the surface.

They had confirmed the rental of a freighter, slightly smaller than the *Asenka*. It would be able to carry all the salvaged cargo and be more stable and manoeuvrable than a dumb barge, a simple floating platform. It would also avoid a standby tug and towing charges. The problem would be ensuring the freighter stayed on station. Jack estimated that in fair weather a series of anchors, supplemented by the raw power of the *Stavanger,* could hold the two ships in position. If there was a danger of them drifting off station, the two ships could simply part until conditions improved. The *Stavanger* was a similar size to the freighter they planned to use but significantly more powerful.

Jack was thinking about the salvage timetable when the phone rang. It was Lesley, the company secretary. 'Jack, caller on the line from Riga in Latvia. Didn't give his name or company... just said he wanted to speak to you.'

Jack waited for the click on the phone to tell him Lesley had put the call through. 'Good morning, Jack Collier here, how can I help you?'

'Good morning indeed, Mr Collier. I think we can help each other,' said the caller with the hint of a Liverpool accent. 'I have a proposal for you that would be to our mutual benefit.'

There was something about the choice of words and confident tone that unsettled Jack. He immediately thought it was a scam call and was deciding whether to end the call or let it continue for a few more seconds. Before he could decide the caller added: 'It could mean your friend doesn't spend the next fifteen years in prison!'

The comment gave Jack a jolt. It must be a scam call. Someone must have heard about the assault and rape charge. It was probably some crude attempt to extort money.

'If you have any information about the charges of assault and rape against Sandro you should go to the police,' Jack almost shouted down the phone.

He was about to slam the phone back into its cradle when he heard laughter from the phone. 'I have no intention of going to the police – it wouldn't be in my interest. What I can tell you is that I can arrange for Anna Kalnina to withdraw her complaint and drop the case. The three of us, you, me and Anna, could arrange to meet, in Riga. I would be happy to describe the proposal and you can decide to accept it or not.'

Jack's mind was racing. All his senses told him this was a scam. But if there was even a chance of Sandro avoiding prison, he felt he had to listen to the caller. He'd just have to be careful. 'Carry on,' was all Jack said.

'You will need pen and paper to make some notes; are you ready?' The speaker paused whilst he assumed Jack would grab a pad and pen. 'Book a room at the Mirabelle Hotel, Old Town Riga for next Thursday evening. It's about one hundred metres from Riga Castle. Go to the hotel bar at 7.00 p.m. Anna and I will be sitting in a corner booth having a drink. I will be wearing a dark suit, pale shirt and tie. Anna will be in a black dress. I will provide details of the proposal at this time. We can discuss it and you can decide to accept it or not. If you do not turn up, I will assume you do not wish to consider the proposal – and the law will take its course. Mirabelle Hotel, Old Town Riga, 7.00 p.m. next Thursday – that's the twenty-second of the month.'

The caller rang off and left Jack in a quandary. He was convinced it was a scam – but if there was a chance, he had to consider it.

Several days later Jack was in Riga. He had flown direct from Manchester and taken a taxi from the airport to the Mirabelle Hotel. It was a few minutes before 7.00 p.m. and Jack was walking into the hotel bar. Subdued lighting, soft music, polished wooden tables and cosy booths surrounded the walls. There were only a few people in the bar and he spotted the couple he had travelled to meet. Initially Jack thought the man was waving at him, but he was beckoning the waiter. Jack approached the booth, gave them both a slight nod of the head in acknowledgment and sat down. He ordered a soda water and decided to let them open any discussion.

'Thank you for coming to Riga and hearing my proposal,' said Tony Levens. His manner, accent and dress confirmed he was British not Latvian.

'A friend of mine has cargo on board the MV *Asenka* – yes, cargo you are due to salvage. One part of his cargo consists of two hundred drums of plastic pellets. The cardboard drums are heavy and likely to be... er, difficult to handle. The problem is that inside the drums are very small plastic pellets – microbeads. In the UK it's illegal to manufacture and sell microbeads and export them. If the contents of the two hundred drums were discovered my friend would be, er, embarrassed.

'The other cargo consists of twenty-three cases of machine parts. They contain the equipment that is used to make the microbeads. The cases are sturdy and should present no problem in salvage.'

Tony Levens paused to take a sip of his drink. He looked relaxed and calm, as though friends were chatting. 'The proposal is that you salvage the two hundred drums and the machine parts and deliver them to the designated bonded warehouse in Riga. You simply do what you are contracted to do. I can assure you there are only plastic beads in the drums and machinery inside the crates. There are no drugs, no chemicals, no weapons. You are free to open any one of the drums or crates, or all of them to check. However, I urge you to be careful. The beads are very small – like specks of dust. They are packed inside heat-sealed plastic bags, with the bags inside cardboard drums.

'Once the drums and crates are delivered to the warehouse, Anna will contact the police in Manchester and withdraw her complaint against your friend. The case will be dropped and your friend will not stand trial, he will not go to prison. Once the case is dropped, your friend will pay Anna €40,000 in cash. It will be a one-off payment. I'm sure you will agree that it's a cheap price for avoiding a criminal record and years in prison. It's that simple – I get what I want, your friend gets what he wants, and Anna gets compensation.'

'What does Anna say?' asked Jack as he turned to look at her.

'Everyone has a price. Mine is €40,000,' she answered.

'Anna, show Mr Collier your passport – so that he knows who you are,' the man ordered.

Anna slipped a hand into a small handbag and withdrew her passport. She handed it to Jack; it was Anna Kalnina sitting opposite him.

Levens suddenly produced a large photo from the seat between himself and Anna. As he turned it the right way up Anna looked at the photo for the first time. She didn't recognise herself at first. Blood and lipstick were smeared across her nose and mouth. Her hair was dishevelled, her eyes looked vacant and her mouth slack. With exaggerated care, Levens turned it back over and offered it to Jack.

'This is the photograph the jury will see at your friend's trial. Yes, it's a photograph of Anna on her arrival at the police station.'

Tony was waiting for Jack's reaction to the photograph. It was instantaneous. Jack's jaw dropped, his eyes stared, and for a moment he appeared frozen. In the dim light it was difficult to see, but colour seemed to drain from his face.

'Please, keep it as a souvenir. I'm sure your friend has already seen it,' Levens said as though offering a postcard.

Anna also noticed Collier's reaction to the photograph. She guessed it would be the same for the police and a jury.

'Do you have any questions?'

'How do I know you will keep your promise?'

'Because it's in our mutual interests to do so,' Levens replied. 'All you have to do is salvage the drums and crates – something you're contracted to do. All I ask is that you are careful not to spill the contents of the drums. If you fail to salvage the drums, and the microbeads are released, my friend will be embarrassed. He will receive a large fine and a slap on the wrist. He will not face fifteen years in prison.

'If you are successful with your salvage, you will no doubt earn a substantial fee. Anna receives compensation and your friend avoids a criminal record and prison.'

Jack turned his attention to Anna but directed his comments to the man. 'What if Anna changes her mind once she has her money?'

'Think about it. Your hotel reservation here is on record. The waiter will remember us. There will be a record of the €40,000. Anna will face the prospect of arrest for… what? Perverting the course of justice, demanding money? It's not in her interest to change her mind.'

'What if you change your mind?'

'The drums will be in the bonded warehouse for weeks if not months before my friend can buy them back from the insurance company. If Anna doesn't have the charges dropped, you simply tell the authorities about the microbeads. My friend gets into trouble, Anna loses €40,000, but your friend still has charges against him. It really is a very simple proposal and, as I say, in our mutual interests for it to happen.'

'What if we change our minds? What if we simply tell the authorities of your proposal and the microbeads? Sandro could challenge the accusations against him, save €40,000, and we wouldn't be complicit in any illegal activity.'

'My friend,' the man said with no warmth in his voice, 'Anna and I would simply admit to trying to reach a compromise with you regarding the charges. We would say Anna wanted to avoid the distress of reliving the assault and rape in court. She would admit to accepting the money as compensation – and saving court time. She would probably receive a reprimand but that's about all. We would deny any knowledge of the microbeads.'

With a condescending smile on his face Levens continued: 'I also suspect documents would appear that indicate you knew of the microbeads, would be paid handsomely for their salvage, and encouraged to submit a low tender in order to secure the job. If you did renege on any arrangement, it would become very messy, and your friend would still end up in jail.'

Jack had spent hours with Sandro rehearsing various 'what if' scenarios. The proposal did seem to be in their mutual interests. However, he still thought it was an elaborate scam and illegal.

'If you don't have any further questions, we'll leave you to have supper. You probably have an early flight tomorrow. Think about it and talk to your friend. I'll phone you in a few days.'

Levens smiled as he and Anna stood and made their way out of the bar. Jack was left with decisions to make.

Chapter 16

The next phase

'The bait's in the water,' said Tony Levens to his business partner, David Moxon.

'Do you think he'll take it?'

'I'm pretty sure he will. You should have seen Collier's face when he saw the photograph. All we need to do now is sit back and wait for them to salvage the drums and the equipment, arrange to buy them back from the insurance company at a discount, and sell them on. We lose a few months but make more money. The outcome is the same.'

'Lose a few months – it's OK for you! I've already spent every Saturday and Sunday morning for the last month as a *pro bono* lawyer at Manchester police stations, listening to the whining of idiots who've been arrested. I had to agree to do six months before my father would arrange it. He also thinks I'm changing my mind about commercial law and considering joining his firm as a criminal lawyer. I've got to keep doing this for months otherwise it will look odd.'

'Relax, we've been through all this before. When the ship went down with the microbeads and equipment on board, we thought it was a simple insurance claim – no problem. When we heard the insurers were requesting tenders to salvage the cargo you nearly shat yourself! At least with Calovarlo we have a chance to make sure our non-hazardous material remains just that. There's no way that he'll risk going to prison – especially after his partner has seen the photograph of the battered face of Anna Kalnina.'

Months ago, when they had heard that the MV *Asenka* had foundered, they had been worried. If the ship had broken up during the sinking, trillions of microbeads could have been released into the ocean. It would be merely a matter of days before their presence was noted. David knew that under European Law all shipwrecks had to be checked and monitored for the release of contaminants. It wasn't the ecological damage that worried them – it was the thought of the cargo being traced back to them.

When they had heard the capsize had been relatively gentle, in calm waters, they had been initially relieved. The chances were that the cargo was undamaged. However, their concern returned when they were informed that part of the cargo was to be salvaged. As owners of cargo on board the *Asenka* they had been informed that whilst the drums of plastic pellets and machine parts had not been identified as primary salvage items, it was possible that they may be salvaged; it would depend upon the *Marine Salvage & Investigation Company* and the ease and speed of salvage. The insurers and salvors would liaise and decide if it was cost effective. It all depended on the time it would take to raise the crates and drums and their potential resale value. What David Moxon and Tony Levens couldn't afford was for the drums to be damaged or punctured during any salvage attempt.

Moxon and Levens had quickly realised they needed to control any salvage operation. They had also decided it was better if the cargo was salvaged and they bought it back from the insurers. In this way no one would ever know of the microbeads. David Moxon was also aware that there were two levers that could be applied to influence company owners: financial mismanagement and scandals associated with their private lives. They would concentrate on these two and he knew just the people to help.

When David Moxon had worked at Salter & Partners, the company had often employed a freelance forensic accountant called Bob Hammond. He was a wizard at detecting unusual financial trends, abnormal payments and dubious practices. If there was anything untoward in the published finances of the *Marine Salvage & Investigation Company,* he would find it. He was also adept at locating unpublished records; it was prudent not to ask how he located this information.

Salter & Partners also used a private detective agency. At the time he was leaving he recalled old John Salter and the other senior partners being in a panic over some issue linked with the detective agency. The office gossip was that the agency had used dubious methods to collect sensitive information. A major damage limitation exercise had been underway with Salter and other senior partners missing his leaving party. He now couldn't remember the name of the company or the problem, so he had decided to phone his former secretary and find out.

David Moxon had never been directly involved in a case with Bob Hammond but had seen him in action and knew of his reputation. Shortly after he arrived at Salter & Partners, he had attended an in-house seminar where Hammond had illustrated common fraudulent techniques and their tell-tale signs. He'd been so impressed he had signed up for another seminar that concentrated on malpractice associated with property development. The case studies that Hammond presented, involving both the private sector and government agencies, were a revelation. He demonstrated how hours of meticulous work, spotting the smallest irregularity, the timing of transactions, incomplete information, and following financial entries through a labyrinth of accounts could uncover the most devious ploys. He really was a wizard, but he didn't look like one. Moxon guessed he was mid-thirties and probably unmarried – no wife or partner would let him out of the house looking the way he did. He had the uncanny knack of looking as though he had slept in his clothes and just woken up. His suit always looked creased, shirt collar ruffled and tie loose. His thin, pale face disguised the stubble on his chin whilst his long, floppy fair hair made him look younger and distracted. However, when he spoke, all the physical features evaporated; when he spoke, people listened.

Moxon and Levens had met Bob Hammond in his Birmingham office and outlined their request; it was simple. They explained that they were about to enter negotiations with a Manchester-based company and were looking for reassurance that the financial practices of their possible partner were sound. They wanted to avoid involvement with a company that could cause them any 'embarrassment by association'. Bob Hammond was sharp and a whole series of questions followed: 'Do you check on the financial practices of all your partners? How did the prospect of the current partnership emerge? What prompted your decision to check on these people? Do you have any evidence of malpractice or suspect any? Why come to me?' It was as though they were under scrutiny.

Moxon knew Bob Hammond was no fool and had done some preliminary research. He judged his explanation was just enough to merit their request. 'The *Marine Salvage & Investigation Company* is only six years old. It's owned by two young men, Jack Collier and Alessandro Calovarlo, and has grown to a multi-million-pound business in record time. They appear to have had some spectacular salvage and financial successes. For example, we understand they bought a state-of-the-art salvage and recovery vessel for a fraction of the asking price. We also heard they salvaged and sold ancient Burmese religious relics for millions; it all sounds too good to be true. That's why we are asking for your help, your reassurance.'

David Moxon had prepared a single sheet of paper with all their details, together with information about the *Marine Salvage & Investigation Company.* Bob Hammond only looked up from the sheet when Tony Levens asked if it was possible to conduct the investigation within the next two weeks. 'I do have other work to do,' was his caustic reply. However, after a few moments he agreed: 'I will undertake some preliminary work. Depending upon what emerges I may have to bring in one or more colleagues. I can assure you that if there is anything untoward in the financial accounts of the *Marine Salvage & Investigation Company*, or those of the owners, I will find it.'

Two weeks later they were back in Bob Hammond's office. It looked as though he was in the same suit and shirt – perhaps he had slept in them a little less restlessly. The same middle-aged secretary served a tray of coffee, milk and sugar without saying a word. As soon as she closed the door behind her Bob handed a slim booklet to both Moxon and to Levens. 'A summary of all my findings, together with corresponding tables and data, has been assembled in the report. I've also attached an invoice for my work.

'My colleagues and I have inspected the published accounts for the *Marine Salvage & Investigation Company*, the company and personal assets as well as the private accounts of Messrs Collier and Calovarlo in minute detail. We have also checked the accounts of those companies that they have dealt with since the company was established. As you pointed out, they do appear to have had some spectacular salvage and financial successes. I'd describe their present state as asset rich but cash poor.'

Hammond paused as though collecting his thoughts: 'I've looked closely at all the transactions that the *Marine Salvage & Investigation Company* has undertaken since it was formed, including the purchase of the MV *Stavanger*. I can find no evidence, whatsoever, of any malpractice. Both their financial adviser and accountant have sound reputations and appear to have guided them wisely.

'What I have discovered is that the purchase of the *Stavanger* prompted orchestrated action against them within the salvage industry. Quite simply their competition within the industry made sure they undercut the company on every tender. This orchestrated action resulted in the severe downturn in their activities in the last year. It nearly ruined them. However, my impeccable sources tell me that this action has been recently abandoned.'

Hammond looked towards his notes and turned a page. 'The *Marine Salvage & Investigation Company* is currently tendering for a lucrative contract with the North Sea Oil Producers Support Group. My sources tell me this is a multi-million, if not multi-billion-pound project including both BP and Exxon. They also tell me it is likely that they will be awarded the contract. From reviewing their accounts, I would expect the company to prosper in the immediate future.

'Their personal accounts and expenditure were extremely active during the first few years of establishing their company, but nothing was questionable. In recent years their expenditure has been geared to investments in the company rather than their personal lifestyles.

'I'm happy to tell you that I've found nothing that would embarrass you if you entered into an agreement with the *Marine Salvage & Investigation Company* or Messrs Collier and Calovarlo.'

It wasn't the news they had wanted to hear – especially about the potentially lucrative North Sea contract. However, if the award of such a contract was in progress, perhaps a phone call to the right person at BP or Exxon could increase the pressure on the unfortunate Mr Alessandro Calovarlo. David Moxon would find the right person and wait for the right moment to make the call.

Chapter 17

Thorpe Investigations

It was an awkward conversation for Moxon. His former secretary soon realised the phone call was requesting a favour she was unable to give. She recalled the fuss in the office about the detective agency, but she hadn't been involved in any of the discussions nor in the typing of letters. She also knew that neither Mr Salter nor his personal secretary would divulge anything. All she was prepared to do was give David the name of the detective agency: Thorpe Investigations based in Manchester. A quick Google search confirmed that the company was owned by Philip Thorpe and that it was based in a recently renovated office block just a short drive from the city centre. A simple phone call set up a meeting with Phil Thorpe.

Thorpe Investigations was on one of the upper floors of a huge glass, aluminium and concrete monstrosity. It looked as though it had been refurbished a few years ago but nothing could disguise the utilitarian construction, cheap materials and shoddy workmanship. The sound of them walking along the corridor leading to the office of Phil Thorpe echoed all around them. The only plus point was that Thorpe's office was light and airy. However, Moxon guessed it would be roasting in summer and freezing in winter. After the brief pleasantries he outlined their enquiry.

'We are considering entering into an agreement with a local company but know nothing about them and are looking for, er, assurance that they will honour our agreement. It's not the type of assurance that can be drafted into a contract, er, more like leverage that could be applied if our partners think of reneging on the deal.'

Phil Thorpe eased his ample frame into his office chair and began to smile as Moxon continued. 'We've employed a forensic accountant to inspect their records and advise on their financial management and viability... er, we are now looking for someone to look into the private lives of the two owners. We would like to know if there is anything that would, er, embarrass us if some aspect of their private life became known.'

Thorpe was silent for a few moments. He clasped his hands together and leaned forwards in his chair. 'Do I assume that the, er, leverage you are looking for should be so great that one or both of these owners would do anything you ask to keep it a secret?'

Moxon blushed. He'd tried to use words and phrases as though it was an everyday request, routine and professional. He'd tried to disguise the fact that they were looking for dirt, a revelation so great that they could control the salvage operation. In a split second, Moxon realised that Phil Thorpe knew exactly what he and Tony were after.

'I'll tell you what I'll do. I'll look into the private lives of your two owners and see if there is anything that you could use as a, er, lever. All I need are the names of the two owners, the name of their company and £3500. If you can give me that now we can meet here, same time, same day, in two weeks' time. I'll either tell you there's nothing you can use or what needs to be done to, er, create your lever.'

Phil Thorpe and one of his colleagues checked on the two young owners of the *Marine Salvage & Investigation Company*. They dissected their private and social life. If the client wanted something discreditable, they knew what to look for and where to look for it. They had done this sort of work before. They were skilled at it and discreet.

As arranged, Tony Levens and David Moxon returned to the office of Phil Thorpe and were eager to hear what had been discovered. Thorpe started by giving them a brief overview of the company, acknowledging that their forensic accountant would no doubt provide all the financial detail they needed. He revealed that Collier and Calovarlo had met whilst studying for their master's degree at the University of Portsmouth. They had formed a marine salvage company and over five or six years had some spectacular successes. They'd earned a lot of money but had invested it in ships, equipment and staff. The purchase of the MV *Stavanger* was the biggest and most significant to date.

'You might want your man to check the purchase of the MV *Stavanger.* It seems they bought a very expensive ship at auction for a fraction of its worth. It appears they have struggled to find work for it and have been under a lot of financial pressure recently. Your accountant may have information that could make this a possible lever.

'We've focused on the private and social lives of Collier and Calovarlo. I can tell you straight away that Calovarlo is your most likely target. We've looked at Collier in detail over the last two weeks – he's as boring as hell. He's a workaholic with little or no social or private life. He leaves for his office just after seven-fifteen each morning and seldom returns before six-thirty. In two weeks of observation, he and Calovarlo have attended a meeting in Liverpool with a shipping company and another one with their law firm McKnight, Lewis and Watts in Manchester. We hacked their phones and...'

'What, you hacked their phones!' exclaimed David Moxon.

The expression on Phil Thorpe's face didn't alter. 'How do you think we were going to find out about their personal and social lives? Ask them to divulge their most intimate secrets? I didn't spend twenty-five years in the Liverpool police without picking up useful skills and contacts.

'The meeting with the shipping company was about routine hull inspections – nothing exciting. The one with the lawyers was a review of ongoing and future contracts; again, nothing exciting. In each of the last two weeks, Collier and Calovarlo had a meal at the Mughal Palace restaurant in Rusholme just south of the city. It seems it's a regular thing; no one joined them. From discreet enquiries, what we observed over the last two weeks is typical of what they do when they are not away on some job.

'We trawled through Collier's phone and laptop records. No incriminating messages or texts, no pornography. Now, here's the interesting bit. Collier has a girlfriend. They've been together four or five years, but she lives and works in Hull. Her name is Penelope Pendleton Price and she's a deputy director with UK Border Force and a highflyer. From the text and email messages, it's a regular relationship – nothing weird. She stays over in his Manchester apartment if she has meetings in Liverpool. From what we have uncovered I'd say that Jack Collier is a nonstarter. He's not a gambler or drinker, he's not a womaniser and he's not into drugs. He's so straight I can't see him falling into a honey trap; he just doesn't seem the type.

'Calovarlo is different. He's tall, dark and handsome – and he knows it. Drives around town in a red Alfa Romeo sports car and is a regular heartbreaker. It took some time to sort out his private life but it's now clear; there's a regular flow of girlfriends through his apartment. The problem is that none of these seem long lasting, a few weeks or a month at the most. From a search of his laptop we can't find anything, er, deviant. However, what we did discover is that at weekends he sometimes goes to the Mojito Nightclub. It's not every weekend and it's not on the same night. What is regular is that he typically picks up a young woman and they end up at his apartment. He drives them home the next day. Sometimes the, er, relationship continues for a few weeks or so, but he then moves on. If you are looking for a "lever" to control one of the owners, I'd say Calovarlo is the man. If you are looking for a plan to, er, ensnare him, I can suggest several. Of course, the advice will incur another fee.'

Moxon and Levens had drawn a blank with Bob Hammond and so they listened to what Phil Thorpe had to say. Over the next hour he outlined several scenarios that could provide the lever they were looking for. In the end they decided on the most audacious, but also the most powerful. Thorpe confirmed that he could provide a key item, at a price, for the plan they'd decided upon. Over the next hour they talked through the plan and agreed the fee.

David Moxon and Tony Levens left the office of Thorpe Investigations and walked along the narrow corridor towards the exit.

'Are you thinking what I'm thinking?' asked Moxon.

'Our two little friends in Riga?' was the reply.

'Do you think they'll do it?

'If the price is right… they'll do it,' Tony Levens predicted. 'It's not even our money,' he laughed.

Chapter 18

B&H Limited

Although the plan to ensnare Calovarlo was working out perfectly, David Moxon still wished he'd never heard of B&H Limited. Months earlier he had been scanning the list of companies applying for bankruptcy when he came across them. Further computer searches, and several hours in the Liverpool newspaper archives, had provided all he and Tony needed to know. It appeared that in the 1950s, Ernest Brocklehurst and Alfred Henshaw had established a company, B&H Limited, to manufacture a variety of Bakelite products in Runcorn in northwest England. They produced small household appliances, parts of home furnishings, electrical items and fittings. The company was successful. It moved with the times and as black and brown Bakelite became less popular it replaced it with colourful thermo and thermosetting plastics.

In the 1990s the company began to concentrate on disposable plastic products for the hospitality and catering industries. It produced disposable knives, forks and spoons, beer and wine glasses, plastic straws and fast-food containers. B&H Ltd was a profitable business and there was little desire for change from the now ageing owners.

The two sole children of Brocklehurst and Henshaw took over the running of the company. However, they soon became absentee owners and regarded B&H Ltd as a cash cow. They made little or no investment. They undertook no forward planning beyond maintaining current production and had little or no day-today involvement. The company suffered in the financial crisis of 2007 to 2011. Stung into action, the young owners borrowed heavily as part of an urgent restructuring exercise to diversify into the manufacture of plastic microbeads. They aimed to satisfy a growing and lucrative demand for them in personal grooming and healthcare products. The new line greatly reduced the previous production of one-use plastics but the young owners judged it to be a profitable area that was likely to expand. It seems that no sooner had they diversified the business than national and international events proved they were right. Public concern over plastic pollution and one-use plastics resulted in an abrupt downturn of orders. There was a return within the hospitality and catering industries to metal cutlery, glass vessels and paper-based food containers, resulting in a reduced use of plastics in these previously targeted industries.

It seemed the decision to diversify into microbeads had been an inspiration. As demand for them increased, they phased out the manufacture of one-use plastics. However, the Netherlands banned microbeads in 2014 and other countries started to follow, with the UK banning them in 2018. In the space of a few years there was no market for their sole product. What's more, B&H Ltd found it difficult to re-enter the single-use plastics business. The market had shrunk, and it was highly competitive. The Covid-19 pandemic in 2020 was the final blow to B&H Ltd. They were declared bankrupt in 2021. The factory was closed and the owners simply walked away, leaving the creditors keen to sell off the business and land to the highest bidder.

The highest bidder had been two local entrepreneurs – Tony Levens and David Moxon. They saw an opportunity to develop the site for either residential housing and offices or warehousing. The Runcorn site was close to the major city of Liverpool and had excellent road, rail, sea and air communication. Tony was able to assemble information on power, water and transport links to the site as well as estimates for various house building or warehousing/office scenarios. David could ensure all legal permissions had been granted for the developments. He could also negotiate short-term loans that would enable them to buy the property and, weeks later, sell it on, repay the loan and make a substantial profit. The planning and assembly of documents was protracted – but the rewards would be significant.

Levens and Moxon were entirely dispassionate about the companies they bought and sold. They had no interest in the history of the place, the building, contents or workers. It was simply the potential value of the site for development. If the buildings could be transformed into alternative accommodation or use it may be a bonus. However, most likely, the building would be bulldozed, sold as hardcore and a brown field site put up for sale – with all the requisite building permissions. Some equipment and furnishings may be sold off but most of it would go for scrap. Speed, costs and profit were their mantra.

Together with the sales agent they visited the B&H Limited site on a wet afternoon; it was a sad sight. The agent parked in the company car park, now half full of fly-tipped rubbish. Heavy metal gates, bolted to the walls and padlocked, protected a graffiti-covered door. There were similar grilles covering the ground-floor windows, but it hadn't stopped the stone throwers and most of the first-floor windows were broken. To Tony and David this was all cosmetic. What counted was the soundness of the structure and the acreage.

The sales agent flicked through an assortment of keys until he found the one to open the heavy metal security gates protecting the main entrance. He then fiddled for another key to the main entrance and led them inside. They had to wait until the power was switched on before the agent could show them around.

Tony and David had visited similar factory sites. What counted now was an assessment of the value of the land and buildings, stock and scrap, potential profit and ease of sale. They both knew it had been merely hours between the decision to close the factory to it being abandoned. Shop floor workers had simply switched off the machines, put down tools, grabbed their coats and gone home. Those in the office had closed the computers, left the files on their desks, switched off the lights and left. It was the fine coating of dust that marked the passage of time.

Tony was prepared for the superficial tour. He had previously reviewed the plans of the whole site. If the buildings were sound, he could have provisional conversion plans for office and residential accommodation drawn up. If not, they would be demolition plans. He had skimmed the report from the liquidators about the value of the stock and raw materials, the machinery and production equipment. It didn't contain any surprises. He'd learned long ago that there was one price for new machinery and new raw materials – and a different price for anything second-hand.

The route through the antiquated offices, dilapidated canteen and grimy stores would have been depressing for many. However, Tony could look beyond the immediate to the possible. It was when they walked onto the main factory floor that his interest was aroused. Ahead of him towered stainless steel panels and large bore pipework, painted valves and glass-fronted gauges. Ventilation ducts snaked away towards massive filters. It was all covered in a thin layer of dust, but the impact was huge. This looked like expensive, modern kit but the notes he had read last night said it was all scrap. Tony turned to the agent and asked: 'I read that all the manufacturing equipment was written off as scrap. This looks like expensive scrap!'

'Yeah, it is,' the agent confirmed. He flicked through the file he was carrying and added. 'They switched from making plastic cutlery to manufacturing microbeads. It was bad timing because shortly afterwards the UK banned them – so did the rest of Europe. They had no market. I guess this kit was expensive, but you can't sell it, nobody wants it.'

Tony was intrigued by the modern machinery in front of him; machinery that was still fully operational. That afternoon he reviewed the high cost of the equipment and volume of raw materials in stock. A few phone calls confirmed the production of microbeads was banned across many countries in Europe – but there were loopholes. Many personal care products containing microbeads were still being manufactured and sold in Europe, including in the Baltic states of Estonia, Latvia and Lithuania where they had contacts.

An idea began to take shape. If they did decide to make an offer for the site, it would typically include the condemned equipment and stock. They could argue there would be a cost in clearing the site – thus a reduced offer. They could then resurrect the facility for a limited production run to use up the existing stock of raw materials. Perhaps the previous workforce could be persuaded to return to work on weekly contracts. They could transform the condemned material into a profitable product. They could even sell off the equipment for a fraction of its original cost. It could represent a significant windfall. Two days after the visit to the B&H site Tony announced: 'Dave, I've got an idea.'

Chapter 19

Doubts forming

Sandro was in a rush. He had slept badly after Jack had phoned him from the Mirabelle Hotel last night and dispassionately described the proposal. They had agreed to meet this morning to discuss it in more detail. Sandro had eventually fallen asleep and then switched off the wake-up alarm when it rang. It had been a mistake because he had then dozed, woken up with a start, and realised he was late.

Sandro had been frustrated by the heavy morning traffic between Manchester and Salford. Once he had parked, he dodged through the traffic as he jogged across the busy road to Wentworth Mansions. Luckily someone was leaving the building and he nipped through the open door and took the stairs to the second floor two at a time. By the time he had walked briskly to the company office door he was breathing heavily. He opened the door with a flourish, gave a cursory wave to Lesley, and went directly to Jack's office. As a courtesy he would normally knock on the door and then walk in. This morning he simply barged straight in and, as he sat heavily in an armchair, asked: 'So, what do you think?'

It was only after he had sat down that he noticed Jack's expression and awkward body language. He assumed this was because the proposal being offered sounded suspect and he was uneasy about it; or was it something else? 'What is it? You don't look happy.'

Jack paused to collect his thoughts and decide what to say

next. 'Sandro, I want to believe you're innocent... I don't know the details of the case – just what you've told me... Last night the mystery guy showed me a photograph of Anna Kalnina taken at the police station. She was a mess...'

The phrase 'I want to believe you're innocent' hit Sandro like a sledgehammer. To his utter disbelief he realised that Jack thought he was guilty – believed he was a rapist. The image of Anna's bloody and bruised face flashed into Sandro's head. It was accompanied by gut-churning emotion and the realisation that Jack's reaction to the photograph was exactly what a jury member would experience.

'Jack, Jack, I didn't do it. I'm sure I didn't do it... I didn't need to do it. I have lots of girlfriends who are happy to jump into bed. I've never forced them to do anything they didn't want to do. But I can see now why Inspector Latchem and Roberta Fox say the evidence is overwhelming and believe I'm guilty. Melton-Barr is just putting a twist on it – saying it was "rough sex" and trying to raise doubt in the mind of a jury.'

Sandro leaned forwards in his chair and put his head in his hands. He stayed in that position, breathing deeply, for several moments before he sat up and looked at Jack. Resignation and defeat were etched into his face. 'I hadn't really understood what Melton-Barr was saying about pleading guilty to the lesser charge of assault "...if the case was going badly". I now realise he thinks I'm guilty. It's just a legal game to him. He's concentrating on this alternative scenario and hasn't mentioned me being set up.'

Jack cursed himself for what he had said. He couldn't imagine for a moment that Sandro would beat up and rape anyone. He stood up, moved to where Sandro was sitting, squatted next to him and put an arm around his shoulder. In a tender tone Jack said: 'I do believe you are innocent. There is no way you would assault and rape anyone.' Then, more business-like, he continued: 'Let's decide what we are going to do. Last night I spoke with Bill Watts and asked him to talk with his colleagues...'

Sandro glanced at Jack but there was no change in the expression on his face.

'I told Bill to be discreet, to talk in general terms with his colleagues, and to look at precedents. I thought his opinion would be helpful.'

The slightest of nods from Sandro told Jack that he accepted this.

'Bill confirmed what Roberta had told you. If the jury were to convict you, and the judge believed the initial evidence was compelling, it's likely you would receive a heavier sentence – heavier than if you had pleaded guilty.'

Jack changed his tone from sombre to encouraging and continued. 'He also told me it's not uncommon for the alleged victims of rape to withdraw complaints; to drop the case. He told me that in the UK last year over sixty thousand rapes were reported to the police. However, more than half withdrew their complaint. Less than five percent went to court and of these about two-thirds were dismissed.'

'Yes, but everyone says the case against me is "overwhelming". I'm also worried that I'm dragging you and the company into this. If I go down, I don't want to take you down with me.'

'Sandro, you're not going to go down for this! Listen, the only people who know about the proposal are you and me, the guy in Riga and Anna Kalnina. We are due to salvage the cargo anyway. Baltic Marine Services say the machine parts and the drums of plastic are a salvage priority. We simply take extra precautions when handling sodden cardboard drums that are likely to collapse. Everyone accepts it'll take extra time. Delivering to the bonded warehouse is routine. If challenged, we are merely the salvors.

'If you decide to go along with the proposal, you can wait until the case is dropped before you pay Anna Kalnina any money.'

'I don't want to go to prison for something I didn't do – even if it means paying her to drop the case. When he phones, tell him I'll do it.'

No sooner had Sandro said 'I'll do it' than the phone rang; Lesley was putting through a call. 'Sandro, a Mr George Cornell is on the line. He says he is a legal representative of Exxon and advising on the tender to provide a standby vessel for the North Sea Oil Producers Support Group. He says it's important.'

Sandro didn't answer immediately but composed himself. 'Good morning Mr Cornell, it's Sandro Calovarlo here; how can I help you?'

'Good morning, I am one of the legal team representing Exxon, a member of the North Sea Oil Producers Support Group. It has been brought to our attention that you have recently been charged with assault and rape. Whilst we make no judgement on the case, we wish to direct you to Section 17, clause 11 of the tender document you and Mr Jack Collier signed. Essentially, Exxon reserve the right to cancel any contract issued if the actions of the company undertaking the tender risk bringing Exxon into disrepute.

'I have been directed to inform you that if a court of law finds you guilty of the charges I have just mentioned, Exxon will consider termination of any contract issued. A detailed letter, confirming what I have just told you, will be mailed in due course. That is all, good day.'

George Cornell had put down the phone before Sandro could even start to reply. He turned to look at Jack and realised the stakes had just got higher.

Chapter 20

The partnership

Tony Levens regarded himself as an entrepreneur despite his initial training as a quantity surveyor. He and David Moxon had accrued their working capital because of a single dubious land deal. Tony had deputised for his line manager during a company meeting where he discovered that a multi-million-pound plan for a major housing development was stalled. At the last minute an elderly farmer had refused to sign; he'd changed his mind about selling his farm to the building consortium. The farm was dilapidated and no longer profitable. However, the owners had decided they wanted the land to remain a farm rather than a housing estate. The building consortium had an option to buy all the surrounding land and had assembled detailed infrastructure and building plans. The acreage of the farm, and its position, were critical to the viability of the project.

Tony saw an opportunity. He naively believed that if he could persuade the farmer to sell the farm it would boost his position in the company. He devised a plan and arranged to meet the farmer, masquerading as a potential buyer. He presented himself as a guardian of the countryside, a guardian who wanted to create a forest of native deciduous trees – oak and sycamore, beech and ash. It was part of his invented vision of a 'long-term, sustainable contribution to the planet'. In his meeting with the farmer and his wife he argued passionately about the need to plant trees, combat climate change and reverse the decline of British forests and wildlife. He explained that grants were available to plant trees, tax relief would limit his costs and he could afford to wait for the trees to become mature. He would 'farm trees' and painted an idealistic and eco-friendly picture – one the farmer and his wife were keen to support and agreed to sell the farm to him.

Tony immediately told his boss about the approach to the farmer and his agreement to sell. Hours later he was driving to a meeting with the CEO of the building consortium and basking in his newfound importance. He was to be disappointed. The CEO ridiculed his ploy to purchase the farm. He outlined the legal pitfalls should the farmer challenge the sale, the ethical issues that would be raised and the adverse impact upon the reputation of the company. In a twenty-minute meeting his hopes were dashed, he was reprimanded and 'sentenced' to six-months' probation.

Embarrassed and dejected, Tony was drowning his sorrows in a local pub. The more he drank the angrier and more resentful he became. It was whilst he was vowing to prove them wrong that a former school friend spotted him. The old friend was Dave Moxon, now a young commercial lawyer. Over the next few hours, and countless drinks, the story about the farm and the housing development emerged. The anger and resentment that poured from Tony's lips served to ignite and fuel those David was experiencing.

David Moxon was the son of Robert Moxon KC, a high-profile criminal lawyer. Robert Moxon had a clear vision for the future of his son. His son would obtain a law degree, eventually join him as a criminal lawyer and take the practice into the future. David did graduate with a first-class degree in law and, as part of his father's vision, he joined a city practice of solicitors to gain experience. However, David realised that commercial law, rather than criminal law, was his passion. Against his father's wishes he joined the commercial law division of Salter & Partners, a highly regarded group of solicitors in Liverpool. Whilst his interest and expertise grew, he became aware that he was doing all the work and his boss, and the senior practice partners, were getting the credit and the bonuses. He began to bridle at the junior role he was allocated and saw little opportunity for advancement and little chance of reward.

Towards the end of the evening, fuelled by alcohol, a plan was formulated. With David's contacts they could borrow money, for hours not days, to buy the farm. Tony could obtain all the details of the farm and land. He could access plans for the infrastructure needed for a housing development as well as the costs of building and projected profits after sales. David could assemble deeds and contracts that would enable simultaneous transactions to occur. They could sell the farm to a rival building consortium for a massive profit. It would be the perfect revenge for both of them and was the start of a partnership between Tony and David.

In the weeks and months that followed, David Moxon and Tony Levens arranged to complete the purchase and subsequent sale. It generated the capital they needed to enable them to resign from their current jobs and create L&M Property Development Ltd. From that point onwards they scoured the northwest of England for properties and businesses where the site was worth more than the business. Tony drafted plans indicating how the site could be developed and David ensured they operated just within the law to secure a deal; they were dispassionate and ruthless.

Chapter 21

Revelations

Sandro walked through the rain towards Themis Chambers and his monthly meeting with Melton-Barr and Samantha Elliot. The forecast had said rain and he was pleased he had brought an umbrella. His leather shoes and the bottom of his trousers were getting wet as he splashed through puddles, but he wasn't bothered. He was entirely focused on the forthcoming meeting. He was keen to hear of any developments, any further disclosures.

Even though he now knew the way to Melton-Barr's office, Samantha still met him in reception and escorted him to the meeting. This morning she looked bright and had a self-satisfied smile on her face. He gave her a weak smile and said:

'You're looking happy.'

'Yes, today could be a very pleasant day. Let's hope you are smiling when you leave.'

Melton-Barr looked awkward as he slowly got out of his chair. His grey hair was ruffled, and he looked tired as he walked to their normal meeting table. He was carrying a slim manila file that he placed in a space before him. It was one of the few empty spaces on the now over-burdened table.

'Sandro, before we start, I need to remind you of certain legal procedures in the UK.' Melton-Barr sat back in his chair as though addressing a seminar group. 'In the event of a reported crime the police will act on the *prima facie* evidence, detain or arrest the suspect and commence the process of collecting evidence.

Eventually a collection of evidence is presented to the Crown Prosecution Service which decides if a case is likely to result in a conviction – if a case will be heard in court.

'This evidence is shared with the accused. It's called the act of disclosure and is part of the litigation process. In disclosure, each party is required to make available to the other party all documents that are relevant to the issues in dispute. Disclosure is intended to ensure that the parties "put their cards on the table" in respect of documentary evidence at an early stage.

'You will no doubt recall early interviews with Detective Inspector Latchem and how she provided numerous witness statements saying you appeared drunk. The police also provided evidence of your saliva and alcohol on the hotel bed sheet. This is all part of the disclosure process. You will also recall I said at our first meeting that whilst we are likely to accept the forensic evidence, we retain the right to check it and offer our own interpretation.

'We sent the bed sheet to a private forensic laboratory and asked them to analyse any traces on it. They confirmed traces of your DNA, bodily fluids and semen as well as those of Ms Kalnina. They also analysed the two areas where traces of your saliva and alcohol could be found. The two traces were intermingled – strongly suggesting they came from your mouth.'

Sandro felt as though he had been punched in the stomach. His defence team were telling him they had found alcohol in his saliva as he dribbled in a drunken stupor. It sounded like cast iron evidence that he had been drinking.

'The private lab we use is exceptional. It was able to isolate the constituents found on the bed sheet and to determine the drink you consumed. Dr Jamie Kunz, who heads the laboratory, likened the process to smelling an expensive perfume. When the perfume is first applied to the skin the complex constituents, warmed by the skin, create the first olfactory impression. It's called the perfume's *top note*. Over time, certain constituents evaporate and others become more volatile; this is the *middle note* phase. The next morning the final vestiges of the perfume can be detected. It's called the *base note.*

'The bed sheet was stored, in police custody, in an airtight plastic bag. The constituents of the trace Dr Kunz analysed identified the drink you consumed were *top note*. It was Russian Shenovnaya vodka, made in St Petersburg, extremely popular – and unavailable in the UK.'

Both Melton-Barr and Samantha were smiling as they looked at him. They were waiting for a reaction, but Sandro couldn't understand the significance of what Melton-Barr had just announced. Eventually he responded: 'If it's unavailable in the UK, how did I manage to drink it?'

'Precisely,' said Melton-Barr as his smile disappeared and he leaned across the table towards Sandro. 'Apparently Shenovnaya vodka is very popular in Russia. Apparently, it has raw, fiery and peppery characteristics and is cheap. However, it's not to UK taste and isn't imported. The Mojito Nightclub doesn't sell it; none of their clientele would drink it. The Wayside Hotel has contracts with a UK supplier for the mini bars, main bar and restaurant. They do not stock or import it. All our enquiries indicate it would be difficult, if not impossible, to buy a bottle of Shenovnaya vodka in this country. It is widely available in Latvia.'

Sandro saw where the discussion was leading. 'Does this mean you are accusing Anna Kalnina of bringing the vodka into the country and getting me to drink it?'

'No, you're missing the point here,' Samantha interrupted with clear annoyance. 'The police have had every opportunity to test the deposits on the bed sheet. They document the presence of alcohol but not the type and name of the drink. They should have checked what liquor was on the bed sheet and provided this as part of the process of disclosure. Judges do not look kindly on incomplete forensic analyses nor non-disclosure of evidence that may be beneficial to the accused. It raises not only the question of doubt but indicates the vodka was imported by a person, or persons, unknown.

'We do not have to prove who imported the vodka. All we have to do is raise further doubt about the interpretation of the evidence that the Crown will be presenting. The police have submitted no evidence that you drank alcohol prior to your collapse. The witnesses to your apparent drunkenness can easily be challenged as we illustrated before. A key part of the prosecution case now looks flawed. I was expecting you to be as delighted as we are.'

'I'm sorry, I didn't appreciate how significant this information could be.'

'There's more,' Samantha announced. 'If there is no evidence of you drinking alcohol before you entered the Mojito Nightclub, and you only drank soda water, why did you collapse and remain almost unconscious for hours? Dr Kunz is currently reanalysing your blood samples and reviewing the associated traces. He is looking for evidence that a drug entered your body whilst you were in the nightclub; a drug that could account for your collapse. There is nothing so far – but Dr Kunz and his team are exceptional.'

Melton-Barr glanced at his notes before continuing. 'Sandro, Samantha has identified what she believes is a pattern of partial and non-disclosure in relation to the evidence against you. You may think this is a legal technicality, but I assure you it is, potentially, extremely important. Let me check a few things before Samantha explains. Did you give Detective Inspector Latchem a list of your recent girlfriends and their contact telephone numbers?'

'Yes, I think it was just before I was released on bail.'

'Apart from statements provided by Isobel Downing, has Latchem commented on any part of the statements that may have been provided by the other women you listed?'

Sandro thought back to the various meetings with the Detective Inspector but couldn't recall any mention of statements from his former girlfriends. He couldn't recall Roberta Fox referring to them either. He answered with an emphatic no.

'So, all we have is the statement from Isobel Downing.'

Sandro recalled damning extracts from the statement and still couldn't understand why Isobel had made it. 'I told Detective Inspector Latchem at the time, and Roberta Fox, that it wasn't true.'

Melton-Barr acknowledged the denial, smiled as he spread his arms in a welcoming gesture, and continued: 'Sandro, I believe you... but do you not think it is strange that the Detective Inspector shared extracts from a statement from only one girlfriend? My colleagues have collected sworn statements from the other women on the list and none make any mention of "weird sexual fantasies" or lovemaking that could be described as "sadomasochistic". Indeed, their comments provide a completely different picture to the one offered by Isobel Downing.'

Melton-Barr glanced at his notes and continued: 'They describe you as "gentle and caring", "considerate and kind", "a proper gentleman" and "generous to a fault". We have checked with Roberta Fox, and she confirms that no such disclosures, relating to statements from your other girlfriends, have been made to her. She confirmed that seeking such statements was to be part of her case preparation – but to date, it had not been completed.'

Melton-Barr sat back in his chair again and launched into one of his explanations. 'Sandro, it's not unusual for an interviewee to give an interviewer what they want to hear – especially to a police inspector who is assembling a case against an alleged rapist. I'm sure Detective Inspector Latchem was delighted to hear of your "weird sexual fantasies" and "sadomasochistic lovemaking" Indeed, it's fairly easy to pose a string of innocuous questions, together with nonverbal cues, which lead to and elicit the statement you want. In my younger days I often tried to do this in court.'

Melton-Barr paused as though choosing his words carefully. 'I'm also aware that statement givers are sometimes offered, what should I say, 'inducements' to make, er, certain comments. One of our investigators believes she has discovered a possible inducement.

'It appears Ms Downing's stepfather was arrested several weeks ago for being drunk and disorderly. He was involved in a brawl in a local pub. It's interesting that shortly after the date of the statement by Ms Downing the charges against him were dropped and replaced by a caution. Our investigators are currently checking the criminal history of the stepfather and whether a caution, rather than prosecution, is a reasonable course of action by the police. This may be yet another example of non-disclosure... or even something far more serious.'

Melton-Barr sat back in his chair and Samantha continued. 'We would have expected the police to take statements from all the girlfriends you listed and to make these available as part of the disclosure process. The fact that they only refer to one statement means that they did not disclose statements that were favourable to you and your claims, or they failed to collect this evidence. This is one example of partial or non-disclosure... or incompetence.

'We've commented before that the police have provided no evidence, made no disclosure, that you drank alcohol in the Mojito Nightclub. You've made a statement that during the evening you bought one soda water at the bar, then two more and two glasses of white wine, for Anna Kalnina, from a waitress. We have interviewed the waitress who was allocated to a group of tables including yours. She confirms you only ordered the drinks you mentioned. We understand no other waitress would have served Table 22. They are allocated specific tables. We also have sworn statements from the rest of the bar staff and waitresses that none of them served you alcohol.

'We understand that only the waitress who served you has given a statement to the police. This is the only disclosure relating to bar staff and waitresses at the Mojito. Do you see the pattern starting to form? We would have expected witness statements to be collected from all the bar staff and waitresses and for these to be included in any disclosure. Those statements that would corroborate your claim that you did not drink alcohol in the nightclub have not been disclosed.

'Let me give you another example. We understand the police searched your apartment looking for evidence of your sexual orientations and alcohol. According to the police report no evidence of a sexual nature was found in the apartment or on your laptop. There was no evidence of consumed alcohol – empty bottles, cans or glasses. However, they did find five unopened bottles of expensive champagne.'

Sandro explained: 'I was given a case of champagne by a grateful client. Four bottles are in a wine rack, one is in the fridge and I took one on board the *Sultano*. It's there if the crew want to celebrate a successful salvage. The bottles have been in the apartment for months – I don't drink but I couldn't refuse the gift. Jack was given a case as well.'

Sandro paused before continuing: 'I don't know why I kept it – just storing it for others I guess.'

Melton-Barr made a note to check the date the present was given. It would serve to illustrate that the alcohol had been untouched for months. 'If the police found no evidence of you consuming alcohol at the nightclub, or in your apartment, we would have expected them to check bars and off-licences on your route to the nightclub. For the last four Friday evenings, a colleague has driven from your apartment to the nightclub at the time you say you made the journey. The average driving time for our colleague is one minute and twenty seconds longer than your journey! How do we know this? We accessed the security camera footage at your apartment and have a clear image and precise time of you leaving the apartment and driving away. We have road traffic CCTV that identifies your car at various points along the route to the Mojito. We also have security camera footage of you parking your car and walking towards the nightclub. The Mojito has security cameras with face recognition software. It's used to identify club members as well as individuals they do not wish to enter. We can identify the precise time you entered the club.

'There is no evidence of you drinking in your apartment, en route to the nightclub or inside it. We would have expected the police to collect this evidence and include it in their routine disclosure. They have either failed to collect this evidence or failed to disclose it.'

'So do you think all these non-disclosures represent a pattern whereby the police are being selective in what they collect, what they present and what they conceal?' asked Sandro.

'We believe it does,' replied Melton-Barr. 'As we assemble more examples it strengthens our argument to have the case dismissed. Oh yes, I should add that security staff at the Mojito monitor their cameras. They check to see if visitors to the club show any signs that they have been drinking or are behaving strangely. We have statements from the security staff and receptionist to say they recognised you and you were behaving perfectly normally. Again, we believe none of this evidence has been collected by the police. It seems they were so sure you were a drunk who attacked and raped a tourist that they didn't bother to look any further; or they withheld evidence that could be beneficial to your case.'

Samantha picked up the conversation: 'The date of the preliminary hearing with the Crown Prosecution Service is fixed for six weeks' time. We plan to attend this meeting and expect to receive any final disclosures at this time.'

Melton-Barr injected: 'The process of disclosure is ongoing, and all such evidence has a date attached. The court can see at what point disclosures were made – and not made. With the evidence we have assembled, we are confident that we can demonstrate that the police have withheld vital evidence that was beneficial to you and have shared only evidence that could be regarded as damning. We will make a formal request for the case to be dismissed on the grounds of partial and incomplete disclosure. We are also hoping, at this time, that Dr Kunz will have more information for us.'

'Do you have anything that may show I was set up – that someone is trying to destroy me? You seem to be concentrating on the disclosures and the alternative scenario.'

Melton-Barr glanced across the table to Samantha as though inviting a comment. 'No, our investigators have explored a number of avenues – former clients, your competitors and girlfriends – but have discovered nothing to suggest orchestrated action against you. We'll keep an open mind but it's not something we are now actively pursuing.'

Chapter 22

Reinforcements

Deputy Director Penny Pendleton Price had finished the UK Border Force briefing in their Liverpool offices by late afternoon. She had then been obliged to have a couple of short meetings with colleagues to whom she couldn't say no. The extra meetings had delayed her journey to Manchester along the M62 and she was now caught up in the early evening rush hour traffic. The stop and start traffic didn't help her emotions which swung from mild concern to gut wrenching panic.

It had started with an extremely brief phone call from Jack last night. She could tell by his tone and language that something was seriously wrong. He hadn't elaborated but merely said he needed to speak to her urgently on a personal matter – but not over the phone. Penny had agreed to meet him at his apartment after her meetings in Liverpool. She had also tried to discover what was so urgent, but he wouldn't say and merely confirmed they would meet that night.

Stuck in traffic, and becoming more and more anxious, she convinced herself that it was about their long-distance relationship. Some months ago, Jack had suggested they move in together, perhaps buying a place between Manchester and her current base in Hull. It would have been an eighty kilometre drive each day for each of them – but not impossible. However, after her recent promotion it had been mentioned that a future transfer to the London headquarters was likely. Penny had felt sure that Jack supported her in her career within UK Border Force. Buying a house between Manchester and Hull just made no sense. At the time she'd had an awkward telephone call with Jack about postponing the idea of moving in together.

She was sure Jack was genuinely pleased about her promotion to Deputy Director. It was what she wanted to do. Equally, she was happy for Jack and Sandro and the way they were establishing a reputation for their *Marine Salvage & Investigation Company*. She also knew he was worried about the looming court case against Sandro and the implications for the company. She replayed last night's telephone conversation in her head. By the time she arrived outside Jack's apartment she was convinced this would be the last time she would visit. She felt awful.

Penny parked, let herself into the apartment block and punched the lift button. She had a key to the apartment and could smell something cooking as she entered. The smells were strangely reassuring. For some odd reason she couldn't imagine him saying their relationship was over whilst they were sitting across a table eating and drinking. However, the look on his face wasn't reassuring. She'd never seen him look so solemn. Her smile evaporated, her body language and expression matched that facing her. With a sinking heart she just came out with it: 'What's the problem?'

Jack didn't say anything but took her hand and led her into the lounge area of the apartment. He motioned for her to sit next to him. Energy seemed to drain from her body as she sank into the sofa; she couldn't bring herself to look at him. Jack was starting to speak but she struggled to concentrate on what he was saying. She missed the first few words: '...may be able to save Sandro from going to prison, but I think I'd be breaking the law.'

Her reaction was instantaneous. The problem was not about them, it was about Sandro! It was about Sandro avoiding a prison sentence and maybe breaking the law to do so. She was suddenly energised and alert and flicked her head towards him. Relief was surging through her body as she struggled to respond. All she could manage to stutter was “Explain?”

‘A few days ago, I had a phone call in the office. It was from a guy in Latvia. He said he had a proposition for me that could avoid Sandro going to prison.’

Penny motioned that she was about to speak but Jack held up his hand to stop her and carried on. ‘He invited me to a meeting in a hotel bar in Riga. Anna Kalnina, the woman who claims Sandro beat her up and raped her, would be at the meeting. He said the proposal “would be to our mutual benefit”. He said if I decided not to attend the meeting the case would proceed as planned and Sandro would go to jail. I met him and Anna Kalnina last night in Riga.’

Penny was worried. Had Jack broken the law? Had he promised to do something illegal? With some trepidation she asked: ‘What does he want you to do?’

‘He says there are two hundred tonnes of plastic pellets on the *Asenka*, cargo we are contracted to salvage. There are four drums per pallet, wrapped in plastic film. The pellets are in cardboard drums that will be collapsing in the seawater. He wants us to salvage them and land them at a bonded warehouse in Riga. He also wants us to salvage twenty-three crates of machine parts; it's the equipment that makes the plastic. None of...’

‘What! There are hundreds of tons of plastic pellets...’ Penny almost shouted before Jack raised both his hands in a gesture asking her to stop talking.

‘In the initial tender documents, the sole cargo for salvage was zinc ingots. Sometime later we were told the drums of plastic and machine parts had been made a priority item for salvage. The video of the inspection shows they are accessible and so we could salvage them. It's what the Riga guy wants; it's part of the deal he's offering.’

Penny was desperately trying to control her emotions as, with steel in her voice, she asked: ‘What else?’

'The guy said that we should salvage the drums carefully so that none of the contents escape. Once the drums are landed, Sandro has to pay Anna Kalnina €40,000 then she will withdraw her complaint.'

In a sombre and dispassionate tone, Penny asked: 'What have you agreed?'

'I haven't agreed anything! The guy is going to phone me in a day or so for an answer. I've talked to Sandro, and he's prepared to go along with it.'

Jack had picked up on Penny's tone and body language. He felt he had to justify his actions and blurted: 'His previous lawyer, Roberta Fox, advised him to plead guilty. She said the case against him was so strong that if he pleaded not guilty his sentence is likely to be higher; it could be fifteen years. The lawyers in London are basing a defence on rough sex going too far – perhaps pleading guilty to a lesser charge of assault. Sandro believes he's looking at a long sentence and will be a middle-aged man by the time he gets out. He's talking of leaving the UK once he's released.'

There was a charged silence between them whilst Jack waited for Penny to speak.

'What were you thinking of Jack? Those drums could be full of anything – drugs, weapons... who knows.'

'He told me they are full of microbeads. They are classed as non-hazardous material. He said I could check any or all the drums – just microbeads he said.'

The word 'microbeads' hit her like an electric shock. It was reinforced by Jack describing them as 'non-hazardous material'. The shock was so complete it was accompanied by a sharp intake of breath as she bounced in her seat. 'Microbeads? Do you know what they are?' she challenged.

Penny pulled her phone out of her handbag. Her fingers scrolled to the calculator and started to punch in a series of numbers. As she did so she began to garble an explanation: 'Plastic pellets, about the size of a lentil or small pea, are used in injection and vacuum moulding to make a variety of products. Depending on the product, they are made from a variety of plastics, and yes, they're all currently categorised as non-hazardous material.

'However, microbeads are something else. Believe me – they're something else! They're tiny spheres, like specks of dust, and banned in the UK, most of Europe and in many countries around the world. Different sizes of microbeads, made from different plastics with different densities, are used in different products. In facial scrubs, their typical size is between 85 microns and 185 microns. If the drums do contain microbeads, let's assume an average size of, say, 100 microns.' Penny paused as she concentrated on punching numbers into the calculator in her phone and read out the result. 'A gram of such a microbead would contain about twenty thousand spheres.'

She continued punching numbers into the calculator. At the end of the calculation, she turned to Jack and handed him the phone. 'Just do the arithmetic Jack! Twenty thousand spheres, times one thousand grams represents twenty million microbeads in just one kilogram. In a metric tonne there would be twenty billion microbeads. That's a cargo of two hundred tonnes or about four trillion microbeads released into the ocean.'

Penny's face was flushed as she grabbed at the phone and punched in more numbers before looking up. 'If you put these microbeads end to end, they would stretch to the moon! They're not non-hazardous material! They are consumed by fish and are killing them. They can't digest or pass them. They are entering the food chain and have been detected in drinking water, human placentas and in human breast milk and stools. Plastic microbeads can attract and absorb harmful chemicals and be a site for harmful bacteria. If trillions of these beads were to be released into the North Sea, it would be an ecological and health disaster.'

Jack was shocked by his ignorance and naivety. In desperation he tried to retrieve the situation and focused on the cargo. 'Sandro, Gunnar and I completed an inspection of the ship a few weeks ago. We were concentrating on the position and state of the cargo we were planning to salvage.'

Jack put his head in his hands as he tried to recall the scene in the hold and the images from the video. 'The sinking wasn't violent and almost all of the cargo is readily accessible. It's going to be an easy salvage. We did look at the cardboard drums and they all looked intact. We've a video of the whole inspection. They could be salvaged easily.'

Penny grabbed Jack by the arm and pulled him round to face her. Looking directly into his face she announced: 'You're not salvaging those drums; don't even think about it! I know you are going to tell me that the *Stavanger* is the perfect ship to do the job. You'll also tell me that your team has all the kit and experience to do it. I'm telling you it's not going to happen, it's out of your hands. Jack, this is an incredibly serious situation. It's potentially a major European ecological disaster. I have to report it and initiate immediate action.'

Jack was chastened by Penny's reaction and amazed at her knowledge of microbeads. In an attempt to help, he recalled what the man in Riga had told him. 'The guy in Riga told me the beads were heat sealed inside heavy plastic bags. There's a single bag inside each cardboard drum. If we don't puncture a drum, the beads should be safe. Once it's landed, the authorities can check the contents.'

'OK, let me think,' said Penny as she opened her thin briefcase and took out a sheaf of lined paper and a pen.

Chapter 23

Plan of action

'What time was the meeting with the man in Riga and the woman Sandro is accused of raping?'

'I met them at seven o'clock in the Mirabelle Hotel bar. It was a short meeting and I phoned you when I got back to my room. You'll have the time on your phone, but it was about seven-thirty.'

'Remind me of the name of the ship that sank and the coordinates.'

Jack almost jumped off the sofa in his eagerness to find the information and was about to bound towards his study when Penny stopped him. 'Do you have a copy of the manifest and the name of the insurers? It will give us a head start on setting up the recovery.'

Jack was back moments later with a large file in his hand. He stood in front of her and read off the information Penny wanted. 'The ship was called the MV *Asenka*, registered in Lithuania. The insurers are Baltic Marine Services based in Riga; I've got their address and contact details here.' When Penny had finished scribbling, he read out the coordinates of the wreck site.

'OK, this is what I think we should do,' said Penny. 'I've got to phone the Director General at Border Force and alert him to the situation; it's what he'd expect me to do. I then need to phone the head of our "HAZMAT" team and tell him there are two hundred tonnes of microbeads sitting inside a recent wreck on the bed of the North Sea. Once he has the name of the ship and the coordinates, he can start...'

'Hey, hang on, hang on,' Jack interrupted. 'Where does all of this leave me and Sandro? What's the guy in Latvia going to do when all this hits the news?'

'Sorry, I should have said... there's a load of things we need to do simultaneously and confidentially. One of these is for me to arrange a meeting with the police in Manchester – with the officer in charge of the case against Sandro. You also need to contact Sandro, tell him what I'm doing and advise him to talk to his lawyers in London as soon as possible.'

Penny hesitated for a moment before continuing: 'Did Sandro know you were going to Riga to talk to this man about his proposal? Think carefully before you answer because the police will ask you.'

'Yes, I told him about the phone call; he's my friend, my partner. We both thought it was a scam but Sandro is desperate… if there was a chance of settling this out of court…'

'OK, I'm aware that people withdraw complaints to the police all the time… but you've got to tell the police everything. Remind me of the name of the police inspector,' she asked as she scribbled on her notepad.

'It's Detective Inspector Coleen Latchem, Greater Manchester Police,' Jack replied.

Penny added the information to her growing list. 'Good, I can ask our duty officer to arrange an immediate appointment for us with her – like tonight! I need to alert her to a possible link between the case she is handling and this emergency in the North Sea. It's likely she will want to start enquiries about the person trying to coerce you into a criminal act. You need to make a statement tonight. My discussion and your statement will be confidential. I can arrange for UK Border Force and the EMSA...'

'Who?' asked Jack.

'Sorry, it's the European Maritime Safety Agency. They coordinate all incidents of pollution within European waters. They are the body that will assess the problem and coordinate any recovery. I've met the Director of the EMSA; he's smart and on the ball. Once he's briefed about the problem, he will ensure it's all confidential and will liaise with both Border Force and the UK police. Your Riga gentleman will know nothing about it.'

Penny paused for a moment to think. 'All new wrecks are monitored for leaking pollutants. The EMSA will have already sampled the water around the wreck. I would have expected to have heard if microbeads are escaping. However, if the manifest is saying they are plastic pellets for injection moulding I suspect it wouldn't set alarm bells ringing.'

Penny paused for a moment to think. 'Jack, can you scan the manifest and send it to me as an email attachment? I also need those pages that identify the manufacturer and the consignee. I can ask my colleagues to track them down.'

Whilst Jack was busy scanning the manifest and other pages, Penny made her phone calls. He returned just as she was making another call; it was on loudspeaker so Jack could hear. No sooner did the ring tones start than the phone was answered. 'Inspector Jackie White here. Can I help you?'

'Jackie, it's Penny here. I've got a job for you and Andy – top priority. Put everything else on hold or delegate. I've just discovered that a recent shipwreck in the North Sea may be carrying two hundred tonnes of microbeads. In the next few minutes, I'll send you a copy of the manifest of the MV *Asenka.* That's spelt Alpha, Sierra, Echo, November, Kilo, Alpha; registered in Lithuania. I'm also going to send you details of the insurer; it's Baltic Marine Services based in Riga. The name of the manufacturer is listed as B&H Limited, Runcorn; the consignee is a Latvian company called Emma Farmaceitiska Fabrika. I probably pronounced that badly.

'Can you trace the manufacturer, the shipper, who arranged the insurance, consignee and so on; we need names and contact details. Email me details of the consignee and I'll forward these to EMSA. I'm going to be back in the office tomorrow. As soon as you get an address for the manufacturers, owners, hauliers and so on we can set up an inspection.

'I'm sorry to drop this on you and Andy but two hundred tonnes of microbeads in the North Sea could be a major ecological disaster. The sooner we get on to this the better.'

Jack scanned and forwarded all the documents Penny needed. He also phoned Sandro and explained what was happening. Sandro's reaction was understandable. 'Jack, the police will think I'm trying to interfere with the case… it's going to make matters worse!'

'No, it's not,' Jack replied. 'I responded to what we both thought was a scam call. As soon as we discovered the details, being coerced into an illegal act, we sought advice from the authorities – UK Border Force – and contacted the police immediately. You've done nothing wrong, you've done everything right,' Jack added.

There was silence on the other end of the phone as Jack wondered what to say next. Then it came to him. 'This could all be part of an elaborate set-up – but I can't see how at the moment. It's obviously something that DI Latchem and your London lawyers will need to consider.'

The confidence in Jack's voice was reassuring and Sandro said he would try to contact Samantha that night or the next day. Somewhat chastened, Jack returned to getting supper. He left the wine in the fridge and replaced it with orange juice. If he was to give a statement to the police, he needed to keep his wits about him.

Jack didn't hear her enter the kitchen but felt her arms around him and her body pressing against his back. The rush of adrenaline was wearing off and she was feeling more relaxed and in control. She'd done everything that was expected of her, and her thoughts returned to Jack. The dark cloud of an impending break-up had faded into the background. In a soft voice she almost whispered: 'There's nothing else we can do until they let us know about a meeting with Detective Inspector Latchem. HAZMAT and Jackie White will get everything underway and will give me an update tomorrow.'

She nuzzled against his neck; the reaction was immediate. He dropped the wooden spatula. With a smile on his face, he turned around and looked into her eyes.

'If there's nothing here that will spoil or burn, perhaps you could show me how pleased you are to see me,' Penny whispered with a coy smile on her lips.

Penny's phone rang twenty minutes later. The shrill alarm shattered the peace, calm and wellbeing that enveloped them. It took Penny a few moments to untangle herself from Jack's arms and legs, and the bed sheet. It was Detective Inspector Coleen Latchem.

'Thank you for meeting me at such short notice; it is appreciated,' said Deputy Director Penelope Pendleton Price as she smiled and reached out her hand to shake that of Detective Inspector Coleen Latchem. Penny then held out her hand to DI Latchem's colleague, waiting for the introduction.

'My colleague, Detective Constable Julie Evers; she's working with me on the case,' was all she said.

It was a frosty welcome but not unexpected. Penny had been escorted to the DI's office whilst Jack had been taken to an interview room inside the police station in Manchester. Penny was in her UK Border Force uniform, complete with crown and single pip on her epaulets. Despite the long day, she looked immaculate and self-assured.

'I had little choice,' replied Coleen. 'A phone call from the Chief Constable is pretty persuasive,' she added.

'I'm sorry they brought out the big guns, but this really is extremely important, and we wanted to alert the Chief Constable, and you, as soon as possible.'

With no show of emotion Detective Inspector Latchem gestured for Penny to take a seat. 'So, what's so important? Why is Jack Collier, business partner of Alessandro Calovarlo, here to make a statement?'

'I can brief you on intelligence I have recently received and upon which UK Border Force is acting. I can also alert you to the actions the European Maritime Safety Agency is currently undertaking. All of this may, I repeat may, relate to one of your ongoing cases – the charge of assault and rape of Anna Kalnina by Alessandro Calovarlo.'

Penny could see DI Latchem visibly bristle at the revelation of a possible link to one of her cases. 'Please continue,' said Coleen through almost clenched teeth.

'Jack Collier is currently making a full statement in relation to a meeting he had last night in Riga, Latvia, with an unknown man and Anna Kalnina. The woman who claimed she was assaulted and raped by Alessandro Calovarlo.'

DI Latchem visibly rose in her chair; there was a sharp intake of breath through her nose and her eyes darted to make contact with those of the Deputy Director in front of her.

'I will obviously leave you to judge the implications of this statement and will respect your decision as to what actions, if any, to take. It's your case.'

Penny could see the DI relax a fraction. She sat back in her chair and her previously penetrating gaze softened.

'Immediately after his meeting in Riga, Jack Collier phoned me for advice. He asked to meet here in Manchester. A few hours ago, he told me there may be two hundred tonnes of microbeads on board the recent wreck of the MV *Asenka* in the North Sea. He was offered a proposal: salvage the microbeads, land them at a bonded warehouse in Riga, pay Anna Kalnina €40,000 and she would drop her complaint against Calovarlo.

'If these microbeads escape from the wreck and into the North Sea, it will be an ecological disaster. In addition to alerting your Chief Constable, and now you, I have contacted the Director of the European Maritime Safety Agency. They coordinate all incidents of pollution within European waters. He and his colleagues will sample the waters around the wreck and make discreet enquiries into the company that was to receive the consignment. The consignee is Emma Farmaceitiska Fabrika, also based in Riga.

'I will keep you fully informed of all developments related to our enquiry. We are currently tracing those involved in the manufacture and sale of these microbeads. I'm expecting an update tomorrow – I'll share it with you. Of course, this incident may have nothing to do with your case involving Sandro Calovarlo, but I felt it only courteous to alert you to a possible link between the shipwreck and your case.'

Within the space of a few minutes the atmosphere within Coleen's office changed from confrontation to cooperation. Whilst Jack completed his statement, Penny elaborated upon the actions UK Border Force and the EMSA were undertaking.

It was late by the time Jack drove them back to the apartment, but they were both energised by the events at the police station. As Jack closed the door to the apartment and turned, Penny was standing directly in front of him. She slid her arms around his neck and with a seductive smile announced: 'I've got a long day tomorrow... but we haven't finished what we were doing before the damn phone rang!'

Chapter 24

Curiouser and curiouser

It had been an early start from Salford to get to UK Border Force's offices in Hull by nine o' clock; it was going to be the start of a very busy day and Penny had much to do. The head of HAZMAT had updated her on their actions and those of EMSA. In the car she had made a mental list of other actions to be taken and information needed. As soon as she got to her office, she instigated these.

It was also a busy day for Detective Inspector Latchem. She and DI Henry Lomas were on their way to Riga to interview Anna Kalnina. Coleen's line manager had decided that she should continue to investigate the rape allegation and any links to the suspected illegal manufacture and export of microbeads. However, the Assistant Chief Constable, the ACC, had overruled him.

'This could easily become a major and high-profile investigation. If the consignment of microbeads on that wrecked ship are released into the North Sea it would become a massive ecological disaster. I don't want Latchem distracted by her current case. I want a fresh new team to investigate. The two teams can liaise.'

What the ACC really wanted was to avoid any potential success by Latchem and to nurture the career of his protégé, Henry Lomas. The ACC kept a close eye on all his junior officers and was aware of the growing reputation of Coleen Latchem. He wasn't about to give her an easy, open goal.

Whilst the police flew to Riga, Penny waded through dozens of awaiting emails and a pile of correspondence. She'd missed lunch and by mid-afternoon needed a break. Penny got up from her desk and began to walk towards the coffee machine; she never made it. Inspectors Jackie White and Andy Wilson were marching towards her office, files in hand.

'Afternoon ma'am,' said Jackie as she and Andy blocked the corridor.

'Please, come,' said Penny as she abandoned any thought of coffee and led them to her office. 'You can tell me what you've got for me.'

A large, flat-topped table, surrounded by chairs, dominated half of Penny's office. Penny sat at the head of the table with Jackie and Andy on either side of her. Jackie placed a slim file in front of her and started to speak: 'Well, it's not straightforward. The manufacturer of the "plastic pellets" is recorded as B&H Limited, Runcorn. It *was* an established company making disposable cutlery, one-use plastics for the hospitality industry and more recently microbeads.'

Penny immediately picked up on the stress placed upon the word 'was'. 'But...?' she asked.

'But B&H Limited was declared bankrupt and closed almost a year ago. I checked on their sales and there's no mention of an order for two hundred tonnes of microbeads anywhere. There was a flurry of activity in the run-up to the national ban on their production but nothing on this scale. I'm currently checking the orders to see if they were fulfilled. It's possible that they falsified the records to beat the ban and stockpiled the microbeads to sell them off later. What's curious is that the person who authorised the shipment is identified as Alice Henshaw, one of the former owners.'

'I've traced her address and contact details as well as the company's managing director, production manager, senior engineer, principal secretary and accountant; they're all in the file,' said Andy.

Just as Penny reached to take the files, Jackie added: 'What's odd is that all of this happened after the company closed and after it was then sold. I've checked and the administrators list a quantity of unused stock and condemned manufacturing equipment in the details of the sale. It's possible that this stock was used to make the microbeads and they were shipped on board the *Asenka* along with the machinery. We'll be able to check when we inspect the factory.'

Andy continued: 'Just a few minutes ago I heard from Calverton & Son, the haulier in Runcorn. They confirm the dates on which two hundred tonnes of plastic pellets and twenty-three crates of machine parts were shipped to Liverpool docks. They remembered it because it was a much bigger transport job than normal. They also told me it was odd because they were paid cash. I'm waiting for documentary evidence of what the haulier told me and loading confirmation from the Port of Liverpool.'

'Well done,' said Penny. 'It's good that we have contact details of key people within B&H Limited, but it needs considerable resources and persuasion to mount this sort of operation. If they did restart production and ship the microbeads the testimony of people like the senior engineer and production manager will be important. However, it's more likely that the former owner or accountant initiated it.

'I'll get onto the Liverpool office and ask them to set up surveillance on Alice Henshaw, the accountant, production manager and senior engineer. When the location of all of them is known we'll detain and question them. Depending on what emerges we can detain others. I'm not bothered about the actual workers for now.'

Glancing at both Jackie and Andy she continued: 'Jackie, I'd like you and Andy to lead two of the teams. I'll ask Liverpool to lead the other two and to inspect the factory.'

The Latvian authorities had been briefed about the alleged rape of one of its citizens and the possible illegal procurement of microbeads by a Latvian company. They had made an interview room available and requested that a Latvian police officer attended the interview with Anna Kalnina. It was Detective Inspector Latchem who started the interview.

'Anna, we've been informed that you met with Jack Collier, co-owner of the *Marine Salvage & Investigation Company* and business partner of Alessandro Calovarlo, in the bar of the Mirabelle Hotel in Riga a few days ago. Can you confirm this meeting occurred?'

Anna was prepared for the question. Tony had told her there was a chance the police may ask her about the meeting; he'd told her what to say. Looking straight into DI Latchem's face she replied. 'Yes, I met him – with Zak Friedman.'

Zak Friedman did not exist; it was a name dreamed up by Tony Levens. He had even made a business card, with false phone numbers and website, for Anna to use if questioned. DI Henry Lomas knew nothing of this and could hardly contain himself. Within moments of the interview starting, he believed he had the name of the person he wanted to track down.

'We also understand you agreed to withdraw your complaint of assault and rape against Alessandro in exchange for €40,000. Is that correct?'

'Yes… but I changed my mind. Zak told me Calovarlo was rich and would pay anything to avoid going to court and to prison. When Mr Collier left, I told Zak I'd changed my mind… I wanted him punished for what he did to me…'

Anna buried her face in her hands and looked as though she was about to burst into tears. Coleen reached out a hand and placed it on her shoulder. It took a few minutes for Anna to compose herself.

'Anna, I know this is difficult but we have to know precisely what happened between you and this person, Zak Friedman. Start at the beginning…'

Anna had already rehearsed her prepared story. 'It was a week or so after I got back home, after the… assault. Zak Friedman came to my apartment… he was unannounced… I didn't ask him to come… he just turned up. He said he was a… er, criminal injuries lawyer who specialised in getting compensation for victims. He'd heard I'd been assaulted and said if I wanted to continue with the complaint in the UK, he would respect my decision. However, he told me that only one or two percent of rape allegations result in a conviction. I told him I didn't believe it… you told me the case against him was overwhelming.'

Coleen visibly winced at the challenge because although she believed the case was indeed 'overwhelming' she also knew only a minute proportion of alleged cases resulted in a conviction. She waited for Anna to continue.

'He told me that Calovarlo was employing expensive lawyers who may get him off. He said I'd have to relive every detail of the… er, assault in court.' Again, Anna covered her face with her hands and waited. 'It's going well… she believes me,' Anna said to herself.

'Would you like a drink? Would you like a break?' Coleen asked.

'No, I want to tell you what happened… Friedman asked me what amount of money I wanted for the case to be dropped – to avoid being questioned in court, reliving the experience. I said €10,000. I don't know why I said that much – the figure just came into my head.'

Anna knew all of this was fantasy – but the policewoman had no way of checking. The final figure she'd negotiated with Tony Levens was €40,000. Anna wasn't a fool. She knew what they were doing was illegal and guessed Levens had plenty to gain if it was successful. If she was going to take a risk it had to be worthwhile.

'He said his commission would be twenty percent… All I had to do was attend a meeting in Riga with Calovarlo's partner. He'd do all the talking. He said if I wanted to back out at any time I could. He said I'd got nothing to lose. If Calovarlo paid up I got the money, if he didn't, he'd have to go to court.'

'So, what happened at the meeting?'

Anna was thinking rapidly. She had to be careful what she said – it had to sound right. 'I was frightened. I sat there but wasn't really listening. At one point Mr Collier asked me about the money, the compensation. I said I wanted €40,000 to drop the case: that's all.'

Coleen asked question after question to check and corroborate Anna's story. However, when it came to any discussion about microbeads, Anna merely said she couldn't remember because she was so frightened. Coleen could feel Henry Lomas's growing irritation as the interview continued. His snorts and gestures eventually had the desired effect when Coleen said she had no further questions at this time and suggested a short break before Detective Inspector Lomas asked her a few more questions.

Within moments of starting to question Anna, Henry Lomas was cock-a-hoop. He was asking questions about Zak Friedman, so he could track him down, when Anna announced: 'He gave me his business card… his website, email address, phone numbers…'

'Do you still have it?' asked Lomas, hardly containing his delight.

'I'm sure I do… I wouldn't have thrown it away… I think I know where it is.'

Anna knew exactly where the business card was stored. Tony Levens had told her it would send any enquirer on a wild goose chase.

Lomas sat back in his chair and smiled. Whilst Latchem would be wallowing in the rape case for months, he had the prospect of a quick result. A criminal case solved; a major ecological disaster averted. It could be a major boost to his promotion prospects.

A few hours later all the euphoria had disappeared. Henry's attempt to get a description of the man was exasperating. According to Anna Kalnina, Zak Friedman was in his mid-twenties or maybe mid-thirties, of average height and weight with no distinguishing features and no identifiable accent. He had 'brownish hair', 'not short, not long...sort of average'. There were millions of men that would match the description.

The Latvian police drove Anna home and she gave Lomas the business card. He transferred all the information to his team in Manchester – who later confirmed the business card was homemade. There was no such criminal injury lawyer, no such website, no such email address and no such phone number.

It took UK Border Force less than twenty-four hours to confirm the location of the four targets. The operation was fixed for 6 a.m. on a Sunday morning. As the second hand swept up to mark the hour, Border Force officers walked up driveways, garden paths and an apartment stairwell. Penny and her team had driven up a grand driveway and were standing under the splendid portico of a magnificent house as one of the team hammered on the door. It took several minutes of hammering before an indignant and flamboyantly dressed woman began to open it. It was an odd sight. The woman had obviously spent several minutes combing her hair and was wearing a luxurious black nightgown dramatically embroidered with colourful dragons. Penny guessed it was silk and expensive.

An officer grabbed the edge of the door and eased past the woman as Penny stepped forward. 'Alice Henshaw: I am arresting you under Section 24 of the Police and Criminal Evidence Act 1984. I believe you have illegally manufactured and sold a quantity of microbeads. As an officer within UK Border Force, I have the authority to enter and search this property, to detain and arrest you; please step back.'

The expression on Alice Henshaw's face changed in an instant. One moment it was haughty and indignant, eyebrows raised and head tilted back. The next the eyes looked shocked, her mouth gaped and her shoulders slumped. Penny took her by the elbow and let her lead them through a spacious hallway and into a lounge. They were followed by another Border Force officer from the Liverpool office. In the few seconds it took to move into the lounge Penny could feel Alice Henshaw recovering from the shock. Turning to Penny she announced: 'This is ridiculous. I demand to speak to my solicitor.'

'You are free to speak to your solicitor at any time – but I suspect he or she isn't in the office at the moment. Perhaps you may wish to wait. Oh, by the way, we have also arrested your former accountant and several senior staff who worked at B&H Limited before you were declared bankrupt, and the factory closed. A search of the factory you previously owned is underway as I speak.'

Penny could see a change in her expression and body language as Alice Henshaw processed the revelation and appeared to think what to do next. Penny was happy to sit and wait. In a few hours she would have a more complete story. Alice looked up to the ceiling as the sound of people searching upper rooms could be heard. Alice had decided how to respond. She relaxed into the softness of the sofa she was sitting on and, in a patronising tone, declared: 'Young lady, I, er, merely facilitated the production of microbeads – there's nothing wrong with that. It's not illegal to make them – just to sell them. I didn't sell them. I allowed equipment that I owned to use up surplus stock; stock that I also owned. If the microbeads were eventually sold, I did not receive any money for them. My accountant will confirm this.'

'Ms Henshaw, thank you for the confession that you "facilitated the production of microbeads". My colleague is a witness to this confession. I don't know who told you it was OK to make microbeads, but they are wrong. In the United Kingdom it is illegal to make, sell or incorporate microbeads into other products. If convicted, you face a prison sentence of up to two years and a fine of up to ten percent of your factory turnover.

'What's more, once you were declared bankrupt the stock, machinery and utilities were no longer yours. They belonged to your creditors. I suspect other charges will be brought against you in due course.'

Alice reacted as though she was a punctured balloon. She simply seemed to deflate and sink into the sofa.

'What I can tell you is this. If you cooperate with my investigation, I will ensure the judge is told of your full cooperation. If you believe you have been deceived or manipulated, you will have every opportunity to explain. There may be mitigating circumstances.'

Penny knew that Alice's full cooperation could make the investigation so much quicker and easier.

'It was Roger's idea, Roger Davis.'

It all came out in a torrent. It seemed a previously unknown man, Roger Davis, had come forward with a proposal. He had told Alice that he represented an Eastern European company that was trying to source microbeads after their supplier had run into production difficulties. Through his contacts he had heard that B&H Limited had previously produced them, had closed abruptly and was for sale. He had offered to fund the production costs and overheads, exhaust the stock of materials to make them, and to cover the cost of transportation. He had offered Alice a one-off consultancy fee to *facilitate* the process.

'I still owned the factory, the equipment and all the stock,' she explained. 'He told me it was a loophole in the law. As long as I didn't get paid for the beads, I wasn't breaking any laws; I was simply disposing of surplus materials.'

'Ms Henshaw, you must have been aware that when you were declared bankrupt, and administrators took over the responsibility for disposing of the remaining assets, you no longer owned them. By using existing stock and assets you were defrauding your creditors.'

Alice Henshaw looked dazed and totally defeated. She led Penny to a concealed safe in a downstairs study and took out a box file containing orders and receipts, lists and dates. She rummaged through and picked out a business card.

'Here it is,' said Alice with a forced smile. 'Roger's business card.'

It didn't take long to discover that the company Roger Davis listed did not exist. It was a fictitious address with an unobtainable mobile phone number.

Initial feedback from the other Border Force teams confirmed much of what Alice Henshaw had told them and what Penny had already discovered. She provided a copy of her report to DI Lomas. He had found the task of trying to find a witness to the meeting between Anna Kalnina and the mysterious Zak Friedman laborious and fruitless. He scoured the reports by Deputy Director Pendleton Price. He sought descriptions of those who organised the production of the microbeads but without success. Rather than a quick result his investigation was becoming a quagmire.

B&H Limited had evolved as a family business. Most of the staff were long standing; many had worked there for over twenty-five years. When, occasionally, a staff member died, retired or left they were typically replaced by a relative of an existing staff member. It was a close-knit group. When B&H was declared bankrupt and closed it was a devastating blow to everyone, especially the older staff members. Whilst some of the younger employees found jobs, often having to move away from the area, most resigned themselves to unemployment and living off government benefits. A phone call offering a few weeks work at B&H Limited, at time and a half plus bonus in cash, was snapped up by many – even though they knew they shouldn't claim benefits and work at the same time. A few simply said no; recent wounds were too fresh.

The senior engineer and a colleague had returned to the factory. They had checked the equipment, confirmed it was operational and supervised the production runs. The production manager had assembled a skeleton team and in just over three weeks drained the existing stock and produced two hundred tonnes of microbeads. Alice and the production manager had organised production and shipping. It didn't take long to list everyone who had been involved.

Chapter 25

Working for the EMSA

Jack wasn't expecting a phone call from Penny but soon realised it was more business than pleasure. Apparently, she had been liaising with the EMSA, the European Maritime Safety Agency, and there was a problem. Everyone agreed that the drums of microbeads should be recovered as soon as possible but there were shortages of vessels and people to undertake the work. Most of the vessels within the EMSA were designed for pollution monitoring and control, essentially clean-up. A vessel and team that was able to salvage the drums was already working on limiting the leakage of contaminants from a partly submerged freighter.

A practical solution was to contract the *Marine Salvage & Investigation Company* to salvage the drums. It seemed the argument was that they were planning to salvage cargo from the MV *Asenka* anyway. They had the ship, most of the equipment and expertise to do so. The EMSA could supply specialist containment jackets to be used during the salvage of the drums. The decision wouldn't alert those who had manufactured and transported the microbeads. A confidential arrangement could be made with Baltic Insurance Services making it the cheapest option. The only other requirement was the presence of an EMSA representative to act as an observer of the salvage.

The *Stavanger* and crew had arrived in Portsmouth on schedule. Sandro had arranged for the planned repairs and maintenance to be completed in half the time, with twice the manpower, at an inflated cost. It would enable the ship to call into Felixstowe on the east coast of the UK for refuelling, collecting the specialist equipment and observer before heading for the wreck site.

Penny had arranged to stay over in Salford the weekend before Jack and Sandro joined the *Stavanger*. It had been a trouble-free journey along the M62 motorway from Hull, and she was relaxing before Sandro joined them for a meal in their favourite restaurant in Rusholme.

'How's Sandro doing?' Penny asked with some trepidation.

'He seems OK, but he's lost weight, and isn't the Sandro we both know. When we're working together, he acts as though nothing is wrong, but I'm sure he's worried about the case.'

'Does he sound more confident in the new lawyers?'

'Apparently the offer to drop the case caused a flurry of excitement but I'm not sure what's happening. There's also some legal manoeuvre that may result in the case being thrown out – but I don't understand the details. However, if the case does go to court, it will all be down to the jury and how they interpret the evidence. I'll show you something.'

Jack rose from the sofa and walked out of the room. He came back a moment later with a stiff piece of paper in his hand; it was a photograph. He gave it to Penny and sat down beside her. He could see the immediate effect it had on her. Her eyes and mouth were suddenly wide open. It was the same reaction as his – and probably the same one jury members would have.

'This is what the guy in Riga gave me. He said it's a photograph of the woman who claims Sandro beat her up and raped her. He said it was taken at the police station.'

Penny didn't say a word but merely stared at the photograph, breathing deeply through her nose.

'I can't help thinking this is more than rough sex,' said Jack. 'Sandro's adamant that he didn't do it, but also says he can't remember. If I was on the jury, and she claimed Sandro did this to her, it would be damning.'

Penny was about to reply when the doorbell rang. Who could it be? They weren't expecting Sandro for another half hour or so. Jack got up from the sofa to answer the door only to find Sandro standing before him.

'Oh, hi, you're early, er, come in,' said Jack before grabbing Sandro's arm and pulling him inside the apartment. 'Penny's here and she's looking forward to seeing you. She can bring us up to date on what's happening with the EMSA before we go to the Mughal Palace.'

Sandro led the way into the lounge and gave Penny a broad smile as he opened his arms in expectation of a cuddle. There was the slightest of pauses before the smile was returned and before Penny started to stand. He'd noticed it, and that she had something in her hand that she dropped over the side of the sofa as she rose. Perhaps he was becoming paranoid, but he sensed a tense atmosphere in the room and in Penny. She was stiff and not relaxed; she felt awkward as they embraced.

There's a sensation when friends embrace. It's based on a familiar series of movements, physical pressures and timescale. Penny broke away from Sandro moments before the unspoken time for an embrace had passed. Feeling suddenly shunned as she broke away, he moved towards the sofa. As he did so, he looked down to the thing Penny had discarded. He recognised it straight away because it had fallen face up. It was the bloody photograph of Anna Kalnina. Sandro stooped to pick it up. As he glanced at it, his expression changed. The smile was replaced with a scowl, his jaw tightened, and his eyes hardened as he looked at the photo and held it out to Penny.

'I think you dropped this,' he said in a flat, accusing tone.

Penny stood motionless and made no attempt to accept the photo.

'Sandro, I showed it to Penny. I was trying to bring her up to date with what you had told me about the case. I was trying to avoid talking about it in the restaurant...'

It seemed Sandro was going to say something in reply, but he paused. He stared intently at the photograph for several moments before he turned to Jack and demanded: 'Where did you get this?'

'The guy in Riga gave it to me – I told you as soon as I got back.'

'When did he say it was taken?'

'Er, he said it was taken at the police station in Manchester.'

Sandro flicked the photograph over. With his arms outstretched, he pushed the reverse side towards Jack. 'There's no exhibit number on the back, no official stamp. It's a different photo to the one Detective Inspector Latchem showed me.'

Whilst both Jack and Penny had confused looks upon their faces, Sandro was suddenly animated. His own rejection and confusion were replaced by eagerness that neither Jack nor Penny could understand. 'There's no trace of tears running down her face and through her make-up, no smudged mascara, the eyes and expression are different; it's a different photo.'

'I don't understand,' was all Jack said.

'When I was interviewed at the police station DI Latchem showed me a photo of Anna Kalnina. She said it was taken at the station and evidence that I had beaten up the woman. I was shocked when I saw it.'

Sandro looked at both Jack and Penny in turn as he admitted: 'Just like you were both shocked when you saw this picture; but it's a different picture. Look, in the one I saw, the one that Latchem says is evidence, you can see the marks that tears had made on her face. There's no trail of tears here. Her mascara is smudged but it's not running down her face. Her eyes are different.'

Sandro looked at the photo again and gestured to a point on it. 'In the photo I was shown at the police station the woman had a split lip and it was swollen. There was also signs of a bruise on her cheek. Look, on this one the lip is split, there's some swelling but not much. There's no sign of any bruise on her cheek. This is a different picture. I think it was taken before she was photographed at the police station.'

'Are you saying this is a fake?' asked Penny.

'No. I'm saying it was taken for the guy in Riga to persuade us to salvage stuff from the *Asenka*... It's part of the set-up.'

'It makes sense,' said Penny. 'I must admit the photograph and her claim about assault and rape is damning; especially when you say you don't remember what happened... But how is it related to the salvage of the microbeads and manufacturing equipment? Jack told me that salvaging the zinc was the main priority and that the drums of plastic and crates of equipment weren't even on the list... You've got to share this new information with the police. You've got to do it now.'

Sandro retrieved the phone number for the Central Manchester Police Station and asked to speak to Detective Inspector Latchem. He was told she was unavailable, but he could leave a message. He left a message saying evidence had come to light that he wanted to share with her. He also phoned Samantha Elliot; she was still in her office in London. Sandro explained about the new photograph, one given to Jack Collier in Riga, and his belief it was taken before Anna Kalnina arrived at the police station. He mentioned the absence of any exhibit number and rubber stamp. He thought this could all be part of a set-up.

'Sandro, this could be extremely important. Can you scan and email the photograph to me at once – both sides? Can you also put the photograph somewhere safe; somewhere we can collect it before a meeting with Detective Inspector Latchem?'

'I've already phoned Inspector Latchem and left her a

message...'

Samantha interrupted Sandro mid-sentence: 'Sandro, do not, I repeat, do not meet with DI Latchem. Do not mention or discuss the photograph with her, do not show it to her, do not leave it with her. Do you understand? I will arrange for a motorcycle courier to collect the photograph tomorrow morning and bring it to London.'

The forcefulness of her reaction was sufficient to stop Sandro in his tracks.

'As soon as I get the photograph I will speak to Reginald, and I will get back to you as soon as possible. If the person in Riga maintained the photograph was taken at the police station in Manchester, and it is significantly different to the exhibit we have seen, it could be of major significance.

'We also need to create an image of the person Jack Collier met in the Mirabelle Hotel in Riga. We have a specialist who can create a "photo-fit" picture from Jack's description. Sandro, this is important. We need to create this photo-fit picture of this man as soon as possible and for our investigators to find him. This could be the single most important part of our case. Can we fix a date and time when our computer specialist can meet with Jack?'

Sandro relayed what Samantha Elliot had said to Jack and Penny. Jack immediately agreed a time and date to meet the specialist in the Salford office, and Sandro scanned and emailed the photograph. The atmosphere in the apartment had changed. It was now charged with excitement and optimism.

During their meal at the Mughal Palace, Sandro's phone rang; it was Samantha Elliot. 'Sandro, Reginald and I have compared the two photographs and considered both the circumstances in which it was given to Jack as well as the lack of any evidence numbers. We believe this photograph may be of major importance and would like to discuss our actions as soon as possible. Can you attend a meeting in London this Friday morning? By then we will have had time for our expert witnesses to inspect the photographs. Our computer specialist, Helen Whiter, will be in your Salford office by mid-morning tomorrow. Together with Jack, she will create a photo-fit picture of the man he met in Riga. Our investigators will start to trace him.'

Sandro was immediately awake and alert. He concentrated for a moment, wondering what had awoken him. It wasn't the alarm clock because it was still too early, and the apartment was quiet. He knew he had slept well and for the first time in weeks felt hungry. He also felt something else – a calmness '*uno stato di benessere',* a feeling of well-being. He realised he'd forgotten the feeling of waking up feeling refreshed, looking forward to the day and feeling confident and happy. Until this morning he hadn't realised the pressure he had been under and how it was crushing him. The phone call from Samantha last night, and the evening with Jack and Penny, had been a turning point.

As he rolled out of bed, he saw his clothes littering the floor. 'This changes today,' he said to himself. Sandro was almost fastidious in his grooming and wardrobe. His father had once told him, 'You don't get a second chance to make a first impression'. At the time, he didn't realise what this meant but he eventually realised and took it to heart. After a long, hot shower he tidied his bedroom, lounge and kitchen. As he left the apartment, he tried to remember the word in English for '*ringiovaniment*' – it was rejuventated.

Chapter 26

Fast-tracked

Sandro was in the office before Lesley and switched on the coffee machine. He was about to open his email when the phone rang. 'Good morning, *Marine Salvage & Investigation Company*, Sandro Calovarlo here, how can I help you?'

'Good morning Sandro, it's Jack's friend from Riga.'

The change in Sandro was immediate; it was as though a switch had been thrown. He could feel his stomach and shoulders tense and the sense of well-being drain from him. The caller didn't wait for a reply but continued: 'My contacts tell me your ship is en route to the wreck of the *Asenka*. I'm sure we are both hoping that over the next few weeks my friend's cargo will be salvaged and transferred to the warehouse in Riga. I know Anna is looking forward to her compensation and you must be looking forward to the thought of avoiding prison.'

The shock of the phone call was so great that Sandro struggled to know what to say. 'I, er, I'll keep my promise.'

'Good, good because I also understand your court case is being fast-tracked. My contacts tell me it's because the Crown Prosecution Service want to demonstrate they are actively addressing the scandal of rape cases taking years to come to court. I'm told it's being fast-tracked because they believe the evidence is so overwhelming it will be an easy win. No doubt the newspapers will love it. "Rich Italian businessman rapes tourist". Let's hope, for your sake, that nothing prevents the salvage. It would be very unfortunate for all of us.'

Without another word, the caller rang off. Sandro's thoughts were in turmoil. It was easy to track the position of the *Stavanger*. There were dozens of free websites that allowed anyone to track a ship in real time via the AIS system, the Automatic Identification of Ships. If a person had the coordinates of the wreck, it was easy to check if the *Stavanger* was on station. It wasn't mention of the ship that was troubling him – it was the news about the case being fast-tracked. He knew Melton-Barr was in discussion with the Crown Prosecution Service about scheduling a trial but there had been no talk of it being fast-tracked. He glanced at the large wall clock and judged that Samantha would be in her office; he phoned her. Afterwards, he realised he had been rude to the receptionist. He'd demanded, forcefully, to speak to Samantha or Reginald. When Samantha answered, he immediately challenged her.

'I've just heard from the man in Riga. He says my case is being fast-tracked. He says the trial will be in weeks! How is it that he knows, and I don't?'

'Sandro, we are always in touch with the CPS, and fast-tracking your case has been raised. However, we have not agreed to this. It sounds like your caller is merely trying to rattle you, to make you more compliant. The defence and prosecution must agree to a trial date. Let me check and get back to you. However, let me assure you: we will not be stampeded into a trial. We were already confident of the defence we were assembling and with the new information about the photograph, we feel there are several lines of enquiry that we wish to pursue before any date is fixed.

'Once we have a photo-fit picture of the man in Riga our investigators will find him. It will open a whole new line of enquiry that can only strengthen our case. I know this will have been a shock to you – but I think it's a ploy to unsettle you. I'll get back to you as soon as possible.'

Jack had alerted Lesley that he was expecting a visitor, Helen Whiter, that morning. Lesley could sense, by the way Jack behaved, that the visitor was important and Jack was anxious. She had seldom seen Jack look so distracted. However, it was mid-morning before Helen Whiter arrived carrying two large and heavy computer satchels, one on each shoulder. She was tiny, the top of her head barely reaching the middle of Jack's chest. Jack invited her into his office, and they sat around his desk.

'Do you need a space to set up your equipment? Sorry the desk is so crowded.'

'Not at the moment. I'd just like to chat to you about the occasions you met the man in question and your impressions. I'd like to get a feel for him before we start to create an image. Where did you first meet?'

'I met him only once, in a hotel bar in Riga, for about ten minutes.'

'Was he standing or sitting?' she asked.

'He was sitting in a corner booth with a woman called Anna Kalnina. We'd arranged to meet at seven o'clock that evening…'

'Could you estimate his build, his physique, during the time you were with him?'

'I'd say he was of average height – much taller than the woman. His legs seemed quite long compared to the woman. I'd say he was probably one metre seventy-five, one eighty, and slight. I remember thinking his legs and arms didn't seem very muscular – even in a suit. I'd guess he was about seventy kilos, not much more.'

'Can you describe the suit and what he was wearing?'

'It was a dark suit. I couldn't tell if it had a pattern or weave; it just seemed dark in the bar. He was wearing a plain white shirt and a striped tie, plain black leather shoes. He looked like a junior banker or estate agent.'

'Do you think he had dressed for the meeting or was he wearing day-to-day clothes?'

Jack paused as he tried to recall the scene in the bar. 'I'd say he was wearing his normal day-to-day clothes. The suit and shirt didn't look crisp. My recollection now is that he'd worn the suit all week and the shirt all day. He hadn't "dressed up" for our meeting.'

The questioning went on and on and wasn't what he was expecting. He'd assumed Helen would be asking about physical features – the shape of his face, colour of his hair and so on. After what seemed like a long time, Jack asked: 'Is all of this relevant to creating a picture of this man?'

Helen smiled and gave a little laugh. 'Yes, more than you may think. It's all part of building up a picture of the man. I'm trying to form an image of him. Was he smart or casual, tense or relaxed? We'll get to the long or short fingernails later.'

Over the next thirty minutes or so the interrogation continued until she believed she had the mental image she wanted. 'I think we're ready to start creating a likeness for this gentleman. I'll set up this monitor on your desk, connect it to my laptop and away we go. We'll start with a bland, non-descript image and gradually refine it until you're happy.'

Over the next hour the questioning continued but was much more directed. 'Was his face longer or shorter... his complexion lighter or darker? Were his eyebrows thin or thick, were they arched or straight? Did they meet in the middle or were they separate?' It was the finer detail, the facial expression, that she wanted to capture.

'That's him, that's him,' Jack said with some urgency.

He didn't want her to change the picture on the screen. Jack had confirmed the shape of the thin, pale face, the clean-shaven complexion and the style of his short, dark hair. It had taken time, but eventually he was confident that the Roman nose, with its prominent bridge, and the almost feminine mouth and pursed lips were as accurate as he could remember. The final touch was the expression: slightly smug. It took more time to create a profile and three-quarter view but after a couple of hours, Jack believed they had a picture that could be recognised. Moments later the images were emailed to Melton-Barr. A short time later three Latvian investigators were leaving their office and setting out to trace the man in the photographs.

Chapter 27

A routine salvage

It was a logical decision. Jack and the EMSA observer would join the team on the *Stavanger* at Felixstowe, a major port on the east coast of the UK where the ship would be refuelled. Sandro would remain in Salford so that he could be in face-to-face contact with both Detective Inspector Latchem and Melton-Barr. He would also handle day-to-day business in the office and respond to any requests from the *Stavanger*.

Captain Erik Sorenson had the *Stavanger* working so smoothly that Jack felt redundant. He chatted to the crew and the divers but was keen not to get in the way. The EMSA observer said little; he just watched and kept in the background. They were approaching the wreck site and Lukas, the dive supervisor, was about to brief the dive teams prior to entering saturation. He asked Jack to introduce the briefing and to provide a voiceover to the video Sandro had taken of the wreck and cargo. The EMSA observer tagged along.

The briefing room was full as Jack followed Lukas inside. Looking around he thought it was interesting that even out of the water the dive teams sat close together. They were tight-knit groups and were all wearing maroon jumpsuits with lots of zip pockets. The name of the company was embroidered on their chests in small letters, and the name of the ship was emblazoned in white on their backs. Lorna, the only woman in the two dive teams, was sitting between Anders and Leif. Gunnar, who had joined the ship in Portsmouth, was sitting beside Greg and Lennie.

It was also noticeable that whilst Lorna and Gunnar were tall and athletic, the other divers were smaller and lithe, mini powerpacks of muscle and sinew. He also noticed that although the dive teams, apart from Gunnar, had been in the Gulf of Mexico for a year, they didn't look tanned. Indeed, they all had a pale, sallow complexion. It was the result of working for months underwater or in decompression, eating or resting. Jack called up a chart that marked the position of the wreck.

'The *Asenka* went down here, about forty-five nautical miles due west of Esbjerg. The captain's report said the ship maintained her trim as she filled with water and simply slipped under the surface; sinking in calm water.'

Jack started the edited video footage Sandro had taken and talked over the images. The scene was familiar to everyone present. The grey monochrome of the slowly moving pictures contrasted with the crisp lines of the ship and flashes of colour as a torch lit the scene. 'Gunnar, my partner Sandro Calovarlo and I checked the hull and couldn't see any major damage or distortion. As you can see, the *Asenka* is sitting upright on the bottom, with a slight list to starboard, and at a depth of just over fifty metres. Your working depth will be a maximum of fifty metres.'

The next clip started as he and Sandro began to inspect the holds. 'Once the hold covers have been removed, the viz should be better. Whilst you're in the holds you'll be protected from any current. We also expect it to suck out much of the muck – again, improving the viz.

'The priority salvage item is the 720 metric tonnes of zinc ingots or rather zinc slabs. They're on standard US pallets with two stacks per pallet. Each stack weighs one thousand kilos; a pallet load of two metric tonnes. I've talked to Lukas and we believe it should be simply a case of slipping lifting straps under each pallet and bringing them to the surface. Some of them are stacked close together so it may be awkward getting the first few out.'

The image on the screen focused on one of the stacks that had toppled, broken the steel bands, and spewed zinc plates on the deck. 'When you come across any damaged stacks, or any you are worried about, we'll drop a cradle so the plates can be shifted by hand. Problem is they weigh over twenty kilograms each. We'd rather you do this than risk a load breaking up en route to the surface. You don't want to be under any of those plates if the lift fails.

'We estimate it will take five to seven days to remove all the zinc. We've then got another five to seven days to salvage the rest because the *Stavanger* needs to be on station by the *Monroe Bravo* oil platform. Depending on the time, and the weather, we may have to abandon the last part of the salvage because the ship can't afford to be late on station.'

As the images of the drums appeared Jack continued: 'These drums of plastic beads are another priority item for salvage. The beads are inside plastic bags, but the problem is the cardboard drums are collapsing. We can't afford to rupture the plastic bags holding the beads. However, we've got hold of some Kevlar jackets and straps that can be wrapped around the drums on the pallet and ratcheted up to support them. It's going to slow down the job, but it'll be the safest approach.'

The video moved on to the JCB backhoe loaders. They looked ghostly grey before the torch transformed the nearest one into vivid yellow and black. 'Assuming we have time you'll have plenty of space to get to the JCBs; they shouldn't be a problem. They're big and heavy but we've got the four slings needed and the lifting positions are marked on the axels. They should come straight up.'

Jack continued as the video swept over the jumble of wooden crates. 'The crates have also been made high priority. We have to salvage them.'

Jack invited questions at the end and between himself and Lukas answered them all. Lukas completed the briefing and gave Lorna a file containing all the details before he and Jack accompanied the team to the accommodation module to begin pressurisation. The divers lined up and, one by one, climbed up the short steps and into the wet well. It was the area where they would put on their diving suits before dropping through the water to the wreck or take off the suits and crawl into the main diving bell and close the watertight hatch.

The pressure inside the diving bell would be increased to match the water pressure at the depth they would be working. This meant that when they opened the watertight hatch between the diving bell and wet well, the pressure would be the same as the water pressure in the North Sea. The gases and proportions they would breathe were also changed so that they were breathing heliox – a mixture of helium and oxygen. The process was called being 'blown down'. The gas mixture would allow them to live and work at depth for weeks. It was called being 'in sat' – in saturation.

Jack still marvelled at the power and sophistication of the ship and the diving system that was at the heart of it. It was a kaleidoscope of colour. Although the cylindrical accommodation module, tunnel and wet well were painted bright yellow, Jack knew that at fifty metres it would look drab grey until torchlight lit it up. A thick, dull orange hose rolled off a huge blue painted drum to feed gases and water and power and data signals to the accommodation module and wet well. The life support umbilical, the entwined red, yellow and blue hoses, snaked from a massive steel basket to the wet well. These would provide the divers with breathing gases, hot water for the dive suits, power and communication. Their lives would depend on the umbilical.

Lorna led her team of Leif and Anders through the heavy hatch and into their tiny world; a world in which they would eat, sleep, work and live together. Gunnar, Greg and Lennie brought up the rear.

It was at this point that all the expensive and complex life support systems linked to saturation diving came into play. Jack found the principles were easy to understand. It was the detail that was complicated. Once inside the accommodation module, pneumatic pumps would increase the internal pressure to correspond to the water pressure at the depth the divers would be working. Breathing normal air at this pressure would kill them, so they breathed a combination of oxygen and helium; it was this mixture, heliox, that accounted for the squeaky voices during radio communication.

The accommodation module was linked by a steel tunnel to a wet well that contained all their diving gear and equipment. It was at the same pressure as the accommodation module but had open access to the sea. Because it was at the same pressure as the accommodation module and the seawater outside, the divers would be dry as they crawled from the accommodation module, via the tunnel, to the wet well. They would put on their diving suits in the wet well and, when ready, collect their equipment and drop through an open hatch to the wreck below.

The first team of divers would work a full six-hour shift underwater and then return to the accommodation module via the wet well and tunnel. They would be replaced by the second team whilst they ate and slept before their next shift. It was a twenty-four-hour operation where their body tissue was saturated with oxygen and helium, hence the term 'saturation diving'. Saturation diving was much more efficient than bringing divers to the surface every few hours.

The dive supervisor, Lukas, was outside the pressurised chamber. He was speaking to Lorna, the senior bell woman, via the onboard communications system to confirm that the pressure chamber containing the six divers had been blown down to fifty metres. He also confirmed the *Stavanger* had arrived on station and the whole rig would be shortly lowered into the water.

Lorna started on the checklist of life support systems that would keep them alive for the next few weeks. Everyone knew that once blown down to fifty metres there was no quick return to the surface. To do so would kill them. The process of decompression would take days; days before they would be able to climb out of the pressurised module and into fresh air. Ensuring everything was safe was vital. Once complete, she was ready to join her team of Anders and Leif.

It was dark on the surface by the time Lorna crawled along the interconnecting tunnel between the pressure chamber and the wet well. It was cramped inside, but it would only be for a few minutes. An array of dials and gauges, levers and switches, buttons and lights surrounded her in the confined space. The warm yellow glow from the painted bulkheads was at odds with the coldness around her. Above and below these displays, pipes and ducting that served the wet well snaked round and around.

Lorna helped Leif and Anders into their diving suits and fitted their distinctive Kirby Morgan diving helmets. A systematic check ensured a mixture of oxygen and helium was flowing through one of the hoses that made up their umbilical. The return gases flowed back through another hose. Lorna checked the voice comms were working and that warm water was flowing through the suits via yet another hose. Helmet lights, portable arc-lights and torches were checked; they were ready to go. Two Bronco Firewires and a supply of rods were strapped to the side of the wet well. Leif and Anders would have to pull the cable and hose feeding the Firewire as well as the umbilical behind them as they started work on the hold covers. It was all part of the job.

As Leif prepared to exit the wet well, Lorna began to unwind his umbilical. Leif held the guide rails firmly as he stepped down the short ladder into the water and down onto the low platform of the wet well. The bulky dive suit and steel-capped rubber boots made it awkward. The good news was that, in the torchlight, the viz was excellent. When he flicked his torch, he could see the for'ard hold cover of the *Asenka* directly below him. The dynamic positioning was spot on. The system controlling the thrusters and propellers was keeping the ship precisely on station. It was only a short drop of a couple of metres onto the ship and he would be ready to start work.

'Leif to Lorna,' he said into the cheek microphone. 'DP spot on. I'm ready to drop onto the wreck. I've collected my cutting equipment and will make my way to the first hold cover. I'll wait for Anders and give you a shout when we are ready to start cutting.'

Dropping through the water onto a wreck or the seabed was a sensation he loved. Inside the wet well it was cramped, and the dive suit was cumbersome. Once in the water he was weightless – it was a great feeling. In the darkness he couldn't see the whole ship, but he didn't need to. All that was important was to do the job. To cut off the port side hold cover wheels and expose a strong point so that they could hoist the cover clear. He and Anders had done it dozens of times. You just had to be methodical and careful. As he waited for Anders, he swept the arc light around. He couldn't see the bow just a dark, grey void all around him. He looked towards the rear tower, but it was lost in the gloom. Inquisitive fish had already found the wreck and were exploring it, but he doubted there would be fish inside the holds. However, once opened, and with sacks of animal feed available, the fish would zoom in on it. Leif was ready. He flared his arms and legs as he sank through the water and then quickly moved into a crouch as he touched down on the deck. He looked back and could see Anders releasing the spare cutting equipment. Anders waited for the signal from Leif before he dropped onto the hold cover to join him.

Leif and Anders started to work their way across the hold cover towards their separate starting points. The current was mild but they leaned into it as they dragged their umbilical and cutting equipment hoses behind them. Between them, resting on the hold cover, was the end of the main hoist cable. Lukas had attached a short length of high tensile steel with shackles at each end. He'd also wrapped around, and clicked on, four lifting straps. Leif and Anders seemed to be working in slow motion as they uncoiled the cables and hoses of the Bronco and let them fall onto the deck. Neither wanted too much hose – it would get in the way, and they would only have to pull it back to the wet well when they had finished. It was all about economy of effort. Working at depth, in six-hour bursts, breathing a mixture of oxygen and helium is tiring. When you must do this day after day, week after week, in six-hour sessions, it's exhausting.

Leif and Anders worked methodically. They each measured and marked the position of two strong points and the wheel axles. It took only minutes to cut through the thin metal sheet and expose the box sections. These offered the strong points they needed. The length of steel cable was threaded around the strong points, formed into a loop and secured with a heavy shackle. The hook at the end of the main hoist cable clicked over the loop before Lukas ordered the cable to be put under tension. When the axles holding the wheels to the hold cover were cut all that stopped it falling into the hold was the high tensile steel cable. Leif and Anders moved clear, braced themselves and gave the winch man a running commentary as he slowly lifted the cover away.

'Hold cover almost vertical... steady, steady...' Anders commented as in the torchlight he could see the gutter on the other side of the hold cover crumbling. 'Slowly, slowly, almost there...,' he shouted.

On the bridge, Captain Sorenson, Jack and the ROV operator had been staring intently at a TV monitor as the tension on the lifting cable increased. At first nothing seemed to happen and then the hold cover suddenly jerked. A tiny puff of sediment erupted from around the edges of the cover as the constrained steel axles and wheels tried to resist being pulled out of their track. Axels and tracks buckled and paint and rust flaked off as the cover slowly moved to the vertical. The ROV operator was concentrating on the screen, and judging the angle of the cover, as the *Stavanger* continued to pull on the hoist cable. He spoke calmly to the winch operator: 'Steady, steady... it's nearly there... steady... any moment now... release!'

The hold cover broke free. Trailing a cloud of sediment, it fell over the side – one gone, five more to go.

Knowing that Jack Collier, the co-owner of the *Marine Salvage & Investigation Company*, was watching, it became a personal challenge for Leif and Anders to remove all the hold covers in their six-hour shift. They missed their target by fifteen minutes, but it was still a feat. Shift over, they secured the Bronco cables to a strong point next to the last hold cover and began to make their way back to the wet well. During the shift, the current had changed direction but it was still mild. However, it was noticeable that actions that had been smooth and precise six hours ago were now forced and laboured. The divers were tired. Once inside they could relax for a while. They would strip off their gear, stow all their kit and crawl along the tunnel for food and rest. In another six hours they were to make a return journey.

Gunnar, Greg and Lennie replaced them. It didn't take long to clear the last hold cover and begin the task of lifting the pallets of zinc. It was perhaps the most arduous shift of the entire operation. The act of removing the hold covers had stirred up all the sediment and debris in the hold. The current, flowing over an open hold, had begun to create a vortex that would eventually suck the hold clean. However, Greg and Lennie faced hours of poor visibility as they began to raise the first pallets.

Chapter 28

Wrong place, wrong time

Lennie had made up a simple tool – an aluminium tube with twin prongs at one end. It allowed him to feed one end of a lifting strap under a pallet for Greg to grab and then together they could position the strap. They were so skilled they could fit lifting straps in the dark. It was just as well because the swirling sediment reduced the viz to ten centimetres. In these conditions the helmet lights were useless. Instead of a dark, grey mist in front of them it was a bright grey mist. Over a six-hour shift, the tool saved valuable minutes and eventually hours of fumbling in the dark.

Greg and Lennie were soon in a rhythm. Once a pallet had been unloaded on the surface, the hoist cable returned to the hold carrying lifting straps. By the time it had arrived, Greg and Lennie had fitted spare straps to another pallet, and it was ready for hoisting. The operation was as fast as the winch man could lift and stow a pallet. They were moving more than four to five pallets an hour: twenty-five in their first shift and twenty-eight in the next. At this rate they were on target to salvage all the pallets well within five days.

Earlier shifts had cleared the pallets of zinc ingots from the for'ard and mid-ships hold and the whole operation moved to the rear. As they cleared the mid-ships hold the viz had gradually improved but it was still poor in the rear. Lennie wasn't sure if the huge rear tower of the ship was blocking the current and thus reducing the effect of the vortex that cleared sediment from the hold. It made no difference; they would have to work by feel in the poor viz.

During the first few days of the salvage Lennie and Greg had checked each pallet to make sure it was sound with straps in the right position. From what they could see and feel the pallets were standard US size, heavy duty and sound. Those handling the pallets on the surface had confirmed it.

The last pallet in the row was hard up against the side of the hold and close to the remaining stacks. It was awkward but Greg could just about squeeze into the space and crouch to grab the ends of the two lifting straps and pull them through. He was doing it by feel because he couldn't see anything. With the end of each strap in each of his hands he struggled to climb out of the narrow space. Greg climbed on top of the stack and grabbed the other two ends that Lennie offered. Together they wriggled the straps into position. Greg slipped the shackle through the ends of the lifting straps, moved away and told the winch man they were clear and the pallet could be hauled to the surface. Neither Greg nor Lennie saw the pallet rise. The viz was poor and they were moving away. Moments later they heard it. There was the distinctive sound of a solid metallic clunk as the corner of a stack clipped one of the hull braces. Then there was silence and both Greg and Lennie relaxed as they envisaged the load making its way to the surface.

The winch man felt it, saw it and heard it. The twin stacks of ingots were just breaking through the surface. Yet another routine lift. Then it was as though a monster fish had broken free from the fishing line at the last minute. It all happened at once. The weight of two thousand kilograms on the hoist cable was suddenly released and it jerked free. There was a muffled twang and a dull splash as the sound of the winch motor changed. He reacted as though he had been hit by an electric shock as the tangled remains of a wooden pallet leapt out of the water and bounced erratically at the end of the cable. The stacks of ingots had disappeared.

'Load lost, load lost... take cover, take cover!' the winch man screamed into his headset.

It was his worst nightmare, a lost load, a load careering to the seabed with his friends directly underneath. Two metric tonnes of zinc ingots, eighty slabs of metal, like blunt guillotine blades, were now raining down on the divers below. A direct impact could maim or kill them. He knew the divers would have only seconds to scramble clear; but where could they go?

'You've got seconds... get clear... get clear,' he screamed, not sure if they could. 'Greg, Lennie... tell me you're OK,' he pleaded, 'tell me you're OK.'

Greg reacted immediately to the alarm, but it was impossible to move quickly. Automatically he grabbed his umbilical, leaned away from the remaining stacks and, swinging his free arm, tried to run towards the space they had cleared. It was like trying to run through dark, grey treacle. If you could have seen Greg, he would have looked almost comical as his arms and legs flailed in slow motion.

'One and two and three...,' Greg counted slowly to himself as he ticked off the seconds.

Experience and simple physics told him the weight would fall about five metres per second in water. He might manage half a metre per second across the deck – but half a metre could be the difference between a solid stack of a thousand kilos crushing him or missing him. It was a life-or-death race as he strained every muscle and braced himself. Greg was just about to count 'seven' when he heard the dreaded 'ding... ding... ding... ding ding ding' of the zinc slabs slamming into the deck around him. Then, almost miraculously, it felt as though a huge hand was wafting him out of harm's way. He was pushed off balance by an invisible force and felt himself falling to the deck.

A solid blow hit his foot. It tripped him and he fell onto the deck, hitting it hard with his knee, hip and ankle. Automatically he tried to roll into a ball and for a split second his leg felt numb but then there was a searing pain in his foot. Terrified, he imagined a stack of ingots had dropped on top of him, trapping him by the leg. In the swirling sediment he couldn't see anything. He was too shocked to speak. Desperately he ran both his hands down his body. Any second he expected to feel the solid mass of a pile of ingots. His foot was free, and he frantically ran his fingers over the outside of his short wellington boot. He felt it but at first couldn't understand it. The toe of his boot had changed shape. The steel toecap had been crushed and now his foot was held in a vice-like grip. The pain made his body quiver. He forced himself to relax, to control his breathing, think and check his equipment. He pulled off his gloves but didn't feel the shock of the ice-cold water. He ran his hands over his helmet, his fingers sliding over the kidney-shaped face plate, along the stainless-steel gas tube and around his regulator. He tried to concentrate. Could he feel any cold water inside his suit? Had the suit been breached? Everything seemed normal. His knee and hip ached but his neck, back and arms were fine.

Lennie, where was Lennie? It was only then that he heard the groans and rasping breathing of Lennie through his earpiece. 'Lennie, where are you? Are you OK? Switch on yer head torch.'

'I've hurt me shoulder... think I've bust me collar bone... got caught by a slab... I'm OK. Gi' me a hand,' was the reply.

Gunnar was already on his way. He'd been inside the wet well when he heard the shout from the winch man. He'd immediately called to both Lennie and Greg to say he was on his way – although later neither recalled hearing the message. Gunnar knew what had happened and how speed could be vital. The adrenalin had kicked in and in a series of bounds he had dropped from the steps of the wet well and onto the deck. He followed the trail of the two umbilicals across the deck and into the hold. There was no viz. He'd heard Greg and Lennie say that it was poor, and they were rigging the pallets by feel rather than by sight. As he dropped into the hold, he could see a faint glow off to his left. He guessed it was a head torch. With the umbilical running through his hands, he found the diver. It was Greg and he was trying to stand. Gunnar grabbed him by the arm.

'Greg, it's Gunnar – what's your status?'

'I'm fine… ingot hit me foot… crushed me boot… foot hurts like bloody hell! Lennie's hurt… help Lennie... I'll make me way back.'

For Gunnar, the training had kicked in. He did a quick buddy check, and everything looked OK. He hadn't seen any damage to the umbilical, Greg's suit hadn't been breached; all looked normal. He made an instant decision and felt confident Greg could make his own way back to the wet well. He would simply pull himself back using his umbilical. Lennie was the priority and he spoke to Lukas.

'Gunnar to Lukas, just checked on Greg; he's OK. Possible damage to his foot but maybe the steel toecap, left boot, crushed. He's making his way back to the wet well.'

Gunnar realised he was breathing too fast and was sounding scared; he was scared. He paused for a few seconds to try and control his breathing. In a more controlled tone, he continued: 'Retracing my route to find Lennie's umbilical... will update as soon as possible.'

At the end of the umbilical Gunnar found Lennie. He was kneeling on the deck and cradling his right arm across his body. The good news was that Lennie's suit looked intact; there was no free flow of gas or bubbles. 'I'm going to check the kit... make sure it's OK before we do anything else,' said Gunnar.

In the poor viz he checked all Lennie's life support equipment was undamaged. A broken arm was a minor problem compared to a ruptured umbilical or a ripped suit.

'It's me shoulder... I've broken something... think the collar bone's gone,' said Lennie through gasps of breath.

'I'll rig up a sling... take the weight off it... and get you back.'

Gunnar unclipped a short scuba strap from his suit, fed one end through the end loop and tightened it onto Lennie's wrist. He clipped the karabiner onto a D-ring on Lennie's jacket. He wound a longer scuba strap around Lennie's upper body to hold his arm against his chest. Getting him into the wet well would still hurt – but it was the best he could do.

'Lukas, Lennie is OK... all his kit is intact... suspected damage to right shoulder and collar bone... making our way back to the wet well.'

It took agonising minutes, and repeated messages of reassurance, before Gunnar and Lennie joined Greg in the wet well. It took even longer to get Lennie out of his drysuit, along the tunnel, and into the accommodation unit. The immediate drama was over.

Chapter 29

A combination of factors

Three months before the accident, and almost eleven thousand kilometres away, the pallet had been stacked with warm zinc ingots. The Santa Rosa Mine and factory, on the outskirts of Lima, Peru, was one of the oldest zinc producers in the country – and it looked the oldest. Work in the factory was hard and unrelenting with the roasting ovens, purification tanks and electrolytic processes working twenty-four hours a day, seven days a week. An acrid smell of rotten eggs permeated the whole factory as crude ore was transformed into zinc metal, purified, re-melted and cast into ingots. The rotten eggs smell was sulphur dioxide, a by-product of the roasting process. When it combined with moisture in the atmosphere it formed sulphuric acid. The Santa Rosa factory was not a place you would choose to work.

Two shabbily dressed workers stood by the conveyor belt of metal rollers as the warm ingots rolled towards them from the foundry. It looked leisurely as, wearing worn leather gloves, they grabbed each end of an ingot, swung it off the conveyor belt, and stacked it on the nearby pallet. Unhurriedly, they moved back to the rollers just as the next ingot appeared. Lifting, carrying and positioning a twenty-five-kilogram ingot may not seem particularly arduous – but try doing that for eight hours, day after day. When the pallet was full, they wrapped steel bands around the pallet and stack. The bands were pulled taut, a securing collar was slipped over them and crimped in place.

Their role was all part of an intricately choreographed handling system. A forklift driver would appear, collect the loaded pallet, and take it to the warehouse ready for shipping. Some days he would merely stack the pallets prior to later transportation. At other times he would load flatbed trailers for the short journey to the Port of Callao. There was money in selling zinc overseas; the price was high. The driver had developed a mental clock. He knew how long it would take to load a pallet and when he needed to deliver a new stack of empty pallets. It's what he did eight hours of every day.

The driver knew it was time to deliver a load of empty pallets. As he manoeuvred the twin forks under the stack, the forklift engine stopped. He sat for a moment unsure what to do next; it had never happened before. He knew there was plenty of diesel in the fuel tank and there had been no odd sounds, no sign of a problem. He switched the engine off and tried to restart; nothing. He tried again and a third time before he gave up and walked off to find the supervisor. It wasn't his job to fix the forklift.

The supervisor was walking close to the conveyor belt and noticed the two men sitting on upturned boxes; they weren't working. He then realised that there were no empty pallets waiting to be filled. A simple breakdown like this could quickly stop the entire factory. If ingots were not cleared from the rollers, they would back up and eventually those in the foundry would stop emptying the casting boxes and preparing moulds for more molten zinc. They could stack the hot ingots for a while, but they would soon run out of space. They would also run out of time to make fresh moulds. Without moulds to fill, the crucible of molten zinc couldn't be emptied. If the zinc solidified in the crucible, it would be costly – and he was paid to ensure this didn't happen.

He retraced his steps and grabbed an old pallet. It wasn't new but looked like a US size, heavy duty pallet. It would allow the men to clear the rollers whilst he sorted out the problem. If necessary, he could get men to carry pallets from the warehouse. The supervisor dragged the pallet to the rollers and let it fall. He simply told the two men to stack the ingots on it whilst he went to find out why no pallets had been delivered. The two men shrugged their shoulders. They were paid to stack pallets. It wasn't their job to move them from the warehouse. They both realised that this old, lightweight pallet wasn't strong enough to carry two thousand kilos of ingots – but it wasn't their job to tell the supervisor his job. They simply stacked the pallet.

The lightweight, one-use pallet had been made from local, immature pine trees. After carrying its first and only expected load, it was scrap. Over months, if not years in the factory it had fulfilled a variety of uses and was now battered and dirty. The filth concealed the bands of sap wood and heart wood that made up the boards that formed the base. The wood surrounding some of the numerous knots had dried out, making them loose. Some knots had dropped out, leaving holes, some remained – jammed in place.

The stacked pallet had eventually joined others on the back of the flatbed trailer and into the hold of a ship: the MV *Asenka.* When the ship sank, the biscuit-dry pallet dropped to fifty metres below the surface of the North Sea and began to absorb moisture. Sap wood and heart wood release and absorb moisture at different rates. When timber is dried out in uncontrolled conditions it develops splits and shakes – jagged cracks across the grain. When it then absorbs moisture, these splits and shakes increase. Although compromised, the boards making up the pallet remain strong under compression, in the direction of the grain. It's the same property used in pit props to hold up the weight of rock in coal mines. However, the boards are weak when subjected to forces perpendicular to the grain. That's why it's possible to snap a twig or a board across one's knee. The knots do nothing to improve the strength of the board; they detract from it.

The old pallet had survived the short journey to the warehouse and onto the back of the trailer. It had survived the loading onto the ship and the sinking. It had remained in the darkness of the hold for months, slowly absorbing moisture and distorting under the constant pressure of the zinc slabs. Sap wood swelled and cracks extended, shakes grew wide as boards slowly distorted. As the *Stavanger* lifted the pallet to the surface, the weight of two thousand kilograms was supported by two lifting straps rather than four wooden battens. It was like lifting a delicately balanced house of cards. The slight collision between the corner of a stack and a hull brace had disturbed the balance. As the pallet rose, the waterlogged base boards started to bend even more. Zinc ingots, no longer supported by the base board, applied increasing pressure to the steel bands holding them in place.

As the pallet rose to the surface the base boards failed, the steel bands slipped through the collar and the stack began to change shape. When the twin stacks of zinc ingots broke the surface of the North Sea the full weight was transferred to a narrow band of wood in each base board; the boards collapsed under the strain. The steel bands slipped through the retaining collars and a whole corner of the stack began to fall away. Once the integrity of the stack was broken, half of the stack followed. The winch man later recalled the scene. He said it was like a batch of fish slithering out of a trap.

As dozens of ingots fell away, the balance of the lift changed. All the remaining weight was supported by a single lifting strap. The strap and remains of the pallet ripped through the remaining stack. In a few seconds, eighty slabs had been cast into the water. They fell like bombs and exploded in a cloud of sediment fifty metres below. Loose slabs peppered the area around Greg, but he was lucky. As the water pressure created by the solid mass of ingots flushed him aside, a single slab caught his foot. If it had landed a few centimetres away it could have snapped his leg or crushed his ankle.

Lennie wasn't as lucky. He'd responded a split second later than Greg. He was forcing himself away from danger when a slab caught him a glancing blow on the side of his helmet. Later he realised the water pressure from the falling slab had pushed his head to one side just before it hit. However, he took the full force on his shoulder and collar bone. The collar bone snapped like a twig and his shoulder was dislocated with the force knocking him to the deck. Moments later, the bulk of a stack of ingots, almost a thousand kilograms of metal, crashed into the deck. A mini wave of water tumbled him across the deck. He was trying to get to his feet when Greg found him.

An intense exchange of messages between Lukas, the dive supervisor, Gunnar, Greg and Lennie confirmed that a potential disaster had been averted by the winch man's quick alarm. They were now in the aftermath of the accident. Lorna was the dive medic in the team. She manipulated the dislocated shoulder back into place and reset the collar bone. Pain killers were starting to work but everyone knew it would be months before Lennie would be fit enough to work. Lorna had cut the wellington boot off Greg's foot and, with his help, had prised the clam-like steel toecap from his foot. She was pretty sure nothing was broken but Greg would have a sore foot for weeks. On the surface they launched the RIB, the rigid inflatable boat, and collected several wooden slats that had broken off the pallet. A detailed examination of the pallet would have to wait until later, but photographs and statements were taken to help the future investigation.

Accidents happen in all businesses but 'the show has to go on'. Within the hour, Anders and Leif were in the rear hold assessing the problem facing them. It seemed one stack of ingots had completely disintegrated and were scattered across the floor of the hold. The other stack wasn't intact but in a large pile. 'Lucky boys,' was all Anders said when he and Leif shone the arc light on the pile. They both knew that had Greg or Lennie been on that spot when the ingots fell, they would be recovering a body. Now they were waiting for a metal cradle to be dropped to them so they could start cleaning up the mess.

In the briefing room a bigger problem was being discussed.

Jack was outlining the problem: 'Assuming Greg is fit enough to work we are a diver short. Lorna is currently monitoring Lennie's condition and whether he needs to be brought to the surface. If he does, that's the end of the salvage. We can get the accommodation module on deck in minutes, but it will take days to decompress. Even if we have a diver waiting it will take more time to blow them down. If they say Lennie can recuperate in saturation, we still have a problem. The rate at which we can recover the cargo will drop, and we may not be able to complete the salvage by the time we have to leave to be on standby.'

'I'm happy to draw up a revised diving schedule,' offered Lukas. 'We could extend the dive time and rotate the divers – but we must be careful not to exhaust them. When you get over tired you make mistakes.'

'There is a simple solution,' Jack announced. 'We could set up a mini blow down using a series of tanks and regulators on a shot line from the surface to fifty metres. The tanks could be attached to the shot line at specific depths. They could hold different mixes and I'd end up breathing the same mix as the divers. I'm qualified, I'm familiar with the kit our divers are wearing and could work alongside Greg. He could take the lead and I'd simply help.'

'Mr Collier,' Lukas said with concern both in his voice and his expression and shaking his head. 'It's a bad idea. I know it's theoretically possible, but I've never heard of anyone entering a pressurised dive chamber from the surface… and I can tell you why. All the dive team have been in quarantine before being blown down. If you were to take in a simple cold virus it would be devastating inside the chamber. We'd have to cancel the salvage and we wouldn't be able to get you and the others out for days.'

Lukas didn't wait for Jack to respond. 'Lorna is good… she's a great paramedic, but she's not a doctor. During the blowdown you start to acclimatise to being in sat; not everyone can cope with it. If you suffer any physical or psychological problems during the descent, or when you get inside the bell, there's limited medical help available.'

Still shaking his head Lukas continued: 'There are lots of guys who have dived deep – but they've had dozens of support divers and a team of medics in case of a bail out. It's also taken months to organise and tons of kit. We don't have the number of support divers we'd need. We may have enough tanks to get you down, but we don't have enough tanks to get you back up. It would be a one-way trip. If you ran into trouble, there's no one to help you. Quite honestly, the risks are huge and simply not worth taking. Even with one diver short I reckon we can still salvage all the priority items.'

Jack was about to speak but Lukas continued. His tone was almost belligerent. 'How many dives have you done in a commercial suit and on heliox? What was your last salvage job at fifty metres?'

'OK, I've only done a handful of dives using an umbilical and they've only been practice dives... but this is not a dangerous wreck site. I'd be in the protection of the hold,' Jack added.

'All dives at fifty metres, inside any wreck, are dangerous dives. I have to say Mr Collier, you wouldn't even be on my long list for the job. You don't have the experience – and maybe not the stamina for this sort of work. You're young and fit but it's unforgiving down there and exhausting. It takes months and years to build up the strength and stamina needed. I want it on record that I'm against you joining the dive team.'

'He's right,' the captain added. 'The injuries to Greg and Lennie are unfortunate but your injury or death would be a disaster. My suggestion would be to concentrate on the primary salvage items and reorganise the existing divers to bring them up. The remaining cargo can be retrieved at some future time and with no additional danger.'

They were right, of course. It was likely that they would be able to salvage all the zinc and come back for the other items.

However, their other ship, the *Sultano,* wasn't equipped for the job. Trying to salvage the remaining cargo using rebreathers simply wasn't feasible. They would have to subcontract the work – which could take months to arrange and complete. It would mean Sandro's case coming to trial before the drums of microbeads were landed. Jack seemed to have no alternative.

'Captain Sorenson, I'd be grateful if you would make a detailed entry of the dive supervisor's concerns and his objection to me joining the dive teams in the ship's log. I'd also be grateful if you would add your own. I'll draft a letter "To whom it may concern" of my decision to join the dive teams and help salvage the cargo of the MV *Asenka*. I appreciate and respect your advice but believe it is vitally important to the company that the salvage is complete.'

There was an awkward silence as Jack scanned the faces of those around him. His gaze stopped at the EMSA observer but he merely raised his hands, signalling he had nothing to say. Jack continued: 'If you'll excuse me, I've got a lot to do. I need to work out how many tanks I need and the gas mixtures for different depths…'

Before Jack could leave Lukas spoke: 'You'd never get into Lennie's suit, and I'd want to check it for damage before it's used again. You're my size and I know my suit is good. I'll get it ready and drop it down to the wet well. I'll also assemble all the tanks we have and work out a sequence of saturation stops down to fifty metres. We can start filling them but it's going to take time. I'm not happy about it – but if you're determined to dive, I'll try and make it as safe as possible.'

'I appreciate it; thanks,' said Jack with a smile.

'Just don't piss in my suit!' joked Lukas and those on the bridge laughed. The tension that had grown in the last few minutes evaporated.

Preparing to dive without Sandro, without a buddy, felt strange; it was also dangerous. Jack knew it was possible to drop down to fifty metres in ten minutes without a stop. He also knew there was an outside chance of a physiological reaction from changing the gas mixture he would be breathing on the surface to the one inside the chamber. The prudent dive plan would be to extend the dive to a couple of hours and descend through various stages to fifty metres. He'd be breathing different concentrations of heliox as he descended. When he joined the divers in the pressurised module, he'd be breathing the same mix at the same pressure. He'd also be cold. The surface water temperature in the North Sea was well under 10°C. It would be much colder at fifty metres. Even in a drysuit and multiple layers of clothes he knew he would be cold by the time he got to the pressure chamber. He also knew that breathing helium would drain warmth from his body six times faster than air. He'd be cooling from the inside out as well as the outside in.

Jack, Lukas and Captain Sorenson met in the dining room. Lukas had several pieces of paper on the tabletop and began to explain his sketch. 'Here's the diving plan from the surface to the wet well at fifty metres. You start with a single tank of heliox – 20/80; twenty percent oxygen, eighty percent helium. However, I don't think you should have the tank strapped to you. Taking your kit off and replacing tanks is fine as an exercise but not in the North Sea, at depth and when you're cold and tired. We can clip a tank to your harness. All you need to do is drop down to fifteen metres for a thirty-minute stop. Thirty minutes at fifteen metres is more than enough to begin flooding your body with helium – so you don't have to drain the tank.

'We'll be attaching a single tank and regs at fifteen metres. It'll be waiting for you. After thirty minutes at fifteen metres, you switch to the new tank, clip the near empty one onto the line, and drop down to twenty-five metres. The mix in the new tank will be fifteen percent oxygen and eighty-five percent helium. Again, all you have to do is drain the tank you're beathing and switch to the full tank waiting for you. You leave the empty tank and take the full tank with you as you drop down the shot line to thirty-five metres.

You simply drain the tanks and then drop down. There will be two separate tanks and regs waiting for you at forty-five metres. Both will be a 5/95 mix: five percent oxygen and ninety-five percent helium. I'm attaching a slate and a torch with each set of tanks. You will need to make a note of the time you start breathing from the tanks and when you leave; it's good practice to monitor your descent.

'I'm suggesting two single tanks at forty-five metres. At that depth you'll get through a tank in ten to twelve minutes. If you can relax, and control your breathing, you may be able to stretch it to close to fifteen minutes. I calculate you need at least twenty minutes at forty-five metres to ensure saturation. Two whole tanks should be more than enough. I'm also suggesting you clip the last tank onto your harness and use that to fin to the wet well. They will have all the external lights on so you should see it clearly. It will be your last tank. You've only got a few metres to swim but it will be cold and dark. You'll also be knackered! Once you're at the wet well you'll be safe.'

Lukas paused before mentioning the next part of the plan. 'You're going to be spending a long time hanging onto a line, getting colder and colder, with nothing to see. It's easy to become disorientated and confused. You're going to have to trust your diving computer, the gauges on the tanks and your own notes. You also need to clip yourself onto the shot line.'

'You want to be able to recover the body if things go wrong,' Jack volunteered.

'I don't expect anything to go wrong but physically hanging on a shot line, for hours, is tiring. If you are clipped onto the line, you can simply relax until it's time to move on,' Lukas replied unconvincingly. 'But if there's a problem, there's nobody who can help you. Lorna and Gunnar will be waiting for you. Remember, there's no scuba gear in the wet well. If you have a problem, she is limited by the umbilical. It will only stretch so far. I've checked all the tanks, regs and torches. I've also checked on the spacing of the tanks and that they are all secure. Whenever you are ready, we can go.'

As he and Lukas did a buddy check, Jack was acutely aware that Lukas was watching him closely. Jack recalled studying other divers about to undertake a difficult dive. Was the diver quiet and withdrawn or too talkative? Was the diver breathing normally or too quickly; perhaps looking 'wide-eyed'. Any of these would cause him to cancel the dive. Lukas was looking for similar tell-tale signs now.

'If you're ready I'll help you into the basket and with the kit,' said Lukas.

With Lukas giving him support Jack put on his fins and stepped into the shallow metal recovery tray. He slipped the harness and wing, the inflatable bladder that would enable him to maintain neutral buoyancy, over his shoulders. Jack fastened all the Velcro strips and clips. Finally, he clipped the single tank to his harness, held onto one of the steel cables that was fixed to the crane hook, and signalled he was ready to go. The winch lifted him gently off the deck, swung him over the side, and dropped him into the water below.

Jack waved to Lukas and Captain Sorenson before the shallow tray submerged and he was clear. He swam on the surface to the steel cable holding the accommodation module and grabbed it. All he had to do was release some air from his wing, start the descent, and let his gloved hand slide over the steel cable. It would lead him to the module and safety. Jack was fully aware that the module below, at fifty metres, represented safety but he had to be patient and methodical. He must follow the planned descent stages and saturate his body with helium. If he didn't, he would be dead.

It was time to go. Jack signalled AOK to those watching, released gas from his wing and sank beneath the waves. He let his gloved hand slide over the heavy cable as he gazed around – but nothing to see. Jack glanced at the dive computer to check the rate of descent. It was OK but he was breathing too quickly and so forced himself to take long and slow breaths. Again, he scanned the water around him, but it was just a grey void. Sunlight was still penetrating the water, but Jack knew the deeper he dived the darker it would become. At forty-five metres he would need a torch to see anything.

Although the current was mild it turned him in the water, like a weathervane, until his body was pointing into it. He didn't bother to fin but merely let the scuba strap take the strain as he dangled off the line and dropped towards the wreck. Tiny particles in the water moved past him as he concentrated on the speed of his descent. It was important that his decent rate was controlled and smooth. Jack forced himself to descend steadily. He reached the first saturation stop at fifteen metres.

Jack checked his dive computer and made a note of the time. He wrote it on the slate above the time he would spend hanging on the line and calculated the time he would leave. Jack had plenty of time. Descending to fifteen metres had increased the water pressure around him. It wasn't a lot, but still crushed his drysuit and the wing; it made him less buoyant. Jack wanted to keep as much air in his suit as possible to keep him warm, so he released a small amount into his suit. He'd juggle the air in his suit and in the wing to maintain buoyancy and keep him as insulated as possible.

Jack scanned the water around him – nothing to see except the steady flow of small particles drifting past him on the current. He was about to unclip the tank he was using but stopped. 'Make sure you're clipped on to the shot line before you do anything,' he told himself.

Methodically Jack clipped the new tank to the harness, clipped the one he was using to the shot line and sorted out the tangle of regs. He felt fine, warm, relaxed and confident. Just another thirty minutes or so to hang on the line before dropping down to twenty-five metres. Jack had completed several deep dives and spent hours hanging on a line as he decompressed through a series of stages and multiple gas tanks. This was different, it was a self-imposed series of stops and probably overkill. However, better safe than sorry.

As he hung on the line Jack's mind wandered. It skipped from thinking of the current salvage and the implications it may have for future jobs in European waters. The captain had confirmed the weather would be mild for the next few days. The first bit of luck they had had in some time! They should be able to clear all the priority salvage items and be on station in plenty of time. He thought of Sandro and the impact the charges against him were having. With luck he could get the drums of microbeads to the bonded warehouse and the charges against him would be dropped. What about Penny? For once he had time to think – with no distractions beyond staying alive!

He now realised that trying to coerce her into buying a house between Manchester and Hull had been a mistake. It was likely that in a year or so Penny would be moved on – a different department, different responsibilities, more promotion. The current arrangement wasn't perfect, but it wasn't bad. They both had space and enjoyed each other's company. Perhaps he should just relax and let things drift along a little longer. He checked his dive computer; time to drop down to thirty-five metres and then to forty-five metres.

As Jack connected the full tanks to his harness, he suddenly realised how cold he had become; his fingers seemed numb. He flexed his hands and moved his arms to get the blood circulating but realised if he drew warm blood to his hands, he was taking it away from his core. Awkwardly he connected the remaining tanks and discarded the near empty tank. He was on the last leg. Jack was relaxed, breathing normally and was about to switch on his torch. He must have dropped through a thermocline because a wave of cold washed over him and the viz cleared. It was then that he saw the glow of lights below him. He smiled at the welcome the other divers were giving him. Gradually, out of the gloom, his yellow-painted steel home emerged – festooned in lights.

Jack realised that by breathing helium his voice had changed. It had a squeaky, distorted, cartoon quality. It suddenly reminded him of a party at university. Some of his friends were breathing helium from gas-filled balloons and everyone was laughing at their comical voices. He would be speaking like this for the next two weeks.

As he scanned the wreck beneath him, he could make out the rails and deck of the *Asenka*. Jack turned his head and realised the massive rear tower of the ship was behind him. He'd been so intent on following the steel cable and scanning the water ahead of him he'd stopped scanning all the water around him. He unclipped himself from the cable and began to fin towards the entrance to the wet well. Jack suddenly realised he was dropping to the wreck at the same rate as he was moving forwards! The water pressure had crushed the air in his drysuit and wing and he hadn't compensated by injecting more air into his wing. It was nothing serious, just a touch on the small suit inflator, and he was back to neutral buoyancy. However, it was a reminder. The North Sea was unforgiving, you had to concentrate. A minor problem at ten metres in the warm Caribbean could rapidly become life threatening at fifty metres inside the wreck.

Light from inside the wet well was shining into the water and Jack could see the shimmering outline of someone waiting for him. He grabbed the safety rail and tried to unclip a fin but struggled. His fingers were so cold he had no feeling in them. He could see his fingers touch the clip – but he couldn't feel it. In desperation he started to swing his arm around and around, trying to force warm blood into his hand. It wasn't working. In a final attempt he jammed his gloved finger under the clip, forced it open and released the fin. In a laboured action he forced it through the water to the person waiting for him. When it disappeared, he started trying to release the other fin and hand it over. It seemed to be taking so long that he felt both embarrassed and angry with himself. Eventually the clip opened and he wriggled the fin free. All he had to do now was climb the short series of steps into his new home. It was harder work than he expected and he was breathing heavily by the time he emerged from the water. Gunnar was waiting for him as he broke the surface. In a squeaky voice and with a big smile he said: ‘Hi boss, good to see you. Let me help you get all this gear off and we can meet the others. It will be brief because Lorna’s team are due to start their shift.’

Jack was relieved to be inside the wet well and slumped onto the steel bench. He felt exhausted and was happy for Gunnar to fuss over him and start removing all his gear. He then followed Gunnar, on his hands and knees, along the interconnecting tunnel. Jack had been in the accommodation module before. It had been empty, and he had only looked around for a few minutes. Now it seemed over-crowded with the divers’ personal gear, clipboards, magazines and books strewn around. The outgoing dive team had eaten but the empty mugs and the smell of food remained. The dive team of Lorna, Leif and Anders took turns to shake Jack’s hand and welcome him aboard before disappearing to start their shift. It was a reserved welcome and Jack could appreciate why. In the aftermath of an accident, the boss turns up. He’s a diver but not a commercial diver. His experience of being in saturation for weeks and working six-hour shifts is non-existent. Will he be an asset or a liability? Will he be checking up on them? There was nothing Jack could do to allay their fears. He simply had to do the job and try not to fuck it up!

Lorna and the team left quickly, and it was suddenly quiet. Lennie was propped up on his bunk reading. Greg had pulled an airline-type mask over his eyes and seemed to be sleeping. It was on seeing Greg that he suddenly realised that this was going to be a gruelling routine. Eat and sleep for six hours, work for six and repeat until the job was done – but Jack was wide awake. The novelty of his new surroundings together with apprehension about the job ahead of him was adding adrenalin into his bloodstream.

Gunnar moved to sit beside him.

'I'll give you a conducted tour and show you how everything works. We've rigged up a bunk for you in the equipment store. It'll give you a bit more privacy and will be quieter. When it's time for your shift I'll give you a safety briefing and outline the job. Greg is steady and reliable – just do what he tells you. It'll be fine. By the way, everyone appreciates what you're doing. There's not many that would take this on.'

Chapter 30

Gruelling routine

Jack slept restlessly and was awake when Gunnar banged on the hatch to tell him it was time to wake up and eat. He simply followed Gunnar and Greg's lead. After eating, the three of them sat together whilst Gunnar worked through the safety procedures and the task for the day. The safety procedures sounded daunting, but the task sounded easy. Just salvage another two dozen pallets of zinc slabs! It was Greg who offered some detail.

'We'll floodlight the stack and position ourselves either side of it. I'll push the end of a lifting strap under the pallet. You grab it, pull it through and lay the end on top of the stack. We want it hard up against the outside batten – between the deck and the pallet. I'll push the end of another lifting strap through, and we bring the four eyelets together. You hold them and I'll slip a shackle through the eyes and secure to the shackle on the line. We stand clear and let them winch it up. We just have to do that for six hours,' Greg ended with a smile, but the challenge was in his eyes.

It was then that they heard the incoming team of divers. Leif eased himself through the watertight door and into the accommodation area. Jack thought he looked dishevelled and scruffy, but his track record was impressive. Anders, who didn't look any better, followed quickly behind him and they both sat across from Gunnar, Greg and Jack. Lorna joined them moments later and gave them an update.

'The boys shifted twenty-six and left you twenty in the aft hold. They've also cleared the awkward stack close to the bulkhead so you should have a straightforward shift. The viz has improved but watch the current. It's starting to drag the load down current as soon as it's in the open. If you can clear the twenty, we can salvage the JCBs on the next shift and move to the drums. I reckon we're back on schedule,' she ended with a smile.

Lorna then moved away to get some well-earned food and much-needed sleep.

Because Gunnar and Greg were relaxed, it helped Jack to relax. However, his anxiety started to increase as he crawled through the link tunnel between the accommodation module and the wet well. Gunnar helped him on with the diving suit and helmet and did a thorough buddy check. Jack then simply mimicked whatever Greg did as he made his way down the steps of the wet well and onto the step. He had seen Greg launch himself off the wet well step and drop to the deck of the wreck below. Jack waited until Greg was clear and gave him a wave before he dropped in slow motion to the deck below.

The job was just as Greg had described – but he had merely mentioned the umbilical. He had to drag it behind him everywhere he went. If he moved, and it was short, it pulled him up with a jolt. However, with Greg talking through every part of the job in minute detail he soon got into a rhythm. Indeed, during the first couple of hours Jack enjoyed the work and felt the rate at which the stacks of ingots were being salvaged was good. It was when they stopped to reposition the arc lights, and had an extended rest, that Jack felt tired – and he still had two hours more work to do! He forced himself through the last hour and was relieved to hear Greg say: 'I think that's enough for our shift. We've cleared the twenty stacks in this hold and can let them clear the JCBs before we start on the drums.'

Jack knew he was tired but hadn't appreciated just how tired. He was happy for Greg to take the lead back to the wet well. He was impressed by the way Greg shimmied up the umbilical and out of the hold. When it was Jack's turn, he struggled to find the energy to pull himself up. He gave himself simple tasks and step-by-step goals: 'Grab the umbilical... hand over hand... rest when you get to the lip of the hold'. Jack flopped over the lip of the hold but didn't have the energy to stand; he took a rest, breathing slow and long whilst he summoned his last reserves. It was only a few metres from the deck to the wet well. He could see the light from inside shining through the water. Greg was already inside, and they would be waiting for him.

'Jack, you OK? Want a hand?' asked Gunnar.

'No, I'm fine... just a bit tired... I'm just below the wet well and climbing up now.'

Even with Gunnar helping, Jack struggled to get out of the dive suit because he was so tired. He simply let Gunnar uncouple his helmet, disconnect his harness and pull off his heavy boots. With Jack pathetically shaking his legs and Gunnar pulling they eventually pulled the heavy dive suit off so he could crawl through to the accommodation module. Jack had found the cold of the wet well refreshing but he knew it was dangerous to linger. He didn't want his core temperature to drop and create another emergency. He simply followed Greg on his hands and knees with Gunnar bringing up the rear.

Lorna, Leif and Anders were sitting in a row waiting for the changeover. Lorna looked fresh faced, clean and bright with a smile on her face. Leif and Anders looked as though they had just woken up and didn't have time to wash, shave or comb their hair. Their expression wasn't exactly surly – more expectant and questioning as they waited for Gunnar to give them an update. There was a subtle change in their expression and the atmosphere inside the pressure chamber when Gunnar announced: 'Greg and Jack moved the twenty stacks of ingots and cleared the way for you to raise the JCBs. There's little or no swell, the viz is good, space clear; apart from the current you should have no problems. If you are able to move the JCBs, we can reposition and be ready to start salvaging the drums on the next shift.'

It looked like the boss may not be a liability! Gunnar looked upwards, towards the surface, and asked Lukas: 'What's the weather?'

'Good weather forecast to continue over the next few days. I'm keeping an eye on it but it won't last forever.'

There was some banter between the incoming dive team and the outgoing, but Jack was too weary to take part; he just smiled. Despite just wanting to stretch out and go to sleep he knew he must eat, rehydrate and talk to Greg about how he was doing. The first opportunity was when they were eating together.

'So, how's the rookie diver doing?' asked Jack.

Greg slowly glanced up and continued chewing a mouthful of food before replying.

'You're doing OK, better than I expected.'

He glanced down to his plate and rocked his head as though deciding what to say next. 'It's all about pacing yourself, economy of effort and thinking ahead. You set off "like a train" and I knew you'd never keep it up. Last hour I could see you were knackered – but you hung in there,' Greg said with a wry smile.

'It's the little things, like where to move to safety after a lift. You moved to safety but away from where you needed to be for the next lift. It meant you had to walk an extra couple of metres. It's not much but in a shift an extra thirty or forty metres is a lot. Try to think what's the minimum you can do to do the job.'

It was good advice and Jack was thinking through his movements as he stretched out on his makeshift bed. He was asleep in seconds.

It was just a gruelling routine: eat, drink, sleep, work and repeat. Leif and Anders raised the four JCBs in just over four hours. They then started on the crates of machine parts. The danger was that they had all moved in the sinking and were in a delicately balanced pile. It was a case of carefully rigging one and lifting it without all the others moving. In their shift Greg and Jack moved about half of them. Leif and Anders salvaged the rest before the end of their shift and started on the drums.

'It's like trying to gift wrap a fuckin' monster blancmange,' Leif colourfully explained. 'The cardboard drums have slumped under the weight of what's inside. They're ready to disintegrate, and the plastic bands round them don't help. If you touch a drum it starts to fall apart... the bands are cutting into the drums... starting to cut 'em in two. It's easy to get the jacket around a stack but as we ratcheted up the straps it was like squeezing out diarrhoea; it destroys the viz.'

It wasn't what Jack wanted to hear. Destroying the viz on every lift would slow down the salvage. Furthermore, there didn't seem to be anything to gain by trying to empty the plastic bags of beads from the disintegrating drum into a wire basket and hauling them to the surface. Simply pulling the drums apart would destroy the viz and add to the risk of puncturing the bags. There seemed to be no option but to persevere, and they persevered.

Greg decided that they didn't need to ratchet the Kevlar jacket too tightly around the drums. The contents seemed to have settled on the pallet and if they wrapped two straps vertically around the drums and pallet it would be safe. However, it took twice as long to raise a pallet of beads against a pallet of zinc ingots.

They had cleared a row of pallets and repositioned the arc lights near a two-high stack of drums. Jack heard it at the same time as he felt it.

Chapter 31

Race against time

It was a sound no diver wants to hear inside a wreck. The dull groan of a ship moving, and the piercing shriek of metal being twisted and torn apart by massive forces. The deck dropped beneath Jack's feet. He was suddenly suspended in the water as the rear section of the ship broke away and dropped a couple of metres to the seabed. The ship was breaking up and they were inside it! It happened so quickly. One moment Jack was braced to step onto the edge of a pallet and wrap the salvage jacket around a stack of drums, the next he was thrown off balance. Adrenalin kicked in as he frantically fanned with his hands and scanned the space around him and his route out of the hold. The twin torches mounted into his helmet picked out the moving scene around him.

The deck rebounded like a springboard towards his dangling feet but didn't slam into them. If he had been standing upright on the deck the force could have crushed spinal vertebrae, broken bones and ruptured tendons. It had been a massive whiplash as the rear tower had broken away and the deck of the rear hold had sprung back. The arc lamp that had been on the deck had been thrown upwards. It was spinning slowly in the water and captured the sight of sediment writhing on the deck. Greg was floating above it.

Even before Jack felt the deck beneath his feet, he realised the danger facing them. The whiplash from the sloping deck springing back had thrown the top pallets of drums upwards and outwards. In slow motion they were now starting to tumble back to the deck

– with Greg in their path. Jack didn't think, he just acted. He forced his boot against the wooden pallet, reached down, grabbed Greg's harness and tried to pull him to one side. For a terrible moment Jack thought he was too late and Greg was too heavy. He could feel rather than see a pallet of drums falling against him. There was no way he could stop it. Instead, he tried to lever his body against it. He forced his shoulder against the mass, tensed, twisted and turned in one fluid, albeit slow, movement. He strained every muscle as he tried to pull Greg's body out of the way. As the pallet slowly tumbled past him, it flushed Greg and the arc lamp out of the way. The viz inside the hold had been destroyed. It was like wading through brown soup; but he was still holding Greg's harness.

'Greg, are you OK?' Jack shouted with the fear clear in his voice.

'What was that? It scared the shit out of me!' was the reply. 'Gi' me a hand to get up.'

'I think the rear tower may have broken away. The stern was a couple of metres above the seabed… the starboard deck was crumpled near the rear tower… I don't think the ship is breaking up… but let's get out of here.'

Jack and Greg hauled in their umbilicals and retraced their steps to the hold opening – but couldn't see anything. First Greg, then Jack climbed up their umbilicals and into clear water, or clearer water. Their head torches picked out the clouds of sediment billowing out of the hold. There was a flurry of questions as Gunnar responded to the drama and as both Greg and Jack made their way back to the wet well. Once inside, Gunnar helped Jack to get out of his commercial diving suit. Jack had already decided. He was going to swim to the wreck and check out the damage before anyone else risked going inside the rear hold. He told Gunnar what he was going to do.

'How much gas do you have in your tank?' asked Gunnar.

'I've got about 120 bar... not enough for me to survey the hull and the damage. Lukas can drop down my rebreather which will give me plenty of time.'

This time no one challenged Jack's decision to survey the wreck. Working inside a wreck was dangerous enough without the fear of it collapsing around them. There was also the awareness that Jack had proved himself. He'd not only lived and worked alongside them but had pulled Greg to safety. The flippant thanks from Greg, and the smiles and slaps on the back from the rest of the team, were all the endorsement he needed.

It took time for Lukas to set up the rebreather, drop it down to the wet well and for Gunnar to collect it. Jack was then in familiar territory – weightless, lithe and swimming free. Fortunately, the current had lessened as he finned towards the rear tower. The crumpled deck that Gunnar had first spotted during the inspection of the wreck had been replaced by a ten-metre gash. It ran from starboard to port, close to the foot of the rear tower, and opened like a crude trench. It looked as though the bulkhead separating the hold from the engine room remained intact but the whole rear tower had dropped away. Jack finned towards the gap and shone his torch into the void. Trunking and cable, panels, pipes and twisted steel barred his way towards the engine room. There was no way he was going to swim inside.

Jack finned above the gash, over the side and down towards the seabed and stern. He remembered the scene during the inspection months ago. The stern and huge propellor had been two to two and a half metres above the seabed. Now a propellor blade had been thrust deep into the mud. It looked as though the whole rear of the ship was now anchored on the seabed. He glanced at his dive computer – time to move on. He finned close to the seabed and shone his torch along the hull. It looked firmly planted – but it had looked fixed before! There was no noticeable distortion in the hull plates, no cracks, the hull looked sound. He paused at the bow and thought the bulbous nose of the ship was higher off the seabed than before. Probably a readjustment as the ship settled once more or the back of the ship was broken. The current gently took him back towards the stern on the other side of the wreck. He scanned the hull, but it looked the same as he recalled.

It was decision time. The smart move would be to postpone the salvage for a day or so and give the ship time to settle. As the current pushed one way and then the other it would cause the hull to wriggle deeper. But that would lose him time. He could tell everyone the ship remained safe – and hope he was right. As he made his way back to the wet well, he decided: they would continue the salvage.

'I've inspected the wreck and the rear tower has broken away from the main hull. It's not complete but there's a ten-metre gash along the entire width of the deck. It looks as though the stern is firmly planted on the seabed. The rest of the hull looks fine. There may be minor settling, but I think it's safe to work inside. I'm happy to go in first,' he added.

'Good enough for me,' said Leif, '…but now we've got to sort out the mess they've left for us,' he added with a smile.

Jack left them to it. It was the sort of challenge they had met a dozen times before – and overcome. All he wanted now was to sleep.

Jack had slept well and was becoming used to the routine. This morning, if it was morning, he realised that although he was tired, he didn't feel stressed. He had an inner calm. The beauty of the job was that it was all consuming. You concentrated on the job in hand and not the dozens of other things bombarding you each day. You were so tired you fell asleep quickly and woke, if not refreshed, at least less tired and ready for the shift. He was strangely relaxed and content as he listened to Lorna and the team. Her report of the clean-up and pallets salvaged was encouraging, despite the slowness caused by the poor viz. All the remaining drums were readily accessible. There had been no further settling – or none of which they were aware. The end of the job was in sight and still on schedule. However, there was news from Lukas that was more worrying.

'There's a cold front sweeping down from Iceland. It's coming in our direction. It's a bit too early to get a definite forecast and timescale. First indication will be an increase in the swell…'

'Great…' was all Leif said but his tone said everything. 'I felt it on the last lift.'

A swell causes a ship to roll as it rises and falls over it. The bigger the swell the greater the movement. The *Stavanger* could mitigate the effect of the swell by pointing directly into it. This would greatly reduce the roll, but it couldn't entirely eliminate the rise and fall of the ship in relation to the seabed. Quite simply, the steel salvage cable would be moving up and down from the ship whilst the wreck remained stationary. The divers would be trying to fix lifting straps and pallets to a cable that could be moving up and down by a metre or more. A skilled winch operator, working with skilled divers, could coordinate a lift that didn't wrench a pallet off the deck and send it swinging erratically as it broke free of the hold. Everyone understood why Leif had said 'Great'.

'I'll watch the weather and give you regular updates,' was all Lukas said.

Jack could sense the change in the weather as he looked down on the wreck of the *Asenka* from the bottom step of the wet well. The viz was poorer than on his last shift and the current was slightly stronger. He could see the tiny particles of sediment scurrying by. He let Greg move clear and pushed off the step to drop to the deck. Perhaps he was imagining a stronger current but he felt he was leaning into it a little more than before. He crouched by the lip of the hold, collected a couple of metres of umbilical and dropped into the hold. It had now become routine. Between them they painstakingly, in poor viz, draped then tightened the Kevlar jacket over a pallet of drums, secured two more straps over it and slid the lifting straps underneath. It was only when he held the end of the straps for Greg that he noticed the increased rise and fall of the lifting cable. The damp hair on the back of his neck tried to rise. He thought about the risk of slipping the hook through the lifting straps in such poor viz and trapping his hand. He'd be dragged towards the surface with a dislocated shoulder! The swell was increasing; it added urgency to the salvage.

They had only salvaged eleven pallets of drums and were almost at the end of their shift when Lukas gave them another weather update. 'Hi guys, just to let you know about the weather... The cold front has picked up speed and is predicted to run south-east towards the Norwegian coast and then south-south-east straight down the North Sea. They are predicting wind speeds Force 6, forty to fifty kilometres per hour, seventeen to twenty-seven knots. Our operating limits are well outside this – so no problem. Just be careful.'

Jack had dived in stormy conditions but never as a commercial diver and never salvaging cargo. He knew that at fifty kilometres per hour, large tree branches move, telephone wires begin to 'whistle', umbrellas are impossible to control and large waves begin to form. He knew the ship and pressure chamber could cope with it. He wasn't sure if he could! By the end of the shift, the hook on the end of the lifting cable was moving more than twenty centimetres. Greg was talking to the winchman as they judged the rise and fall and coordinated the lift to reduce the jolt on the cable. It wasn't just the rise and fall. They were now under the edge of the hold and the winchman had to manoeuvre the pallet to one edge of the hold so that it didn't catch the other edge as the current caught it. It was all painfully slow.

Chapter 32

On station

Jack wasn't disappointed that it was Anders and Leif who raised the last pallet of drums to the surface. He'd listened to the conversation between Anders and Lorna as he described the effects of the increasing swell on the rise and fall of the lifting cable. Jack simply admired the combined skills of the divers and the winchman as they coordinated the lift and prevented it being wrenched from the wreck, swinging widely in open water and then caught in a growing current.

Inside the main chamber he was starting to feel the slight pendulum swing as the current swung them one way – before the sheer weight of the chamber swung them back. He also noticed a change in the mood of those inside the pressurised chamber. Normally they would eat, relax, chat a little and then sleep. Now there was little talking and no sleep as they envisaged the tricky operation being undertaken just a few metres away. Everyone knew these were the last few lifts and almost the end of the salvage. They could relax when it was all over.

It ended with no drama as Leif announced: 'That's it… last load gone… put the kettle on… we're on our way back.'

The mood had changed dramatically as Lorna, Anders and Leif crawled from the wet well into the main chamber; it was almost festive. Everyone knew that even with a Force 6 approaching and rough seas above, they were all safe inside their steel shell – dangling fifty metres below the surface. Lukas would be organising their lift back to the surface and the decompression sequence. It didn't take long for Captain Sorenson to announce that, despite the increasingly rough seas, the final pallet of drums had been transferred to the freighter and the whole salvage was en route to Riga. In a few days' time they could walk on deck, feel the wind on their face and the sun on their back – well, in a Force 6 gale maybe not much sun. They'd also have a healthy bonus and several weeks ashore before re-joining the ship, on station, by the *Monroe Bravo* oil platform in the North Sea.

Jack knew it was less than five hundred nautical miles from the current wreck site to the harbour in Aberdeen and that it would take them about thirty hours. He also knew that it would take more than thirty hours for all of them in the diving chamber to decompress. If they went to Aberdeen they'd have to sit in the harbour until the divers could safely leave. The obvious answer was to make their way to the Fortes area, two hundred and forty kilometres due east of Aberdeen and be on station early. Once the divers had decompressed, they could be flown to Aberdeen by helicopter and be replaced by the relief divers.

It was only when Jack checked with Sandro that he discovered their new helicopter, a Eurocopter EC225, wouldn't be available until hours before their standby duty officially started. As a result, the *Marine Salvage & Investigation Company* would be perilously close to being in breach of contract; not the start they wanted. Sandro had explained that the complicated leasing agreement for the helicopter, the reconfiguration of the interior and addition of heat-seeking search electronics and rescue and retrieval equipment, as well as air crew training, had gobbled up all their built-in time reserves. However, Sandro also announced that he would be flying out to the *Monroe Bravo* oil platform with other oil rig workers and transferring to the *Stavanger* by boat so that he and Jack could be present at the start of standby duty. Their helicopter would bring the replacement dive teams and take the current teams, as well as the two of them, back to Aberdeen. He could fit it all in between meetings with his London lawyers.

Jack now had no choice but to pass the days decompressing as the *Stavanger* made its way to the Standby point adjacent to the *Monroe Bravo* platform and the Eastern Trough Area Project. The one hundred and fifty square kilometre speck in the North Sea represented the most expensive piece of real estate in the world. The sums of money being spent and the income being generated was astounding.

Chapter 33

Expert witnesses

Sandro found himself following a routine when he met with Reginald Melton-Barr and Samantha Elliot in their London offices. He would deliberately walk to the end of the platform at Manchester Piccadilly railway station to reach the farthest carriage. It was farther to walk but the carriage would be less crowded. He would also have farther to walk to the barrier when the train arrived in London. He'd take his time getting off the train and let all the other passengers scurry for buses and underground trains. When the surge of commuters had cleared, he would stop at one of the fast-food stalls to get a large coffee, in a paper cup, and sip it whilst he walked the fifteen minutes to Themis Chambers. He'd smile and wave to the receptionist, knowing that she would signal his arrival to Samantha. He found the routine calming, as though he was in control and not being swept along. His first few visits to Themis Chambers had been anything but calming.

The smile from the receptionist was as expected and moments later Samantha escorted him along the well-worn route to Melton-Barr's office. In recent visits Melton-Barr had looked tired and his manner had been reserved. Today he was transformed. There was a smile on his face, his eyes flashed, and he seemed to bounce around the huge office. However, it was Samantha who placed the two photographs of Anna Kalnina on the table in front of Sandro. She spoke first.

'Sandro, we have some excellent news for you – well in time for the next disclosure. We asked one of our expert witnesses to inspect these two photographs: the one given to your business partner in Riga and the police exhibit. We have his report; it's highly technical, but it confirms our initial thoughts. The photograph of Anna Kalnina, given to Jack Collier in Riga, was not taken at the central police station in Manchester. What Jack Collier was told was a lie.

'The police use cameras with a high-definition setting; tens of millions of pixels form each photograph. They use a certain type and weight of paper with a particular surface finish and a type of printer that has small separate tanks of ink that combine to give the best quality image. The characteristics of the exhibit photographs produced by the police in Manchester are consistent and readily identifiable. Our expert confirms the authenticity of the police exhibit – as you would expect.

'You spotted that the photograph given to Jack didn't have an exhibit number and there was no official stamp on the back. Our expert witness has proved that the image of Anna Kalnina was printed on a completely different type of paper and using a common colour cartridge. Our expert went into detail about the difference in the number of pixels in the two photographs and provided analysis of the inks used. We are confident that his testimony will be rock solid. The photo given to Jack was not taken by the police.'

Samantha pointed to the photograph Sandro had sent to her by motorcycle courier. 'You spotted the lack of any smudges to Anna's mascara and that there were no tracks of tears through her make-up. Our other expert witnesses analysed the injuries to Anna Kalnina's face in the two photographs. We have her report here. She is convinced that the two photographs were taken hours apart.

'She notes the change in the colour of the blood around her mouth and nose. It's oxidized and has become darker; this occurs naturally over time. Although her lip has been cut, and started to swell, there is no bruising as shown in the official police photograph. There is also no bruising on her cheek. That's only apparent in the police photo. Our expert maintains that the bruising evident in the police photograph would take hours to form. Finally, her expression is very different in the two photographs.'

Samantha held up the photograph given to Jack Collier in Riga. 'The clear conclusion is that someone took this several hours before Anna Kalnina arrived at the police station. We believe it was taken as part of a plan to coerce you into an illegal act of salvage.'

Samantha sat back in her chair looking very pleased; but she had one more thing to say. 'The laboratory that we use has identified five different sets of fingerprints on the photograph. From what you have told us it is highly likely that there are prints from you, Jack and Penny on it. I'd expect the prints of the man in Riga to be on it as well. Once we find him, and match the prints, we have him.'

Samantha paused with her body language clearly expecting a response from Sandro.

'I can see that, but how does it change the charges against me? The guy may have been trying to get us to salvage microbeads and Anna Kalnina may have been trying to get money out of me, but the charges still stand.'

It was Melton-Barr who replied: 'Sandro, we are pursuing several new lines of enquiry, and they already offer more points of doubt. Remember what I said at our first meeting – "Whenever there is doubt there cannot be a conviction". We have people working to identify the man who gave Jack Collier the photograph. Once identified, we may have more evidence to challenge the charges against you.'

The rest of the meeting was a disappointment to Sandro. Samantha paraded a succession of refined arguments and supporting evidence, but none were new; none seemed to be the killer blow that would get the case dismissed.

Samantha was bringing the meeting to a close and starting to list the ongoing investigations and avenues still open to them when the phone rang. Melton-Barr got up from his chair and moved to answer the phone. His expression made it clear he was not happy to be disturbed. 'I asked Angela to hold my calls. I told her we were not to be disturbed.'

However, rather than dismiss the call, Melton-Barr listened and, before thanking the caller, said he would check with his colleague and client. As he returned to the table there was a look of concentration on his face. Speaking to them both he said: 'That was the Crown Prosecution Service. They wish to provide us with the latest disclosures and are happy to accept any we may have. They also say important new information has been obtained about the case; information they are happy to share once it has been verified. They have invited us, all of us, to a meeting in Manchester to consider it.

'This is most unusual and could mean anything from strengthening their case even further to dismissing it; from offering a deal to a disputed point of law. You heard me say I will discuss it with my colleagues and get back to them.'

Melton-Barr eased back in his chair, interlinked his fingers and rested his chin on his knuckles, deep in thought. 'In my opinion, there is nothing to be gained by avoiding the meeting. We will have time to consider their disclosure and will need to decide what disclosures we make at this time. We could delay any meeting a little to give us more time; time to strengthen our case. The key questions are do we wait until we have seen all their latest disclosures before we present all of ours? Do we present everything we have, challenge their failure to disclose and go for a dismissal? In my opinion, it would be prudent to hear what they have to say before we do anything. However, I wouldn't wish to delay our disclosure too long – since delay and partial disclosure is the basis of our call for a dismissal.'

Chapter 34

New lines of enquiry

When Melton-Barr announced they were 'pursuing several new lines of enquiry' it was an understatement. Several investigators were frantically trying to trace the man Jack had met in the Mirabelle Hotel bar and who had given him the photograph of Anna. The hotel did have CCTV and did save the digital files – but only for a month before they were wiped. When the bartender was shown the photo-fit picture, he couldn't recall the man, nor the trio of people in a corner booth. It was weeks ago, and they had dozens of customers every day.

The investigators checked hotels in the immediate area for any British businessmen who had stayed there before and after the meeting. There were dozens but none that matched the artist's impression Jack Collier had helped create. They checked car hire companies in case the man was merely passing through Riga, but without success. The easiest way to trace him would have been to give the photo-fit to the British police. They had access to face recognition software used at airports and seaports. However, Melton-Barr wanted to retain this information until the last possible minute.

He had also told the investigators not to visit the offices of Emma Farmaceitiska Fabrika where Anna worked. He didn't want to take the risk of alerting Anna or her elusive friend. Just when they were about to give up, one of the team, in desperation, suggested, 'Why don't we check on Kalnina's friends and workmates – but outside the office? They may be able to recognise him – worth a try?' It was a simple idea that brought a result in twenty-four hours. The website for Emma Farmaceitiska Fabrika posted pictures of the senior management team. The three investigators simply took two each, followed them home and knocked at their front door or apartment door. Four of the management team identified the man in the photograph as Tony Levens, co-owner of L&M Property Development and a man currently conducting a business deal with their company. Within the hour, a message was sent to Reginald Melton-Barr; it prompted more frantic activity before the next meeting with Sandro.

Samantha removed a copy of the photo-fit picture and a single photograph from a folder. She placed them on the table in front of Sandro. The resemblance between the photo-fit picture and the photograph was uncanny. He'd never seen the person in the photograph, only the description by Jack and the photo-fit. It was him, it must be him. The photo-fit had even captured the facial expression in the photograph. For a moment, Sandro was shocked into silence as Samantha explained: 'His name is Tony Levens, co-owner of L&M Property Development Limited in Liverpool. Earlier this year Tony and his partner, David Moxon, purchased B&H Limited in Runcorn...'

'What... Who?' exclaimed Sandro. 'Did you say David Moxon? Is this the same person – the lawyer I first met in the police station after I was arrested? The *pro bono* commercial lawyer who steered me towards his father's law firm and who was "sitting in" on the discussions with Roberta Fox? This is...'

It was time for Samantha and Melton-Barr to be taken aback. They quickly glanced at each other before Melton-Barr responded. 'I'm confident the name David Moxon has not appeared in any documentation I have seen to date. I was aware you had been advised by a duty solicitor, but the name of that person was never listed. Samantha, do you have any recollection of this person's involvement in the case?'

'No, I'm certain that his name has never appeared in any of the documents. However, I'll search just to be sure… let's just check.'

Samantha moved away from the table and began pounding at a computer keyboard. Within the minute, two smiling faces appeared on the computer screen: the two co-owners of L&M Property Development Limited were staring at them.

'Is this the David Moxon you first met at the police station in Manchester and who claimed to be a *pro bono* lawyer?'

In a calm tone that belied his boiling fury Sandro merely said 'yes'.

It was Melton-Barr who took up the discussion: 'Sandro, the involvement of David Moxon could be a game changer in our case. The businessman and lawyer are the same person and could indicate premeditation. It's simply too much of a coincidence that the co-owner of L&M Property Development Limited was waiting for a potential client at the police station just when you were detained. It's too much of a coincidence that his business partner was the person who tried to coerce you and your partner to conceal an illegal act. Tell me what you know of David Moxon.'

Over the next hour, Melton-Barr and Samantha questioned Sandro about every occasion he had met David Moxon and his likely contacts. They compiled dates and times, the nature of each meeting and those present. Melton-Barr was aware that at this stage the list didn't have to be complete – they had enough to start their investigation.

Samantha revised the detailed timeline, from the purchase of B&H Limited in Runcorn to the loading of 200 drums of microbeads onto the MV *Asenka* and the meeting with Jack Collier in Riga. Ongoing investigations were filling the gaps in their knowledge – from how and when the microbeads were manufactured to meetings between Tony Levens and the owners of Emma Farmaceitiska Fabrika. They established that the Latvian company used microbeads in the production of cosmetic and personal hygiene products: facial scrubs and toothpaste, shower gel, make-up and sunscreens. They also established that L&M Property Development Limited, through the bankrupt B&H Limited, had agreed to sell the manufacturing equipment to them and arranged to ship everything to Riga on board the MV *Asenka*.

Everything was pointing to a conspiracy to coerce the *Marine Salvage & Exploration Company* into an illegal act. Fortunately, an act that had not been undertaken.

Chapter 35

Mutual disclosure

Sandro's defence team had agreed to meet in his office at the *Marine Salvage & Investigation Company* in Salford. It would allow the team to provide Sandro with an update on their investigations, and to review the latest disclosures, before travelling to the meeting with Detective Inspector Latchem. It was Melton-Barr who set the scene.

'This so-called mutual disclosure is merely the excuse for the meeting. Samantha and I reviewed all the materials; they add volume, but no new or substantive evidence. There must be something else.

'Everything presented so far suggests that the police believe they have a strong, an overwhelming, case against you. It is my belief that the police will present more disclosures that *have only now become available,* and which have only now been forwarded to the CPS. I suspect we are about to be ambushed by this so-called new evidence and invited to reconsider your plea.'

'What new evidence?' asked Sandro in alarm.

'Who knows?' replied Melton-Barr; his relaxed and off-hand reply suggested it was of little concern. 'I believe we have addressed all eventualities and this announcement, if it occurs, is merely a ploy. They will be hoping for a reaction from you – be sure you don't give them one,' Melton-Barr stressed. 'It's my guess that the CPS rep will respectfully decline to comment on any new evidence at this time… but will outline the case against you. They may even comment on the specific charges against you. Again, these will be scare tactics to encourage you to change your plea. The CPS would be delighted to get a guilty plea with a minimum of time and cost.'

They speculated for several minutes about what form any new evidence could take before Lesley, the company secretary, announced that the taxi had arrived. It was Samantha, almost as an afterthought, who announced: 'Oh yes, we've received a report from the MPA Clinic about your assessment. According to Dr Esther May and her colleagues, you are extremely fit and well balanced, with all measures taken well within normal ranges. They could find nothing that would prompt a sexual attack.'

The meeting was scheduled to take place in the briefing room within the Greater Manchester Police headquarters. The building was a huge glass, steel and concrete rectangular box that looked as though it had been dropped into simple landscaped gardens. It was surprisingly close to the busy city centre. The venue for the meeting, the main briefing room, wasn't ideal but it was the biggest room available and could accommodate Sandro's defence team, a member of the Crown Prosecution Service, Detective Inspector Latchem and her colleagues Detective Sergeant Alan Herman and Detective Constable Julie Evers.

Melton-Barr and Samantha had already worked through the disclosures that had arrived from the Crown Prosecution Service days before. They contained nothing of significance, nothing that could have initiated the extraordinary meeting. Sandro should have been buoyed by the confidence of Melton-Barr. However, he was subdued during the taxi ride to the Greater Manchester Police headquarters. He didn't speak as they made their way to the meeting room or when invited to help himself to tea, coffee or water.

DI Latchem interrupted the informal chats and asked if they could all take their seats so the meeting could start. She thanked them all for attending and asked each person to introduce themselves and state their current role with respect to the investigation. To Sandro it all seemed highly bureaucratic and he was eager to hear if Melton-Barr's belief that new evidence would be presented was correct.

DI Latchem read out a long statement that summarised the case against Alessandro Calovarlo. It was emotionless, factual and damning. When mention was made of the photograph of the victim, Sandro could visualise the picture. He tried to imagine the reaction of the members of a jury listening to these charges and seeing this evidence; it sounded overwhelming. If he had not heard it all before and knew how Melton-Barr would challenge and interpret the evidence, he would have been dismayed.

'All of this evidence has been disclosed to the defence,' stated Coleen Latchem as she drew the statement to an end. 'However, new evidence has been collected which we can now share with the defence team. We are not expecting an immediate response, but it is obviously something that they will need to discuss with their client. I apologise for the timing – but our enquiries are ongoing and will remain so.'

DI Latchem stood up from her chair, picked up two files from the table and gave them to Melton-Barr. He smiled, with no warmth, and thanked her.

'The first item is a statement from Anita Woods, a former girlfriend of Sandro Calovarlo, that provides a second account of his violent sexual behaviour. In the account Ms Woods describes her relationship with Sandro Calovarlo as *transactional* – even though she doesn't use that word. Mr Calovarlo pays for expensive weekend breaks in hotels, meals, drinks, expensive clothes and jewellery and so on in return for, I quote, *satisfying his energetic sexual fantasies*. Later in the same statement she states that the form of these sexual relations was *too much for me*. She ended the relationship after a few weeks. The comments from this witness mirror those from Isobel Downing.'

Sandro listened in disbelief. He recalled his brief relationship with Anita. She was an attractive young woman but forever drooling over a dress or a pair of shoes, wanting to visit some restaurant she'd heard of or talking about a gig she wanted to attend. At first Sandro was happy to indulge her. After a few weeks he concluded she regarded him as an easy touch. As soon as he stopped buying the shoes and buying tickets, she lost interest in him.

'Our investigation into the second item is ongoing but we wish to alert the defence at this time. In recent months we have become aware of a new synthetic, recreational drug that is circulating in the nightclubs of Manchester, Liverpool, Leeds and Sheffield. It's called DanZe and is similar to MDMA or Molly. It's cheaper than ecstasy because it's typically contaminated with bulking agents. A characteristic of DanZe is increased energy, heightened empathy, feelings of pleasure and increased impulsiveness. In those patients who have taken DanZe, an increase in ketone levels has been recorded as well as a drop in glucose levels.

'Unfortunately, the collapsed state of Mr Calovarlo prevented early blood tests. By the time blood was taken for testing any trace of DanZe had been lost. Our investigations to date have confirmed that DanZe is readily available in the Mojito Nightclub in Manchester. Previous statements indicate that Mr Calovarlo visited the men's toilets shortly before he collapsed. At the present time we are trying to determine if Mr Calovarlo purchased the drug, DanZe.

Still standing, DI Latchem closed the file and turned to the representative from the Crown Prosecution Services. 'At this time, I would like to invite Julian Ross from the CPS to offer any comments he may have.' She then sat and waited for Ross to speak.

'Thank you, Detective Inspector.' There was no way Julian Ross was going to comment on this new, yet speculative, evidence. He'd wait until the police provided firm evidence of drug purchase. However, he was happy to summarise the judgement of the Crown Prosecution Service in relation to the evidence presented to date. 'We have reviewed the evidence in the case against Alessandro Calovarlo and judge it does provide a realistic prospect of conviction. Furthermore, we are of the opinion that it is in the public interest to prosecute.

'In terms of the severity of the charges against Mr Calovarlo, at this time, we will be recommending charges of grievous bodily harm and rape. If convicted of GBH the maximum jail sentence is five years. Rape is an indictable offence and carries a maximum of life imprisonment.'

Julian Ross turned his gaze directly at Sandro and in a cool, unemotional tone continued: 'We would like to proceed with this case as soon as possible and would like the defence team to agree to fast-tracking this case. We believe a date for the trial in two months is realistic.'

Julian Ross resumed his seat, packed away his documents and turned his head towards Coleen Latchem. She, in turn, turned to Melton-Barr as though inviting a response. Samantha had been watching Sandro throughout. She had noticed the impact the statements were having upon him and gave Melton-Barr the slightest of nudges. With a look of indifference Melton-Barr turned casually to make eye contact with Samantha. She flicked her eyes towards Sandro and Melton-Barr gave the briefest of nods. He was aware that Latchem had got the reaction she was after.

Sandro felt he had been plunged into deep, dark water. An all-enveloping wave of cold washed over him as the phrase *maximum of life imprisonment* rang in his ears. He felt paralysed. Melton-Barr had confidently talked about the case being dismissed. Maximum of life imprisonment was a long way from the ten to twelve years that DI Latchem had predicted. If Sandro had been subdued as he entered the meeting room, he was now shell shocked. All the colour drained from his face and he looked visibly distressed.

In contrast, Melton-Barr was delighted at the outcome of the meeting and was struggling to keep the smile from his face.

However, after being alerted by Samantha, he immediately recognised the impact of the comments on Sandro and made an instant decision.

'Detective Inspector Latchem, a moment if you please. I wonder if we could suspend this meeting for a few minutes whilst I confer with my client. It is possible that after a brief discussion I may have additional comments to make that could influence the nature of the charges my client is facing.'

It was a vague request, delivered in an awkward manner, but just what Coleen was hoping for. She had seen the effect of the announcement of life imprisonment from the CPS and its dramatic effect on the accused. She struggled to supress a smile and graciously agreed to suspend the meeting. She offered her own office to Calovarlo and his defence team.

Between them, Melton-Barr and Samantha marched Sandro from the meeting and along the corridors to Latchem's office. Once inside he grabbed Sandro's arm and turned him, so they were face to face. 'Sandro, that performance was designed to unsettle you; and I can see it worked.'

Years of experience with clients told him Sandro wasn't listening – he was still processing the so-called new evidence and implications of a life sentence if found guilty. He took Sandro by both his arms and shook him to get his attention. Sandro had a vacant look on his face, his mouth hung open. Melton-Barr grabbed him by his biceps and squeezed as hard as he could. He had to break the trance and get Sandro's attention. 'Sandro, look at me, look at me!' he demanded aggressively.

Sandro focused on Melton-Barr's eyes and closed his mouth.

'Are you listening to me – answer yes or no,' he said firmly.

Sandro was back in the present and answered 'yes'.

'This case will never reach court – I stake my reputation on it.'

Samantha clasped Sandro's face between her open hands and

spoke to him confidently. 'I don't need to check because I know the answer. The only way a sentence of life imprisonment is handed down to a person accused of rape is if they kill the victim. I too believe this case will be dismissed.'

Melton-Barr took up the conversation. 'Forget about Anita Woods and Isobel Downing – we can deal with them easily. We already have evidence that the stepfather of Isobel Downing was charged with being drunk and disorderly, and assault; charges that were subsequently replaced with a caution. I suspect the charges were dropped in return for her statement against you. We're working on it. I wouldn't be surprised if Ms Woods hasn't received similar incentives.

'Sandro, I'm sure I know the answer to these questions, but I need to ask them anyway. Did you purchase DanZe, or another recreational drug, at the Mojito Nightclub?'

Sandro had regained some composure and was listening attentively to Melton-Barr. 'No, definitely not.'

'Was there anyone in the toilet at the Mojito Nightclub when you were there?'

'No, definitely not.'

'Did you see anyone leaving or entering the toilet at the time you were there?'

'No, definitely not.'

'Did you knowingly take any drug or substance whilst at the Mojito Nightclub?'

'No.'

'I haven't heard of DanZe but we will investigate. If you didn't buy and take it, there will be no evidence to the contrary. Sandro, this is a speculative claim about DanZe being available. The police will be frantically trying to find a drug dealer who will testify that he sold it to you. They will not find one.

'Sandro, I was going to wait until I had written confirmation but new evidence has come to light that will destroy the case against you and implicate others.'

Whilst he had been talking to Sandro, Melton-Barr was urgently assessing his client's mental condition. He thought he had prepared Sandro for the ambush and scare tactics – but obviously not well enough and he needed to be sure.

'There's one other thing. Do you remember us talking about partial and non-disclosure? Today was the perfect opportunity for Detective Inspector Latchem to provide evidence similar to that which we have collected. The CPS have a continuing duty of disclosure, but are reliant on the police to provide this evidence. The evidence that we have collected presents a completely different picture to the one she is painting. The CPS and the courts take a very dim view if they believe there has been partial or non-disclosure. You may think it is a technical point but let me assure you. This technical point is likely to have the case dismissed.'

Melton-Barr looked again at Sandro and formed a judgement. His client looked more in control and he decided he didn't need to hand over disclosures from the defence at this time. It could wait a few more days.

'Sandro, Sandro, look at me,' Melton-Barr demanded. 'I know that what Detective Inspector Latchem announced and what the CPS have said has unsettled you but do you trust me? Do you trust my judgement?'

Sandro felt the same fear he had experienced when he was trapped under a slab of rock in a worm hole and when he had lost the shot line on a wreck and was drifting to his death. It washed over him and was in danger of obliterating everything else.

'Yes, I trust you.'

'I'm waiting for what may be a key jigsaw piece in our puzzle. It should be arriving in the next few days. Do you think you can hang on until next week whilst Samantha and I review all our evidence and provide what I expect to be our final disclosure?'

Still shell shocked, Sandro agreed.

'When we return to the meeting, I want you to appear calm and relaxed – OK? Don't look at your feet. I want you to alternate looking at Ross and Latchem. I want you to show them you're in control.'

They retraced their route back to the meeting room where the rest of the people were waiting for them. Melton-Barr thanked them for suspending the meeting and asked if it could be reconvened at a convenient time next week – perhaps Wednesday. 'At this time, I hope we will be able to bring our discussion to an acceptable conclusion.'

Chapter 36

Kunz Laboratories

Two days before the meeting in Manchester with Detective Inspector Latchem and Julian Ross of the CPS, Melton-Barr was in his office in London. He was responding to a message left by Jamie Kunz, the owner of Kunz Laboratories.

'Good morning Jamie... you left a message saying you had something for me,' said Reginald Melton-Barr as he eased his ample frame into his office chair and clicked the phone onto loudspeaker so that Samantha could hear.

'Yes... let me find it.' Dr Jamie Kunz shuffled a pile of files on his desk until he found what he wanted. He smiled, sat back in his own chair, and opened the file. 'The Calovarlo case,' he confirmed. 'We've been intrigued by the aldehyde and ketone spikes in his blood trace as well as the dip in his glucose level. I've been talking to some of my contacts, we've been doing some research and undertaking further analyses.'

'So, what have you got?'

'Patience Reginald, patience... don't spoil my fun. We started looking at the effect and metabolic residues of products like Rohypnol and GHB...'

'The date rape drugs,' Melton-Barr confirmed.

'Yes, but there was no evidence of these in the blood and urine samples, and they wouldn't account for the abnormality in aldehyde, ketone and glucose levels. However, one of my contacts at Porton Down, the chemical weapons research centre, gave me a lead.'

Jamie sat even further back in his chair and began to share the information he had collected. 'The Americans were having problems sedating battlefield casualties in Afghanistan. Intramuscular morphine is relatively slow acting and there is always a risk of an overdose. When soldiers are screaming in pain it's easy to give them another shot – a dose too many! They developed AmilSed, it's short for American Military Sedative, an oral, transmucosal sedative to replace morphine. It comes in lozenge and liquid form. If the casualty is conscious, they can suck the lozenge, if they are unconscious, a small amount of fluid can be squirted into their mouth. It's absorbed readily, acts in a few minutes, and is highly effective for two to six hours...'

'Come on Jamie, spare me the lecture. What have you got for me?'

Jamie sighed down the phone in a gesture of defeat. 'When AmilSed is metabolised in the body it depletes glucose levels and produces aldehydes and ketones. If Calovarlo ingested AmilSed he would be unresponsive or unconscious in minutes. It's unlikely he would begin to recover for at least two hours or more.'

There was now urgency in Jamie's voice. 'One of the benefits of AmilSed is its short half-life, the rate at which it decays in the blood stream once administered. This is why we couldn't find any evidence of it in his blood or urine. By the time the samples were taken it was too late. However, when we analysed samples of his saliva and alcohol on the bedsheets, we found traces of AmilSed. He was drugged.'

'Would you take it deliberately... to get high?'

'Definitely not! You'd only take it in desperate situations to relieve pain – or to become unconscious for hours.'

'So how do you think he took it?'

'We'd already checked the victim's dress for the suspect's DNA and semen. When we re-examined the dress we found a small pocket in the waistband – and a trace of AmilSed. The victim had the drug in her possession at some time.'

This was the *magic bullet*. This could be the single piece of evidence that would blow the case wide apart.

'OK, OK, how easy, or difficult, is it to get hold of this drug?'

'Not sure, you'd have to ask the US Military, but I suspect you would get the run-around or simply "no comment". Every patrol in Afghanistan would carry lozenges and ampoules. Soldiers would acquire a back-up supply, supplies would get lost, it would be sold on the black market. My guess is that if you wanted it, and had money, you could get anything in Kabul.'

'Thanks Jamie,' said Melton-Barr as his mind raced. 'I'd be grateful if you could email your full report to me on Wednesday morning, together with your invoice. The timing is critical – first thing Wednesday morning; no earlier, no later.'

Samantha had been listening intently and knew the significance of the timing. They would be in Manchester when the report arrived.

'I can print out Jamie's report in Sandro's office to take to the meeting but it will be too late to include it in the current disclosures.'

It was clear from Melton-Barr's expression and hand gesture that he was thinking about both the disclosure and its timing and his next move.

'Samantha, could you send a copy of our latest disclosures to the Detective Inspector asap. Could you also confirm the meeting with Latchem, the representative from the CPS, Sandro and the two of us for this coming Wednesday?'

Chapter 37

Disturbing disclosures

Detective Inspector Latchem was wading through the witness statement of an armed robbery in Stockport, south of Manchester. It was yet another big case to add to all the others on her desk. They had consistent descriptions of the two attackers and their car and blood traces from the suspects on broken glass. They even had fingerprints from the partly burnt-out car which had been dumped several miles away. A gardener had been watering a newly planted hedge and put out the fire before it took hold. She looked up as Detective Sergeant Alan Herman walked towards her desk carrying a thick file.

'Latest disclosure from Melton-Barr KC. I've gone through it and you're not going to like it.'

'Leave it on the desk. I'll get to it as soon as I can'.

DS Herman put the file down and remained standing; he didn't walk away. 'There's a couple of other things you need to know. The ACC has asked to see the case file, and the latest and previous disclosures. It seems he's taking a special interest in the case; it's unusual.'

Coleen Latchem nodded her head, mumbled her thanks and felt uneasy. She put the armed robbery to one side and picked up DS Herman's notes as he explained: 'Melton-Barr is challenging each piece of evidence we've collected. At first, I wasn't unduly bothered. We've been involved with enough cases and enough barristers to see how evidence can be interpreted. The physical evidence of the assault and rape is powerful. Look at page nine, about halfway down.'

Coleen flicked the pages and focused on the mid-page paragraphs as Herman continued. 'Anna Kalnina works for Emma Farmaceitiska Fabrika, the company importing the microbeads. She was working for them at the time the MV *Asenka* sank and at the time of the meeting in Riga with Jack Collier.'

Coleen was suddenly on high alert and her mind raced. She thought out-loud as she started to integrate the new information. 'When we originally spoke to Anna, she made no mention of Emma Farmaceitiska Fabrika. She said she worked for an agency as a temp, a clerical and secretarial assistant. I remember her giving us the name of the agency but I'm certain she never mentioned working for Emma Farmaceitiska Fabrika. It's too much of a coincidence… assault and rape allegation, a meeting with Collier and pressure to salvage cargo from the wreck…'

'I checked the transcripts. In all the interviews with Anna Kalnina there was no mention of the, er, Emma company.'

'Alan, contact Anna Kalnina in Riga and arrange for her to travel to Manchester. Tell her it's routine, tell her it's about the forthcoming trial and preparing her testimony. Don't rattle her, don't say anything to upset her but try and get her here as soon as possible.'

She thought that was the end of it – but Alan didn't move away.

'There's more. Melton-Barr included a letter to you that wasn't included in the disclosures. He's demanding the case be dismissed on the grounds of partial and non-disclosure. He's provided two long, annotated lists. One claims to prove our failure to disclose evidence beneficial to his client, quote, *through incompetence or design*. The other provides evidence favourable to his client which he claims the police have failed to collect – again, quote, *through incompetence or design.* It's a strong argument. I've seen cases dropped before now that didn't have half of these allegations in them.'

'OK, leave it with me. Once I've read through it all we can decide what to do next.'

The armed robbery was forgotten. A charge of partial or non-disclosure was serious and career threatening. What she had to do now was establish the link between Anna, the mystery man in Riga and the cargo being salvaged. She also had to work through Alan's note and the letter from Melton-Barr to assess his claims; she would have to respond. She also needed an update from DI Lomas. Suddenly it felt like the case was starting to fall apart and she was in danger of dropping one of the balls she was juggling.

She also wondered who had prompted the ACC to review the disclosures in the Calovarlo case; she was sure she knew.

Chapter 38

Last-minute evidence

When Anna entered Latchem's office inside the Central Manchester Police headquarters she immediately sensed a change in the atmosphere. There was no friendly welcome from Coleen, no smile from Julie Evers and no relaxed, informal chat. It was immediately business-like with Detective Inspector Latchem saying they needed to ask her more questions surrounding the alleged assault and rape. Anna thought there was an emphasis on the word 'alleged' – but maybe she imagined it.

'We'll conduct the interview in another room because we need to record your comments under caution in case they are needed at some time in the future.'

The three of them walked in silence to an interview room. Anna sat quietly whilst Coleen switched on the recording equipment and then started the interview; Anna was nervous – especially after a repeat of the police caution. It was nervousness that Coleen was trying to generate.

'Ms Kalnina, could you tell me who you currently work for?'

Anna wasn't expecting the question. She was immediately on her guard and answered carefully. 'I work for the Garīdznieks Sekretais Agencia in Riga. I do general clerical and secretarial work.'

'Yes, we know that's the agency that arranges your work, and that takes a fee, but which company do you currently work for?' Inspector Latchem's tone and expression suggested she knew exactly who she worked for. Anna broke eye contact and looked down at her hands. She was rolling them together. She had to discover how much this woman knew but couldn't afford a lie.

'Emma Farmaceitiska Fabrika.'

'How long have you worked for them?'

'Almost a year.'

'Did you have a meeting, at your workplace, with Tony Levens of L&M Property Development Limited in which he made a proposal?'

Coleen had made a series of telephone and video calls to senior staff within Emma Farmaceitiska Fabrika. She knew the date a meeting had taken place between Levens and Kalnina. She knew it was some form of project but that was all. The timeline confirmed that L&M Property Development Limited had already exported the microbeads and manufacturing equipment to the cosmetic company by that date. She also knew when Calovarlo was being coerced into salvaging material originally judged to be not worthy of salvage. What she didn't know was of a link, if any, between Calovarlo, Levens and Kalnina.

This was a critical point in the investigation. The latest disclosure meeting was only days away and the ACC may call her into his office at any time. He'd already informed her that DI Henry Lomas was to be transferred to the Serious Crime Division with immediate effect – 'to work on an important project'; yes, she also believed in fairies at the bottom of the garden! Lomas's stalled case, and the elusive Zak Friedman, had been dumped on her desk. The ACC had told her dismissively: 'It's all straightforward… just a case of wrapping it up… DI Lomas has made excellent progress…' Coleen had worked through the case file and was certainly impressed by the notes Lomas had made. He was 'pursuing positive lines of enquiry' and 'hoping to make an arrest soon'. He'd also eliminated the 'threat of an ecological disaster'. It all made Lomas sound like the maestro conducting an orchestra of police units, UK Border Force, EMSA and the Latvian authorities. It was only when looking beyond the rhetoric that she realised that UK Border Force had prevented the disaster and Lomas was no closer to apprehending Zak Friedman than he was on day one.

Coleen had to get a result here otherwise she was going to flounder under all the other cases. There was steel in her voice when she announced: 'Your alleged attacker is charged with grievous bodily harm and rape. If convicted, he could be sentenced to fifteen years in prison or even life imprisonment. Is there anything you want to tell me?'

Anna made no reply.

'We have evidence that Tony Levens illegally exported plastic microbeads from the UK to Latvia; to the company you work for. We know you spent a weekend showing him around the city. Tony Levens is going to prison. The only question is "do you join him?" I'm giving you one chance – and this is it. Tell me exactly what happened between you and Levens and between you and Calovarlo and I will tell the court you cooperated fully. Believe me, it's in your interests. If you continue telling me lies, this interview is over and you will be charged; it'll be too late.'

Coleen was giving the performance of her life – because her future within the Manchester Police Force depended upon it. She had to tread a fine line between what she knew and what she could finesse from Anna. She also knew that the taped interview would be available to the CPS and Calovarlo's defence team. She had to avoid anything on the tape that would damage her case.

Anna had decided weeks ago – if it all started to go 'belly up' it would be damage limitation time. There was no way she was going to risk going to prison and would happily drop Levens and his friend in it. What she had to do now was make out she was coerced into it, but first some tears – to get Latchem on her side.

Anna let her emotions rise to the surface; tears sprang easily from her eyes and she hid her face in her hands. It was easy to act as though she was trying to control her sobs as she waited for a consoling hand – but it didn't come. Anna had rehearsed what she was going to say, if the need arose, and looked up through still tear-filled eyes.

'She's on the verge of providing the missing pieces of information. I can sense it,' Coleen told herself. She just had to tip her over the edge, over the edge but not into an abyss. In her softest, warmest voice, and in a practised confessional tone, she placed her hand on top of Anna's. 'Start from the very beginning,' was all she said.

Julie Evers reached across the table and gave Anna a tissue and a sympathetic smile. 'It's going to be OK,' Anna said to herself and started to tell her version of the story. 'The first time I met Mr Levens was in the office… in Riga. I met him in other places later, with my girlfriend Karolina, Karolina Balodis… lots of times. He told us what to do.'

'Good, tell me about the first meeting.'

'Mr Levens was a visitor – I saw him arrive and meet the boss. They were making a fuss of him even though I'd no idea if he was a supplier or a customer. It was after lunch when the office manager asked if I'd do her a big favour. It seemed there was a problem, and Mr Levens would have to spend the weekend in Riga. She asked if I'd look after him, show him the sites, over the weekend. They'd give me two extra days pay and €200 for expenses.'

Anna manufactured a brief smile as though recalling the weekend. 'I showed him around the sites… he was good company… we got on well. I think it was Sunday afternoon when he asked if I'd be interested in working on a project in Manchester… well paid and generous expenses.'

Anna repeated the smile as she continued her story. 'At first, I was flattered. When he asked if I had a friend I trusted and who would be interested in working with me for a few weekends in Manchester I was intrigued... I thought it might be a sales event, marketing, something that might lead to another job.'

Anna paused as though collecting her thoughts – indeed, she was collecting her thoughts, and making sure she was careful what she said. 'He said me and my friend could earn and share €20,000. I told him, "There's no way I'm smuggling drugs!" and stood up to leave. I thought the only type of project that involved that much money would have to involve drugs.'

The sudden thought of drugs hidden inside the drums of plastic beads ratcheted up Coleen's anxiety but she maintained a neutral, knowing expression. 'What happened next?'

'He jumped to his feet, spread his arms and said something like, "No, no, it's nothing like that,' and asked me to sit down so he could explain. I'd already decided not to be any part of it but he went on. He said he and his partner had a business rival. I remember him saying, "Property development is a very competitive and ruthless business." He said they were both after the same property and his rival was spreading rumours about him – saying he couldn't manage the deal or something. He said his rival was playing dirty so he and his partner were going to play dirty. Mr Levens said all he wanted were some... sexy photographs of the businessman that they could threaten to show to his wife. They wanted to persuade him to back out of the deal.'

'What was your reaction?'

'I started to get up again to leave. I wasn't about to become a prostitute, even for a share of €20,000. He stood up as well, to stop me, and said he wasn't explaining it very well... asked me to let him finish and then decide what to do... that he wasn't asking me and my friend to be drug carriers or to jump into bed with the guy – but to play-act. He wanted it to look like, er, a sexual encounter, to look as though the other businessman had been unfaithful.

'Mr Levens was quite embarrassed at the time... said if I let him explain I could talk it over with my friend... we could decide if we wanted to do it or not.'

Anna hadn't been embarrassed but intrigued by the thought of earning so much money so easily... but she had to give the impression she was reluctant.

Coleen Latchem noted the change in Anna. The emotion that had threatened to overwhelm her had disappeared. Her account seemed to be cathartic and Coleen was happy to let her talk. She could always come back to points, and clarify, later.

'So, what was the plan?'

'Mr Levens's rival was an Italian called Alessandro Calovarlo. It seemed he often went to a nightclub called the Mojito in Manchester on a weekend... problem was he didn't go every weekend or on the same night, but once or twice a month. I was told he always went on his own, typically picked up a young woman and at the end of the evening took her home – to a nearby hotel or his apartment. He said it was impossible to take pictures inside the Mojito that would embarrass him – that'd provide any "leverage". He used the word "leverage" a lot.'

Anna suddenly seemed reticent; reluctant to continue – she wanted DI Latchem to work for the information she was getting.

'The plan, what was the plan?'

'The plan was for me to pick him up and... at the end of the night, take him back to my hotel.'

Anna hesitated over what to say next. Coleen let the silence continue – perhaps what Anna was about to say was incriminating or embarrassing...

'How were you to get him back to your hotel?'

'Mr Levens was going to give me "knockout drops" that would make Calovarlo so sleepy that he'd only vaguely know what was happening...'

It was one revelation after another. It was turning the entire case on its head. For a moment, Coleen stopped listening: was Calovarlo drugged?

'…showed me how to slip the knockout drops into his drink… said he'd be too drowsy to drive and so we'd take a taxi back to the hotel. Once back in the hotel room, Karolina and I would undress him and take photographs as though it was a three-some. We'd leave him asleep in the hotel room, give the, er, camera card to Mr Levens and then be taken to another hotel before flying back to Latvia the next day.

'Mr Levens said he'd pay all the expenses, each weekend, until we were able to get the photos. If they were convincing, we'd share €20,000 when Calovarlo withdrew from the deal. He reassured me that all me and Karolina had to do was play-act. There were no drugs to carry, no sex, just a business rival that he needed to be, er, compromised – that's the word he used a lot… "compromised". The way he explained it, it sounded like a story from a novel rather than a porn movie with me playing a leading role.'

'Tell me about the conversation you had with your friend Karolina.'

'We talked over the plan that evening; at first, she was sceptical.' Anna had been trying to judge the reaction she was getting from DI Latchem and DC Evers. It looked as though they believed her. 'She said something like "Who pays €20,000 for a few titillating photographs? I'd do it for two hundred" and laughed. The more we talked about it, the more daring and erotic it sounded… Karolina can be crude and at one point said: "I can think of a few positions that would surprise his wife. We don't need him smiling at the camera, just looking as though he's enjoying it, his face between my boobs." We were laughing and joking at the thought of earning so much money.'

The smile had disappeared from Anna's face as she turned to face Coleen. It was time to convince her. 'Mr Levens seemed to be a nice guy and if he was being screwed by a rival, perhaps there was no harm in helping him out... €20,000 would change our lives. For me it would be the deposit on an apartment. Instead of paying rent for my tiny flat I could be paying the same amount as a mortgage for my own home. For Karolina it was a no brainer. With her share she said she would quit her job, go to university, live cheaply for three years and still have money left over. With a degree she could get a job that paid two or three times what she was earning now. If all she had to do was simulate having sex with a sleepy stranger, she said she'd do it.'

Momentarily Anna stopped talking. She thought she was making it too easy. It would be more convincing if she was more hesitant and told the story piece by piece.

Coleen wasn't sure if the pause was caused by the recollections of her meeting with Karolina or what she was about to say next. She just wanted to keep Anna talking. She didn't want to interrupt and knew the tape was recording everything. She and Julie could go through it a dozen times and cross-check everything. She rehearsed some of the body language positions a psychologist had once told her encouraged disclosure. She wasn't convinced it would work but was prepared to try anything. Surprisingly Anna began speaking again.

'We started to think through all the practical things and what could go wrong. We calculated the cost of return flights and transfers, hotel rooms and food. We rounded everything up and agreed we'd ask for this in advance of every weekend. Karolina said we could borrow her boyfriend's camera and tripod. He'd show us how to take time-delayed photos, even video. We also talked about how we'd protect ourselves and ensure Tony Levens paid up.

'I suggested we tell Karolina's boyfriend what we were doing. It seemed to be sensible insurance. We also decided that we'd ask her boyfriend to join us for the weekends in Manchester and to be around if a problem arose. It wasn't that we didn't believe Mr Levens. It was just for additional insurance and reassurance. If we made €20,000, we could afford to pay the expenses for her boyfriend… The next morning, I told Mr Levens that me and Karolina would do it. We'd take the sexy photos. We just needed to know when it would start.'

'When did you start?'

'We didn't. Just before the first weekend in Manchester he changed the plan. He said simple photographs of me and Karolina in bed with Calovarlo wouldn't be enough. He said he needed something much more, er, persuasive; something that the Italian couldn't ignore or brush aside. We met him in a quiet bar in Riga and he explained…'

A possibility suddenly occurred to Coleen; could Tony Levens be the elusive Zak Friedman? It would make so much sense – and resolve the case that had been dumped on her. She put the thought to one side and quickly returned to listening to Anna.

'He'd heard from an insider that Calovarlo was close to convincing the owners of the property to sign a contract with him. There was only, er… due something or other to do; it'd only take a couple of weeks. He said that the revised plan was still play-acting but was more physical and would involve the police. He described the new plan in detail and offered us €40,000 if we'd do it. He just told us what he was asking us to do was "a bit riskier" – that's why he was prepared to pay more. I wasn't sure if taking sexy photos was illegal, but I was sure drugging a person so they could take them certainly was.'

The repeat mention of 'drugging a person' made Coleen's stomach churn. It was looking more and more as though Calovarlo was a victim and not the suspect… but Anna was continuing.

'Even for a share of €40,000 I wasn't happy about going through with it. The play-acting that Levens described was much more than a few titillating photographs and would be all the "leverage" Levens needed. We told Mr Levens that we'd need to talk about the new plan… it was so different to what we'd agreed.

He told us to talk it over and tell him what we'd decided the next day. I didn't want to go through with it – even for all the money rather than half. When Levens left I told Karolina I was frightened and didn't want to do it... but I didn't want to let her down. I didn't want to destroy her dreams.'

It had been Karolina, not Anna, who had baulked at the new plan. €20,000 was more than Anna's take-home pay for a year and she wasn't going to let this opportunity slip by. She just switched what she and Karolina had said.

'What did Karolina say?'

'She said she was also frightened by the new plan… that she didn't like what we'd be doing – but for a share of €40,000 she'd do it. I remember her saying, "Where else are you and me going to get a share of €40,000? We're talking about a few hours of distasteful work. One person loses a deal, another person makes one. Think of the forty thousand as our commission. You can bet your life that Levens is making ten times what he's giving us!" It was convincing.

'She went on, with a determination that surprised me… something like: "Think about it. You don't have to have sex with the guy. You don't even have to like him. All you've got to do is play your part. I'll play mine. If we're caught, we just say we were playing an erotic game as a favour to Mr Tony Levens. My boyfriend would back us up. There's no way we'd be prosecuted. The worst would be a caution and a telling off. For the reward, I'm prepared to take the risk.

'I felt trapped. If I pulled out now, I'd risk losing Karolina as a friend, destroying her dream of going to university and a better life. She made me realise I'm only an office assistant, a temp with little chance of promotion. She also said if I pulled out, Levens may get me fired… I couldn't afford to lose my job. She convinced me that an opportunity like the one Levens was offering comes along once in a lifetime.'

Anna sighed deeply. 'A share of €40,000 would change our lives. I said I'd do it.' Anna was suddenly quiet. She'd done it. She'd made it all sound convincing – just as she'd planned. She just had to sit quietly for a few moments as though the confession had drained her.

'Anna, from what you've told me so far, I think there could well be mitigating circumstance in your case. It sounds as though Tony Levens coerced you and Karolina into doing what you did. It's not just the money offered but the subtle pressure of a company client gradually ensnaring you. Let's have a short break. Julie, can you get Anna a glass of water?'

Just as Coleen was about to walk away from the table she turned and asked: 'Oh, before I forget, can you confirm that Tony Levens called himself Zak Friedman… that it was Levens who gave you the fake business card at the time of the meeting with Jack Collier?'

Anna realised she couldn't deny it. She just said, 'Yes'.

Chapter 39

Final jigsaw pieces

It took more than a few minutes for Coleen to brief DS Herman and to begin the process of arresting Karolina Balodis and her boyfriend and confirming that Levens was the elusive Zak Friedman. Julie and Anna were waiting for her as she re-entered the interview room.

'Tell me about the new plan and what Levens told you to do.'

Coleen could see Anna's shoulders visibly relax as she raised her head and gazed, unseeing, into the distance beyond Julie Evers. Anna recalled every moment, every detail of the hours inside room 107 at the Wayside Hotel. She also decided to give DI Latchem just the bare bones; she'd keep the juicy flesh of the night to herself.

'I just followed his instructions. I was to go to the Mojito Nightclub and spot Calovarlo when he turned up – if he turned up. On the first two weekends he didn't. However, Levens phoned me that Friday night… said Calovarlo was on his way. I spotted him as soon as he walked into the lounge. I already had a drink in my hand and followed him to the bar. I just waited in the shadows until he was being served. It was easy to bump into him, drop my glass and appear flustered. Just as we'd expected, he bought me a replacement drink.'

Anna looked up as she continued her story – 'just the bare bones,' she told herself.

'It was a bit awkward at first… but he was easy to talk to. I told him I was in Manchester on a weekend break, by myself, and enjoying seeing all the sites I'd read about. I told him a girlfriend had told me about the nightclub and since I enjoyed dancing, here I was. I think he found me attractive… I was trying to get him to like me. We started dancing… we were enjoying ourselves.'

Anna stopped talking and remembered dancing with Calovarlo. It was like being in the Reivas Nightclub in Riga on a Saturday night. The pulsating lights were synchronised with the boom, boom, boom of the music. For fractions of a second the light bathed the dance floor in colour and then in darkness. It created the effect of people frozen in poses as they danced to the music. It went on and on. She remembered it was hot and airless and she could see Calovarlo was sweating. His shirt was sticking to his body. The music never stopped; it went on and on. When the DJ mixed to another track it was an opportunity to take a break and return to their table, have a drink and rest.

'He bought drinks...'

The memory of the moment was etched on her mind. A waitress with a very short black skirt and big boobs was standing by a column near their table. Calovarlo asked her if she wanted another drink. He looked hot and there was a sheen of sweat on his face. 'Same as before,' she'd replied. She remembered that when he ordered he had to lean towards the waitress and shout into her ear… the music was so loud.

'…a soda water for him and a pinot grigio for me. I saw him drop a £20 note on her tray… told her to keep the change.'

In the nightclub she was happy for the break… they'd been dancing a long time. Just before she sat down, Calovarlo said he had to go to the loo, said he'd be back in a minute. It was the chance she'd been told to wait for as she watched him weave his way towards the toilets.

'He said he needed to go to the toilet. I watched him disappear through the dancers. Mr Levens had given me a tiny glass bottle, he called it a phial, of knockout drops. I had to put them in his drink. He'd made me practise opening it...'

Anna recalled exactly what she'd done as Calovarlo made his way to the toilets. She'd patted the waistband of her dress; the knockout drops were still there. It was so simple, so smooth. She slipped her fingers into the small pocket in the waistband, took out a tissue to blow her nose and put the tissue back. At the same time, she palmed the phial in her fingers, hid it under the table and snapped the top off with her thumb.

'...said I had to be careful not to drop the glass top.'

Anna remembered her heart thumping in her chest as she waited at the table – would he come back before the drinks arrived? She need not have worried... the waitress came back with the two drinks, put them on the table and moved away. She was off to find more orders and get more tips. Levens had made her practise. She had to reach across the table with two fingers and a thumb – holding the glass phial in her other fingers. As she grabbed the top of the glass of soda water, she poured the knockout drops in; it took only seconds. When Calovarlo came back she lifted her glass in a toast to make sure he drank. She'd said '*uzmundrina*', cheers, they'd clinked glasses and Calovarlo had taken a long gulp.

'I'd been told that it would take only minutes for the knockout drops to work and that I should get him back onto the dance floor. Levens told me that dancing would get the stuff into his bloodstream quicker.

'I was surprised how quickly it happened. One moment his arms were waving, head rocking and hips twisting; the next he stumbled to the floor and seemed to collapse. I didn't know what to do... a bouncer forced his way through the dancers and sat him up on the floor. He asked me "Where yer sittin?" and I told him the table number. I remember being surprised by the other dancers – nobody offered to help me... they just carried on... as if people collapsing around them was normal. Another man arrived and they dragged him back to our table. One of them said, "It's time to go home… need a taxi luv?"'

Anna had walked behind the two bouncers, self-consciously, as they carried Calovarlo out of the nightclub to the row of waiting taxis; but no one seemed to care. As the two men struggled to get him inside the taxi, she wondered how she would get him out.

'When we got to the hotel, the taxi driver got him out and the hotel receptionist got him to the room. He looked terrible… I thought he might die… especially when the receptionist wedged him with pillows to stop him choking on his own vomit!'

'What did you do once you had Sandro in your room?'

Using Calovarlo's first name suddenly made him seem more real. Until now Anna hadn't thought of him, or talked about him, as a real person. It was easier to do what she'd done to a non-person. It was only when the Detective Inspector repeated what she'd said that Anna returned to the story.

'Mr Levens had given us mobile phones, said they were untraceable, and I phoned Karolina. She just said "*esmu ceļā*", she was ready and on her way. I'd left the door ajar so she just pushed it open and closed it behind her. I remember that she looked sporty – as though she was going to the gym. I hadn't seen the grey jogging bottoms and white trainers, or the grey Nike T-shirt before.

'She was already wearing surgical gloves and carrying the plastic pouch and a towel. She gave me the towel and pouch… Mr Levens had gone through it all with us and we were just following his instructions.'

'What were your instructions? What did you do?'

Anna remembered exactly what she'd done. She had unpacked the pouch and given Karolina the white all-in-one protection suit. It felt flimsy and was awkward for Karolina to put on; they were anxious not to rip it. A pair of white elasticated shoe covers were next, then a face mask and safety glasses. The suit had a hood and she tightened it with drawstrings; they were ready.

She remembered Calovarlo being heavy, but with both of them pushing and pulling they managed to get him sitting on the edge of the bed. 'Hold him still and I'll get behind him,' said Karolina. She crawled onto the bed and knelt behind him, using her knees, arms and thighs to hold him in place. '*Gatavs*?' she asked; Anna nodded – she was ready.

Anna recalled the deep tingle inside her as she stood directly in front of Calovarlo, nodding and bracing herself. She knew what was coming. Karolina cupped his limp right hand in hers, forced his fingers to curl, hooked them in the top of Anna's dress and pulled down as hard as she could. It was a cheap dress. Anna didn't want to pay much for a dress she knew would be ruined. The flimsy material stretched and ripped. Another tug and it was completely ripped open. It hung from her shoulders like two lengths of cheap curtain.

Anna remembered how excited she had felt. Calovarlo's shirt had fallen open and exposed him to the waist. His skin looked smooth and tanned. Thick, black, curly hair snaked across his chest. As she looked lower, his body hair seemed shorter and softer. It ran in two different directions and met in a line in the middle of his belly. The short-sleeved white shirt was tight around his biceps. More black hair curled on his tanned forearms and on the back of his hands.

'We sat him up on the edge of the bed, Karolina behind him and me in front. She cupped his hand – like a claw – and ripped the dress off. She did it again and made him rip off my bra. His nails scratched my chest and breast... they oozed blood but weren't painful...'

Anna pulled a face as though wondering what to say next. Coleen and Julie waited expectantly.

'I want to tell you everything – just as it happened and how I remember it… I can't remember which hand, but she used his hand to rip off my panties. His fingernails scratched me again.'

Anna recalled that the scratches looked far worse than they felt; it was exhilarating. When Karolina slipped Calovarlo's fingers into her waistband Anna could feel herself becoming aroused and unable to speak. She was breathing deeply and simply nodded. With his hand in hers, Karolina tore off her panties. His nails had made another bloody scratch on her hip but she didn't care.

Coleen and Julie just sat quietly, waiting for Anna to tell her story – there was no rush.

Memories of the night were flooding back. She remembered it took her a moment to compose herself before she knelt on the carpet in front of them. She had to clamp her thighs together to control the deep tingle inside her. It was in danger of exploding. Anna had looked into Karolina's eyes: they were set and determined. She had asked, *'Vai tu esi gatavs?'* …are you ready? Anna was ready, she nodded her head, closed her eyes, braced herself and clenched her teeth.

'Levens said we had to make it look convincing. Karolina punched me in the face – twice. She made my nose bleed, she cut my lip.'

The blow had knocked Anna off balance and she had put her hand to the floor to stop herself falling over. She could feel the warm blood starting to trickle down her nose and fall onto her chest. *'Mesties ceļos'* – Karolina ordered her to kneel up. Anna clenched her teeth and braced herself again. The second punch seemed even harder and Anna could taste blood in her mouth and panicked; had she broken her teeth? Anna brushed her tongue over them but none were loose. *'Tas ir izdarīts'* – it's done said Karolina.

Blood was running from Anna's nose and over her lips and there were drops of blood on her chest. Karolina grabbed Calovarlo's wrist and rubbed one of his fists against Anna's mouth and the other against her chest.

'We'd been told to make sure there was my blood on his hands as well as my DNA. Karolina let his hands drop and held his head firmly between her hands. Mr Levens said it had to look convincing… I leaned forwards, held his arms, and kissed him hard. I smeared blood and lipstick onto his lips and face. Then Karolina gave me a towel – not for me, but to catch any splashes of vodka. Mr Levens said we had to make sure he drank it all.'

'So, you and Karolina forced Calovarlo to drink vodka. Is that correct?'

'Yes, Mr Levens said he had to appear drunk.'

Anna had wrapped the towel around Calovarlo's chest and exchanged places with Karolina. Once she had him balanced it wasn't difficult to keep him in place. All they had to do then was get him to drink the half bottle. She remembered that he didn't want to drink at first but the more they got down him the easier it got. It took time to get him to swallow the small sips they poured into his mouth. Karolina had put her hand over his mouth and pinched his nose until he swallowed.

'What happened once you had managed to get him to swallow all the vodka?'

'We took his trousers off.'

The knockout drops must have been wearing off because as he swallowed the last of the vodka, he started moving his arms and legs and mumbling. It was time. Anna held him upright whilst Karolina undid his belt and unzipped his trousers. There were hidden buttons and clips… it was awkward working out how his trousers were held in place. They'd been told to use one of his shoes to kick off the other – so that one of his trousers legs was off and his legs were free. Anna remembered thinking that he had nice clothes. They had to wriggle his trousers down to his knees and got one leg free; the one that was shoeless. Karolina pulled down his briefs until they were caught on his foot; he was exposed. Anna could feel the warmth of his body through her chest, arms and thighs. She could look over his shoulder and see what Karolina was doing. Karolina prodded him with her finger saying, "You're a funny little thing... let's see if we can make you bigger". Anna noticed Karolina's voice had changed; it was husky; she was as excited as she was. Calovarlo just grunted and mumbled as though he was trying to reply.

Anna slipped her arms around his chest and clasped her hands. Her neck was still on his shoulder. From nowhere came the memory of a school trip to the National Museum. She must have been about twelve or thirteen and had to pick a statue and say why she liked it. Her friends had already decided they would pick Michelangelo's *David.* At the time they weren't interested in the sculpture, just the chance to see a naked man, even if he was in stone.

Anna's thoughts returned to the hotel bedroom. The image of the lithe and muscled man with a mass of pubic hair and a tiny penis flooded back to her.

'What happened then?'

'Karolina got him, er, excited… we had to get his, er, body fluids… to make it look convincing.'

Anna recalled feeling embarrassed but Karolina didn't seem to care. She began to rub and squeeze him as she whispered into his ear. If he'd been awake, he would have reacted straight away – but it took minutes before he started to become aroused. At first, Anna peered over his shoulder to see what Karolina was doing. When Levens had described what they had to do it had seemed sordid. Now Anna was aroused and began to rhythmically squeeze him with her arms and thighs as she watched Karolina's pumping fist and heard her heavy breathing. Anna was urging him on – 'come on, come on, yes, come on', and could see he was responding to her goading.

Anna stole a glance at Karolina… she recalled that she was

enjoying it as well. Her eyes were bright and wide open, her pale face was flushed and sweat glowed on her forehead. The sweat was misting up her safety glasses. Anna found it odd that her boyfriend was just down the corridor, and she was performing like a porn star with a man she met only minutes ago... It took a while to work him up. She felt his body tense as they drove him to his climax. For a few seconds she felt him shudder and then relax. Karolina caught the semen in a gloved hand and held it safe.

They let go and let him topple onto the bed where he lay on his side; Karolina had finished with him. It was Anna's turn and Karolina reminded her: 'You'll have to roll him on his back. Just lay on top of him so that you get his DNA all over you. Push your knee between his legs and try to rub yourself against him.' It's what Levens had told them to do.

'We'd got his blood and DNA on me... we had to get, er, his semen on me as well. I lay on top of him and made sure I had stuff on me.'

Anna couldn't forget what happened next. As she started the simulated love making, her embarrassment and awkwardness suddenly switched to desire. It was so sudden and so shocking that she froze for several seconds. It suddenly didn't matter that Karolina was watching. A basic animal instinct took over and she began to writhe on top of him; but the passion was short lived.

Moments later Anna climbed off the bed and stood before Karolina. 'Looks convincing,' was all Karolina said. Anna's dress was in shreds, there were weals and bloody scratches on her body, blood and lipstick smeared around her nose and mouth. There were patches of moisture and semen on her stomach and thighs. The patches seemed to shine in the bright bedroom lights.

Anna knew that Karolina had two things to do. She collected the remaining semen from the gloved hand and, as Anna stood obediently in front of her, forced it inside her. They were almost done.

'We just had to take a photograph. Levens wanted a photo of me… said it should be full face, head and neck… only found out why later.'

'The photograph, we need the photograph,' Karolina had exclaimed as she wiped her hands and retrieved the camera from her bag. Anna stood, almost naked, with her back to the bedroom wall and waited patiently for Karolina to take the picture. 'Look frightened, look shocked… look terrified…' she said as the camera shutter clicked. She took lots of full-face photographs and methodically checked them to ensure they captured Anna's face and expression before taking more using the flash. Carefully she returned the camera to her bag.

Anna just stood by the wall, unmoving, as Karolina methodically checked and rechecked the scene before moving to the door. The empty vodka bottle went back inside the pouch. It was followed by all the other protective clothing – including the rubber gloves. 'Give me your phone and I'll call Mr Levens,' said Karolina. 'I'll tell him everything went as planned. He can come and collect the SIM card.'

'When we'd got the photographs, Karolina went back to her room.'

Anna had moved to the door, opened it and peaked out. The corridor was clear, Karolina had returned to her room and her waiting boyfriend. Anna moved to the bed, sat next to Calovarlo and forced herself to wait ten minutes. He seemed fast asleep and appeared to be breathing evenly. She was certain he would sleep until someone woke him up, but it was time for the next act. Two high-pitched screams broke the silence as Anna bolted for the door, flung it open and ran towards reception.

'I waited… then screamed and ran to reception… You know the rest.'

Coleen sat back in her chair – the dam had indeed been breached but it would take hours more careful questioning to document all that had happened. She only had a couple of days to do it in. She recalled Sandro Calovarlo's claim when she first interviewed him. He claimed it was a set-up – and he was right.

Chapter 40

A fairy tale

They met in Sandro's office like before. However, this time when he and the defence team drove to police headquarters in Manchester, his mood was entirely different. Sandro was smouldering with resentment. He and the defence team were escorted to the meeting room where only Detective Inspector Latchem, Detective Sergeant Herman and Detective Constable Evers were waiting. Julian Ross was absent and Melton-Barr was surprised. He had expected him to be smug and gloating after what happened at the previous meeting. He also wondered why Latchem was smiling. It wasn't a self-satisfied, triumphant smile… more contented and relaxed. She turned immediately to greet him.

'Reginald… I hope you don't mind me calling you Reginald,' she said but carried on regardless. 'I'd like to make a short statement before the meeting starts. I think it will…'

Melton-Barr raised his hand – signalling her to stop. 'Detective Inspector, may I call you Coleen? I also have a short statement to make… I did request the meeting and I think you will find what I have to say, er… informative.'

Coleen gave a mock bow and gestured that the meeting was his. Melton-Barr walked to the head of the table, took his seat and placed several thick folders in front of him. Coleen looked around the table; she made eye contact with everyone before looking at Melton-Barr and saying, 'Reginald, over to you.' It was the cue he was waiting for and he rose to his feet. In his usual tone and manner, he began speaking.

'I would like to tell you a fairy tale.'

Suddenly his tone and manner changed as he addressed his audience.

'Boys and girls, if you are sitting comfortably, I'll begin. Once upon a time there were two very naughty boys…'

Subtly, his body posture changed. He crouched slightly and turned his head towards Coleen whilst theatrically shielding his mouth from the rest of the audience. In his normal voice, but in a conspiratorial tone, he confided:

'We will call them David and Tony.'

Melton-Barr then reverted to his role as storyteller as he continued. *'David and Tony were schoolfriends who decided to make their fortune buying and selling land; land upon which old and abandoned buildings stood. One day they found an old factory and decided to buy it.'*

Again, Melton-Barr turned conspiratorially to Coleen and confided: 'The company was B&H Limited in Runcorn. They made microbeads before they were banned in the UK.'

A smile flickered over Inspector Coleen Latchem's face. She was aware that microbeads had been manufactured at the old B&H Ltd factory and that Levens and Moxon had exported them on board the ill-fated MV *Asenka*.

'The two naughty boys made a plan. They would secretly get the machines in the factory running, continue making things and then sell the machines, the things they made and the factory for bags of gold.'

Melton-Barr's audience were now expecting the theatrical aside to Coleen. They were not disappointed. In an increasingly confident and authoritarian tone he announced: 'David and Tony persuaded the former owner of B&H Ltd, Alice Henshaw, to facilitate the illegal assembly of a skeleton workforce, fraudulently use existing raw materials to illegally manufacture microbeads, and then illegally export both the manufacturing machinery and two hundred tonnes of microbeads. The recipient was to be Emma Farmaceitiska Fabrika in Riga.'

'Catastrophe,' Melton-Barr announced theatrically. *'The old ship taking their precious cargo to a new land sank in the ocean. The two naughty boys were very sad and afraid. They were sad that they wouldn't receive their bags of gold. They were also frightened that a handsome young nobleman, who could swim under water, would find their treasure, and discover how naughty they'd been. So they devised another plan.'*

Melton-Barr scanned the faces of his audience and knew he had their complete attention. Coleen Latchem knew the story so far and wondered how much more he knew.

'It was a catastrophe. David and Tony's insurance company informed them that the *Marine Salvage & Investigation Company* would be salvaging cargo from the wreck. They couldn't risk the drums of microbeads being damaged, released into the ocean and traced back to them.'

Melton-Barr reverted to his fairy tale: *'The naughty boys' plan was to find a simple village girl and arrange for her to make friends with the handsome young nobleman. When they had made friends, she would slip a magic potion into his drink which would make him very sleepy. When he was asleep, she would hurt herself and tell the king's men that the nobleman did it. The king's men would be very cross and would tell the nobleman he would be punished. The naughty boys promised to give the simple village girl a small bag of gold for helping them.'*

Melton-Barr directed his comments directly at the Detective Inspector. 'Tony recruited Anna Kalnina, an office worker at Emma Farmaceitiska Fabrika and other accomplices to compromise Alessandro Calovarlo. David and Tony supplied Anna with a powerful sedative, AmilSed, which we believe was slipped into his drink at the Mojito Nightclub in Manchester. Traces of AmilSed were found in the waistband of Anna Kalnina's dress. It was also found, mixed with Alessandro's saliva, on bedsheets. Details of the analyses, from Kunz Laboratories, are provided in the latest disclosures.'

Coleen interrupted and confidently continued the fairy tale. *'Anna and her accomplice, Karolina Balodis, forced Sandro to swallow half a bottle of Russian Shenovnaya Vodka. It's a brand that is not available in the UK but widely available in Latvia. Our forensic team also found traces of this vodka in Sandro's saliva.*

'It was Karolina Balodis who inflicted the facial injuries on Anna Kalnina. Together they ripped Anna's clothing and transferred DNA, blood and semen between Anna and Sandro to simulate the effects of the assault and rape that was claimed.'

Sandro reached across the table and touched Melton-Barr's arm. Melton-Barr smiled at the gesture and returned to his story.

'The two naughty boys thought they were very clever. One of them, David, had volunteered to work at the local prison so he could help people arrested by the king's men. He wanted to be at the prison when the nobleman arrived – as he knew he would. When the nobleman did arrive, David offered to help him. He didn't really want to help him but to know what was happening.

'David Moxon is indeed a lawyer. He arranged to work *pro bono* at the central Manchester police station so he could intercept Alessandro Calovarlo and direct him to a legal practice where he could gain access to confidential information about the case.'

Coleen took up the fairy tale and even adopted a similar theatrical I tone. *'The other naughty boy, Tony, went to a friend of the nobleman and showed him a picture of the village girl. In the picture she was hurt and covered in blood. The naughty boy said, for a bag of gold, he would tell the simple village girl to say the nobleman didn't do it. It would set the nobleman free.*

'The photograph of Anna Kalnina's injuries, given to Jack Collier, was taken in her room at the Wayside Hotel. This was before she arrived at the central Manchester police station. We both know it is not an official police photograph and will, no doubt, have the fingerprints of Tony Levens on it.'

Melton-Barr locked eyes with Coleen Latchem and they both smiled. The last few moments had revealed that both of them knew most, if not all, of the story. Melton-Barr continued: *'It was the king's men and the friend of the nobleman who could swim underwater, not the naughty boys, who were clever. The friend of the nobleman found the treasure inside the shipwreck and took it to the king's men. The naughty boys were arrested and thrown into a dark dungeon. They quicky confessed to what they had done and begged for forgiveness.'*

It was like a double act as Coleen Latchem continued. 'UK Border Force arrested David Moxon and Tony Levens this morning for illegally manufacturing and exporting microbeads. It is expected that other charges will be made against them and numerous other individuals.'

When Melton-Barr looked around the room there were only smiling faces. DS Herman had a grin on his face and DC Evers was silently clapping her hands.

'Boys and girls. There's a happy ending to the story. The king's men found out what happened and would punish the naughty boys and those who had helped them. The handsome young nobleman was released from prison and joined his friends to celebrate. All the treasure was found and the nobleman's friends were rewarded.

'They all lived happily ever after.'

Melton Barr finally dropped his storytelling voice and concluded: 'David Moxon and Tony Levens are currently helping the authorities with their enquiries. The European Maritime Safety Agency have confirmed that all two hundred tonnes of microbeads have been recovered safely.'

He leaned forwards to tap the pile of files in front of him. 'You will find detailed evidence supporting everything I have said this morning in the disclosures before you. I expect all charges against my client, Alessandro Calovarlo, to be dropped and a fulsome apology to be offered. I'm happy to respond to any questions you may have.'

Coleen continued to smile as she scanned the room and looked directly at Sandro. 'Anna Kalnina is currently inside this station and has been charged with making false accusations of assault and rape against Sandro Calovarlo. Other charges against her and her accomplice, Karolina Balodis, are likely to follow.'

Coleen turned to Melton-Barr. Smiling she continued: 'Thank you for the fairy story and I'm glad it had a happy ending. I'm pleased to tell you that all charges against Alessandro Calovarlo have been dropped and the ACC will be writing to him in due course. I'd be grateful if you could give me a couple of days to work through the disclosures. I'll get back to you as quickly as I can.'

Coleen got up from the table and walked to where Sandro was sitting. As she got closer, he stood, unsure what to say or do. She clasped his hands in both of hers. 'I had to run with the evidence I had – but I now know what really happened. It was a set-up but it is a happy ending.'

'Grazie,' was all Sandro said.

Postscript

The Latvian police raided Emma Farmaceitiska Fabrika and confirmed an order had been placed for two hundred tonnes of microbeads from B&H Limited. They also confirmed the purchase of manufacturing equipment for microbeads, also from B&H Limited. Police investigations continue.

David Moxon and Tony Levens were taken into police custody and face a series of charges related to illegally manufacturing and selling microbeads, perverting the course of justice and extortion.

Anna Kalnina, Karolina Balodis and Karolina's boyfriend were charged with attempting to pervert the course of justice and blackmail.

Alice Henshaw pleaded guilty to fraud and was fined and given a suspended sentence for two years. The workers who had returned to B&H Limited to manufacture a quantity of microbeads were also fined and given suspended sentences for one year.

Detective Inspector Coleen Latchem received a commendation from the Assistant Chief Constable for her role in preventing a miscarriage of justice.

The European Maritime Safety Agency drained fuel oil from the wreck of the MV *Asenka* and found no evidence of contaminants in the surrounding water.

Deputy Director Penny Pendleton Price has been transferred to UK Border Force Headquarters in London. She will join the anti-terrorist squad.

Alessandro Calovarlo phoned Dr Esther May and arranged to meet for champagne and soda water in London.

The MV *Stavanger* moved to its station as a dedicated standby vessel, close to the *Monroe Bravo* oil platform, in support of the North Sea Oil Producers Support Group.

Here's a chance to read the first chapter of the next book in the Jack Collier Series.

Chapter 1

A blow against the West

The digital timer counted down and triggered the release of the spring-loaded plunger. It smashed the glass phial; the chemicals were combined and the thermite process commenced. Nothing on earth could stop it now. The positioning and strength of the thermite device had been discussed at length by electrical and structural engineers, chemists and explosive experts. Computer simulations had been created to determine the ignition sequence and optimum level of destruction. It was to destroy the Backup Command and Control System to the Western-owned oil production platform but not to prompt a major response; that would come later.

The chemicals combined and the reaction started along the long core of the device. It generated heat, lots of heat, very quickly along the centre of the tube. As the milli-seconds passed, the core got hotter and hotter until it glowed. The surrounding mixture ignited and the temperature increase was exponential. In seconds it rose through one hundred degrees centigrade, three hundred degrees and the plastic sleeves around the wiring and data transmission cables were bubbling and smoking.

As the first whiffs of smoke and rising heat were detected, sensors were triggered. In the Central Control Room, bright LED lights flashed on the main display board and a warning screen burst onto the main monitor. The Chief of the Fire Team and the Acting Platform Controller were alerted at the same time. There was no panic, sensors were triggered all the time, but it had to be checked out. Immediately, the Acting Platform Controller initiated action: 'Chief, smoke and heat detected inside the Backup Command and Control Centre, Level 3, Grid A6. Repeat, smoke and heat detected Grid A6, Backup Command and Control Centre. Investigate immediately.'

At six hundred degrees centigrade, the long steel mesh canister that was clipped across the main wiring harness and fibre optic feed was glowing red hot. Black pungent smoke was billowing through the cabinet air vents and into the remote, backup control room. Smoke and heat sensors had triggered the gut-wrenching 'Awooga, Awooga, Awooga' siren which deafened everyone close by and alerted everyone on the platform. Vents from the tanks of carbon dioxide above the building released a flood of CO_2 through ceiling vents to smother any flames. However, the thermite device would even work under water; it didn't need oxygen to complete its task. It just got hotter and hotter.

The standby Fire Team were already suited up. Harnesses and breathing apparatus were clicked on in seconds. As helmets and gloves were pulled on, the Acting Platform Controller, sitting before the main console in the Command and Control Centre, punched a button to speak to the now scrambling Fire Team. Before he could speak, the temperature at the centre of the thermite device exceeded two thousand five hundred degrees centigrade. Metal melted, plastic and fibre optic cables vapourised alongside the crackle of burning. The resultant gases expanded dramatically. The sides of the heavy steel cabinet that had contained the backup platform command and control system began to deform under the internal pressure. The cabinet door latch and hinges failed at about the same time. The cabinet door blew open and vented a super-heated cloud of gas and pungent smoke into the room.

Those who designed and constructed the thermite device knew that the building housing the Backup Command and Control System was designed to withstand violent North Sea weather. The computer simulation they had created confirmed the building could absorb the modest blast that would be produced. Two clear plastic windowpanes simply popped out of their frames and the single door blew open. The black smoke pouring out of the building was whisked away by the wind and flood of CO_2. All communication between the Central Command and Control Centre and the backup centre was lost.

A second, much more powerful, thermite device had been placed inside the cabinet that housed the main wiring harness and main data transmission and control cables. The cabinet was housed inside a side room within the Command and Control Centre of the whole platform. It ignited within thirty seconds of the first detonation with devastating results.

There were eleven people inside the main control room when the thermite device ignited and its temperature soared. Pungent black smoke again billowed from the cabinet as the sound of crackling increased to a crescendo. More sensors were triggered and more klaxons blared; clouds of pressurised CO_2 poured into the control room as the front of the cabinet began to glow red hot. There was panic inside the control room before a shower of white-hot metal and super-heated gases swept all before the expanding blast. It resembled the pyroclastic flow of a small volcano. The walls, roof and floor of the control room and the bowser of CO_2 above it were all transformed into deadly shrapnel. The blast killed all the night shift – one-third of the senior management team, the team that provided the leadership and managed the *Monroe Bravo* oil production platform.

The oil platform was still working but without any control. The strategically positioned thermite devices had destroyed both the main and the Backup Command and Control Systems but not the basic operation of the platform. Power to the pumps and lights, compressors and turbines still worked. Automatic safety valves and well shut-down sequences had been circumvented. Thousands of barrels of hot crude oil were still being pumped through a thirty-inch steel pipe from the seabed ninety metres below into the separation plant and then into the shore-bound pipeline. Liquified natural gas, at 1800 psi, was still being pumped at over one hundred kilograms per minute through an eighteen-inch diameter pipe that was one inch thick. The pipeline disappeared over the side of the rig and through miles of pipework to distribution points on shore… but not for long.

When the Fire Team reached the backup site, they knew what to do; they practised weekly. Two men grabbed the hand grips around the nozzle of the adjacent foam bowser and ran towards the building; thick black smoke was still billowing out of the windows. Colleagues frantically threw the concertina of hose aside and hit the lever to emit the foam. A torrent of foam sprang from the nozzle and through the open doorway as the Fire Team began to douse the fire. On the other side of the platform a simultaneous flash of light and explosion rocked the night. Anyone who was on the platform, and who was exposed, felt the pressure wave as it vented its force between the steel grated levels and into the night.

'Jimmy, Bob, Ron… with me,' shouted the Fire Chief as he turned and started to run towards the next fire.

Thirty seconds after the main control room was neutralised, a third thermite device ignited alongside the main crude oil riser. It had been positioned on a flange, below the steel housing that allowed heavy mud to be pumped down the drilling shaft. The mud, under huge pressure, forced the crude oil back to the seabed; it could make the well safe. The housing and valves were made of specialist steel, able to withstand massive internal pressures and high temperature before failing. It really didn't matter if the device was above or below the housing. Within seconds the thermite mixture would soar to over two thousand degrees, melt the steel pipe and anything nearby and ignite the crude oil.

The effect wasn't immediately spectacular. Crude oil began to spray from the main riser at an angle as the thermite device melted the steel pipe. Some oil shot through the metal grating of the main drilling floor above but the majority was deflected onto the floor below. Within seconds it had doused everything within sight with hot crude oil. The volatile gases that had been trapped inside the oil, thousands of feet below the seabed and under immense pressure, were suddenly free. There was a dull boom as the volatile gases ignited and a fire ball shot between the floors of the platform and into the surrounding air. The Fire Chief and his two colleagues were lucky. Had they been on the same level as the fireball they would have been incinerated and blown off the platform and into the cold waters of the North Sea. For an instant the fireball sucked all the oxygen from the air around it, but the heavy metal grid that created one of the levels of the platform had shielded them from the worst of the blast and the heat.

In the aftermath, a blue flame began to flicker around the housing that had supported the main riser. Although the bulk of the crude oil was hot, it was far below the flashpoint at which it would ignite. The white-hot molten metal would change all that. It boosted the temperature of the oil close to it and set it alight. These flames heated the surrounding oil to flashpoint. A blue light writhed and flickered over the surface of the oil spewing over and through the steel grating floor, through the floors below and onto the sea. The light began to change colour to orange as pungent, billowing black smoke erupted. The hotter the oil got the more it burned and the thicker the smoke.

The volatile gases inside the pressurised column of crude oil that was bursting from the ruptured main riser expanded dramatically. They transformed the solid column of oil into a massive spray which then erupted like a Bonfire Night Roman Candle – but on a gigantic scale. As heat soared into the night sky, fresh oxygen was drawn into the fire to change the oil platform into a funeral pyre. With an almost endless supply of crude oil, it wouldn't take long for the floor grating above the flames to glow red hot, to buckle and collapse. Those on or near to the main riser when it exploded were incinerated or blown from the platform into the sea. It would be like falling over thirty metres onto burning concrete. The outcome would be inevitable. If, by a miracle, they survived the fall, the cold water would kill them within minutes.

Captain Erik Sorenson was on the bridge of the MV *Stavanger*, enjoying the quiet time of his watch. There was a dull hum within the ship as the engine and thrusters maintained their standby position. The sea was calm and hundreds of lights reflected off the water from the towering silhouette of the *Monroe Bravo* oil platform. The dive teams were *out of sat*, the injured diver had been seen by a doctor and would make a full recovery, they were on station early and the co-owners would be leaving in a few hours. Life on the *Stavanger* would soon be back to normal.

He didn't hear the first explosion but saw the flashing sensor, relayed from the rig. He walked across the bridge, unclipped the night vision binoculars from the rack, and was in the process of scanning the area when the second device exploded. This time he heard the dull bang and saw the dramatic effects; he reached to hit the 'All men on deck' button. There was a problem on *Monroe Bravo.*

Just as men rushed to their station and onto the bridge the third device severed the main oil riser and the platform began to burn; red LED lights on his monitor went out.

'*Stavanger* to *Monroe Bravo, Stavanger* to *Monroe Bravo,* report on the situation,' Captain Sorenson demanded; there was no reply.

He repeated the request three times before he spoke to the skipper of the MSV *North Guard.* The *North Guard* was a huge floating platform anchored several hundred metres away from *Monroe Bravo.* In addition to acting as a store, supply ship and maintenance workshop, it was a fire killer. There were sixteen water cannons on board the *North Guard* that could send jets of water seventy-five metres and pour one hundred and eighty-thousand litres of water per minute onto a fire. The cannons were so powerful they could punch holes through concrete. They could also wash men off the platform. The problem was that the *North Guard* was slow to manoeuvre. It was designed to support firefighting taking place on the platform. Whilst it had enormous capability, it would take time to get in place. Time was something *Monroe Bravo* did not have.

'*North Guard, North Guard* this is *Stavanger*, acknowledge,' stated Sorenson.

'*Stavanger*, this is *North Guard*, over,' was the reply.

'*North Guard*, fire on *Monroe Bravo*. No response from Platform Controller. I am launching a RIB and fast rescue craft to search for men in the water and those abandoning the rig. Will restrict search area to south-east – down current. Will proceed to east-south-east of rig and deploy water cannons. Will move away at your request, over.'

'Message received and understood. I am unable to contact *Monroe Bravo*,' was all the captain of the *North Guard* said.

Captain Sorenson turned to his officers and was about to address them when the fourth device exploded. It was on the other side of the platform and two levels down. It was attached to the high-pressure liquified gas pipeline. A pipeline that stretched from the platform, down to and along the seabed, to the onshore control point. It ignited thirty seconds after the device attached to the main crude oil riser. At first it was like the ignition of an oxy-acetylene blowtorch. Witnesses later described a deafening 'pop' that could be heard over the sound of the fire above. A small jet of liquified natural gas broke through the ruptured wall of the pipe and immediately burst into flames. It was followed, moments later, by a deep rumble that quickly changed to resemble the start of a jet engine. The roar increased in intensity and pitch from the low rumble to a deafening scream.

The full jet of intense flame hit the first floor of the four-storey accommodation block like an express train. A whole section of the first storey collapsed before it could be melted. Internal walls simply couldn't withstand the onslaught. They were blown away or incinerated as the white-hot flame bored through the building. Even when the flame broke through, the devastation continued. Nearby metal support beams began to glow and distort as the weakened structure couldn't support the weight of the storeys above. As the accommodation block sagged, more storeys were fed into the resultant inferno. There were thirty-seven people inside the accommodation block when it was incinerated.

The jet of intense flame from the ruptured high-pressure gas pipeline not only destroyed everything in its immediate path, but anything close by. The intense heat caused cables and lines, plastic pipes and anything that could burn to smoulder and burst into flame. This included the main umbilical that supplied the diving bell with a mixture of oxygen and helium. The surfaces of the rubber hoses were already bubbling in the heat and would burst into flame at any moment. When this happened, pressurised oxygen and helium would explode in another fireball. Gas supplies to the divers below would be cut off.

A crane in the path of the searing heat began to feel the effect of the oxy-acetylene-like flame; it was later estimated to be close to three thousand degrees centigrade. The lattice of steel plates that made up the jib of the crane began to glow red hot. Steel plates began to buckle as the jib bent under the weight it was holding. Link after link of the chain slowly disappeared into the North Sea.

The crane was supporting a pressurised diving chamber containing nine divers *in sat.* They had been blown down to ninety metres days before to conduct repairs and maintenance on the rig in eight-hour shifts. Two other divers were close to the seabed, working, and one was in the wet well when the crude oil from the main riser burst into flames. The divers in the water could see the increasing glow in the water above them.

'Danny, Danny… look up… what the fuck's that?' sounded Archie in alarm.

Archie had never seen such a glow before but knew exactly what it was. It wasn't the glow from an arc light or a torch that had fallen over the side. It was too big for the flare burning off excess gas. It was a fire, a massive fire on the platform above. Before Danny could call the dive supervisor, they heard from him.

'Emergency, emergency, emergency – drop everything – return to the wet well immediately. Repeat, we have an emergency. Archie, Danny, return to the wet well immediately. Confirm.'

'On our way,' was all the divers said as they dropped their tools, grabbed their umbilical and started to pull themselves back towards the wet well. They were 'moon walking' on the seabed, hauling on their umbilical, as they hopped and skipped towards the wet well. Through the dark, Danny could see the glow of lights from the diving bell. As he got closer, he saw it slowly drop to the seabed. The short steps he was expecting to climb were driven into the sand and mud. The whole bell then slowly toppled over onto its side. From the lights around the diving bell, he could see the chain slowly disappearing behind it – but could he get inside?

'We're going to have to dig a hole so we can squeeze inside,' was all Archie said as he fell to his knees and began to scoop away mud and sand with his hands.

Danny glanced upwards to the dull orange light before falling to his knees and digging frantically.

Future Reading

If you enjoyed *Non-Hazardous Material* you will probably enjoy earlier books in the Jack Collier series.

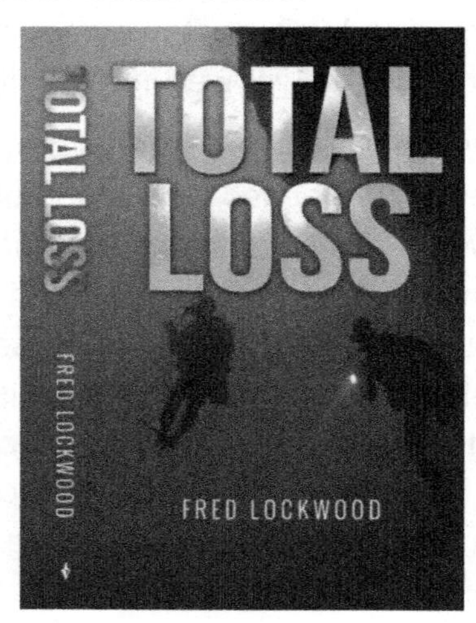

Total Loss (2016) traces the lives of three groups of people before they intersect dramatically when an ageing freighter sinks off the coast of Kenya. A routine marine inspection of the wreck by the fledgling *Marine Salvage & Investigation Company*, established by Jack Collier and Sandro Calovarlo, brings them together.

The Sacranie brothers and sister, who own the vessel and have cargo on board, risk their secret being uncovered. Soloman Mbano, a powerful underworld figure in East Africa, is desperate to salvage valuable merchandise he is transporting and to do so at any cost.

The action above and below water is relentless. *Total Loss* takes you from Liverpool to Dar es Salaam, from Dubai to Delhi, from the depths of the Atlantic to the warm waters of the Indian Ocean.

Two heavy, sealed plastic tubs are salvaged from a light aircraft in a remote part of the Celebes Sea, off the coast of Indonesia. Within hours of informing the authorities, strangers are asking about the whereabouts of the salvors and their boat.

Jack Collier and Sandro Calovarlo, co-owners of the fledgling *Marine Salvage & Investigation Company*, are thrust into a deadly "cat and mouse" game. They face ruthless opponents, both above water and below, who want to retrieve the tubs ... at any cost.

Overdue (2017) will take you from the Celebes Sea to the Caribbean, from Jakarta to Salford, and a whole new world in-between.

In *Missing, Presumed Lost* (2018) a sailboat is lost during a sudden, violent storm off the coast of Croatia. On board was a battered briefcase – but where is it? People inextricably linked to the briefcase cannot ignore its disappearance and must recover the contents or destroy them.

Jack Collier and Sandro Calovarlo, co-owners of the *Marine Salvage & Investigation Company*, accept contracts to locate the wreck and then salvage it. They become unwittingly involved in an attempt to recover the briefcase or destroy it.

The stakes are high. Is it Jack, Sandro, or the briefcase that becomes … *Missing, Presumed Lost?*

A modern-day treasure hunt locates the wreck of a freighter, sunk by the Japanese in 1941. The *Unlisted Cargo* on board has special significance for a religious community in Myanmar, a community that previously placed this cargo into the safe keeping of the British over seventy-five years previously. It is also of interest to international art criminals trading in antiquities and, for different reasons, both the Myanmar and British Governments. All are determined to get their hands on it.

In the corridors of power, the possession of the *Unlisted Cargo* becomes a battle of wills with high stakes. Within the criminal group their actions are not personal – it's merely business. Who will be successful in securing the contents of the wreck? Will it be worth the price?

A derelict ship is towed from a South American backwater to be scuttled to create an artificial reef of the coast of a Caribbean Island. This previously neglected part of the island, and a new dive centre, are set to benefit – but at a cost to a local entrepreneur.

The entrepreneur is determined the artificial reef project will fail and has ingenious ways of funding his plans and destroying those of others.

The bizarre death of divers on the newly scuttled ship and a series of unexplained accidents around it cause the wreck and dive centre to be shunned. *The Marine Salvage &Investigation Company*, that stripped out and prepared the ship for sinking, is charged with *Gross Negligence*. The dive centre is also under investigation and both could face financial ruin.

The remains of a ninth-century wreck, which may contain ancient Chinese artefacts, is discovered in shallow water in the Quirimbas Archipelago, Mozambique. A Chinese-led archaeological expedition contracts the *Marine Salvage & Investigation Company* to provide onsite support.

Whilst marine archaeologists excavate the submerged wreck site, corrupt officials and a ruthless coastguard captain collude to steal any Tang Dynasty porcelain and ceramics that have survived. They also eliminate witnesses and anyone who stands in their way. Unknown to all are the political decisions that will dictate the fate of any recovered items.

Accidents and deaths decimate the teams associated with the expedition. Who will survive? What will survive? Who will decide?

Printed in Great Britain
by Amazon

20048492R00173